Lake House Secret

Debra Burroughs

Lake House Books
Boise, Idaho

First eBook Edition: 2014
First Paperback Edition: 2014

THE LAKE HOUSE SECRET by Debra Burroughs,
1st ed. p.cm.

Visit My Blog: www.DebraBurroughsBooks.com

Contact Me: Debra@DebraBurroughsBooks.com

ISBN-10: 1502526336
ISBN-13: 978-1502526335

DEDICATION

This book is dedicated to my amazing husband, Tim,
who loves me and encourages me every day to
do what I love – writing.

TABLE OF CONTENTS

ACKNOWLEDGMENTS

*I would like to acknowledge my awesome Beta Readers,
Cathy Tomlinson, Janet Lewis, and Buffy Drewett,
who inspire me and help me with their words
of encouragement and critique.*

*I want to also acknowledge my brilliant Editor,
Lisa Dawn Martinez.*

i

CHAPTER 1

"THAT STUPID WOMAN!" Jenessa Jones sputtered as she slid behind the wheel of her compact car and slammed the door shut. "I can see I'm not getting *that* job."

She jammed her key into the ignition and turned it. The engine of her twelve-year-old Toyota moaned a few times, trying to turn over.

"No, no, no!" she screamed, banging the palm of her hand against the steering wheel. "I don't need this today."

The blistering July sun of Central California made the inside of her car feel like an oven. Her long, dark hair began sticking to the perspiration that trickled down her neck and onto her white silk blouse. She rolled her windows down to release the suffocating heat.

She had gone to the job interview dressed in her navy blue business suit, hoping to make her best impression, but she could tell by the interviewer's questions, and apparent lack of interest, that the woman was simply going through the motions, like she had already made up her mind who she would hire.

Whispering a prayer and crossing her fingers, she tried the engine a couple more times. Success! The engine finally roared to life and eventually settled into a steady purr. Flicking on the air conditioner, switching the fan to the highest speed, she pulled out of the parking lot to head for home.

Jenessa had been a reporter for a newspaper in Sacramento for the past five years, that is, until almost nine weeks ago when her boss gave her the news that the paper was forced to downsize and he was going to have to let her go.

"Sorry, but more people are finding their news online these days and it's killing us," he had said.

Since getting the axe, she had sent out almost a hundred resumes and gone on countless interviews but, to her dismay, there had been no job offers yet. Reaching the point of desperation, she couldn't afford to be picky.

Although nabbing another job as a writer would be her first choice, at this point she'd take a job as a secretary, a bank teller, or a store clerk if she had to. Her bachelor's degree in journalism and her seven years of experience working for newspapers were getting her nowhere. At this point, even waiting tables or cleaning hotel rooms was not beneath her.

She'd already burned through the little bit of savings she'd had and was running out of cash fast. The current month's rent was already a few days past due, plus she was late on last month's—actually, she hadn't paid last month's rent at all.

To add to her misery, now her car was giving her trouble and there was no money to repair it. It would be near impossible to go on any more interviews without transportation.

She parked the car in the lot of her complex and climbed the outdoor stairs to her third-floor apartment. As she approached, her portly apartment manager was standing in front of her door in his t-shirt and shorts, taping a piece of paper to it.

"Mr. Morelli?"

He whipped around to face her, obviously startled by her unexpected presence. "Hi there," he said, offering her a weak, rueful smile. "I'm really sorry, Miss Jones, I have no choice but to give you a three-day notice of eviction." He glanced back at the note he had attached to her front door and motioned toward it.

"No, please...just a little more time," she pleaded. "I'm sure I'll have another job soon."

"Sorry, but I have to do this, Jenessa—company policy. If it was up to me, I'd keep carrying you a little longer, but I have to answer to the owners, you know." He tapped a chubby finger on the notice a couple of times before walking away. "You have three days— bring your rent current or you've got to move out."

Jenessa pushed through the door and rushed inside, fighting back angry tears. She was doing the best she could. Things just weren't going her way. In fact, they seemed to be going from bad to worse. She wished she could talk to her mother.

She peeled off her hot jacket and flung it over a chair. After kicking off her shoes, she untucked her silk blouse that had stuck to her sweaty back and plopped down on her old sofa, stretching her legs out and crossing them on the coffee table. She sunk back, closed her eyes, and rested her head against the cushion, hoping for some relief.

What was she going to do now? Perhaps her sister Sara could loan her some money, or maybe Aunt Renee, although, she cringed at the thought of asking either one of them.

After leaving home at seventeen, Jenessa had always been self-sufficient, never asked anyone for anything. Her mother had insisted on paying her college tuition and her father went along, but beyond that, she took care of herself. Now, her life was in a downward spiral and she didn't know what to do to stop the momentum.

She wished she could call her mom and cry on her shoulder, ask her what to do, but her mother had passed away a couple of years earlier. Her father's face, stern and aloof, popped into her mind, but there was no way on earth she'd ever ask him for help of any kind.

Her cell phone began to ring and she dug around in her purse until she found it. "Hello."

"Jenessa, this is Aunt Renee."

Taken aback by the perfect timing, Jenessa took a moment to respond. Maybe it was more than a coincidence that her aunt was calling. Maybe things were finally going to turn around. "I was just thinking about you, Aunt Renee. How are you?"

"Honey, I have some bad news."

Great! Just when I thought things couldn't get any worse.

She squeezed her eyes tight and steeled herself. "What is it?"

"It's your father, dear. He had a heart attack this morning and," she paused and cleared her throat, but there was still a tightness in her voice as she continued, "I'm afraid he's passed away."

Jenessa's mouth fell open. She wanted to say something, but no words would come. She was frozen. She loved her father, the way all good daughters should love the man they call Dad, but the two had become increasingly distant. For the past twelve years they had been almost like strangers, even on the rare occasion when she had gone home for a visit.

The last time she saw her father was at her mother's funeral, and even then, he walled himself off from her. Tears blurred her vision now as she peered down at the small framed photo of her parents that sat on her end table.

"Jenessa, did you hear me?"

Renee Giraldy was her father's younger sister. She lived in Hidden Valley, where Jenessa's parents and younger sister, Sara, also lived, and where Jenessa had gone to high school. Aunt Renee had been married three times, each time to a man more wealthy than the one before.

Her last husband had died of a massive stroke while on a business trip in Europe. She had once shared with Jenessa how much she regretted not having been with him when he'd passed away. She rarely cared to go traipsing all over Europe while he met with clients and suppliers—she had gone twice, and that was enough.

"Yes, I heard you." Jenessa shook her head, trying to clear the daze. "Sorry, I don't know what to say. It's such a shock."

"For me too, hon."

"What happened?"

"From what I've been able to gather, he was at his office working, dictating to his secretary I believe, when he began to have chest pains and slumped over on his desk. She phoned nine-one-one, but it was too late."

Too late.

The words pressed down on Jenessa like an elephant sitting on her chest. She struggled to suck in a deep breath. Reconciliation of any kind with her father would be impossible now. Guilt rippled through her. Why hadn't she tried harder?

Her father, David Jones, had been an attorney in Hidden Valley. He had moved the family there from San Francisco to start up a new practice when Jenessa was fifteen. She had been heartbroken, inconsolable, leaving her friends and the home she had grown up in.

He had tried to comfort her, her sister too, telling them that he was doing it to give his family a safer, better life in that small town, nestled in the central valley of California. They would make new friends, he had promised, and they would have a larger, nicer home than before. His sister Renee had lived there for years and had often encouraged him to take a leap and move his family there.

"I guess I shouldn't be surprised," Jenessa said. "He was always one to keep things bottled up." Unfortunately, in that way, she took after him. "Perhaps the stress got to be too much for him."

"You're probably right." Aunt Renee sniffled. "I know you and he didn't get along all that well these last few years, Jen, but I know he loved you very much."

"He sure had a funny way of showing it." Jenessa pinched her lips shut. She hadn't meant to sound so cold and had blurted it out before her brain could filter her response.

Aunt Renee's words had yanked up painful, buried feelings and the comment had unexpectedly slipped out from a dark and wounded place. Jenessa was instantly thrown back to the years her father had been cool and distant, ever since she screwed up and made that one mistake—that one *very big* mistake—when she was seventeen.

No matter how much she wished it, Jenessa couldn't pull her icy remark back in. "I shouldn't have said that," was all she could offer.

"I understand, you're upset. We all are, hon. When can you come home?" Aunt Renee asked.

Jenessa hadn't told anyone in her family that she had lost her job at the paper. She'd hoped to get another before she ran out of money, before she disappointed her father one more time.

She hadn't even told her best friend, Ramey St. John, who still lived in Hidden Valley. She and Ramey had met in Spanish class after her family moved there. They were in the same grade and became best friends.

"I can leave as soon as I get a bag packed." It was a two-hour drive down Highway 99, assuming her old Toyota was up for the journey. "I'll call you when I get close."

"Sara and Ramey will be glad to see you, hon, and so will I. Drive safely."

Ramey would be glad, but Jenessa doubted Sara would.

Jenessa hadn't visited her hometown very often after she'd left at seventeen, but she did stay in contact with Ramey, and her sister too, somewhat. She and Sara had been close until Jenessa left, but her sister had blamed her for the rift between her and her father. She also blamed Jenessa for their mother's death.

But sweet Ramey was always there for her. Ramey had become more like another sister than a friend to Jenessa. She had been raised by a single mother who had become an alcoholic and a recreational drug user over the years, making Ramey's home life miserable and sometimes dangerous. Jenessa often invited Ramey to come and hang out at her house, to spend the night most weekends, and the girl became like a third daughter in the family.

The thought of seeing Ramey again was a bright spot in an otherwise sad situation. Sara? Well, she'd have to see how that went.

After changing out of her suit, and into a comfortable pair of jeans and a t-shirt, Jenessa began packing. With no job and no way to make up the back rent, she crammed all her clothes into suitcases and every other thing she wanted to take with her into boxes.

She loaded her trunk and back seat with all the belongings she could fit, carefully setting a framed picture of her mother on the front seat beside her purse. The manager could have her old sofa, dining set, and well-worn bed—Jenessa wasn't coming back.

She filled the car's tank with gas and made sure the radiator was topped up with water before she hit the road. Relieved that her car started when she turned the key, she looked over at the picture of her mother and brushed her fingers gently over it. Her mother was of Mexican descent, and the photo drew attention to her short dark hair and warm brown eyes.

Jenessa shot a glance to her own image in the rearview mirror and smiled—she loved that she had her mother's espresso-colored hair.

"I'm coming home, Momma."

Over the next couple of hours, as she drove on the busy highway, Jenessa thought about her father. As a child, she remembered thinking how tall and strong he looked. He was six three, slender build, with dark blond hair and pale green eyes. Aunt Renee had the same golden hair and green eyes, which had been passed down to Sara, as well.

Though Jenessa had inherited her mother's beautiful dark hair, she had her father's light eyes. When she was a little girl, her dad used to tell her they were the color of her August birthstone, the peridot.

Flying down the highway, Jenessa's thoughts wrapped around memories of their family trips to fun places in San Francisco—the aquarium in Golden Gate Park, boating and fishing in the bay, and eating crab out of cups from the street vendors at Fisherman's Wharf. David Jones had been a good father, and they were a happy family—at least back in those days.

"Oh, Dad," she sighed, "why did we ever have to move to Hidden Valley?"

As she passed the second exit into Stockton, a chill rippled over her and she fought back the tears that were beginning to blur her vision. It was at this spot on the highway that her mother had died. The week after Christmas, her mom had come to Sacramento to visit her and to bring her Christmas gifts. Jenessa had gone to Hidden Valley for Thanksgiving that year, and it had not gone well with her father, so she'd refused to come down for Christmas.

After staying a couple of days with her daughter, Lydia Jones had headed back home. A thick fog had settled into the valley that afternoon and Jenessa's mother ended up in the middle of a twenty-car pileup. The police report had said she'd died immediately upon impact, her small SUV crushed between two semi-trucks.

The news had devastated Jenessa. She *was* to blame. If she hadn't been so stiff-necked, if she had given in to her mother's request to spend Christmas in Hidden Valley, she would still be alive. If only she could turn the clock back and undo it. But if she could do that, she would turn the clock back more than twelve years and undo it all.

As soon as she'd received word of her mother's death, Jenessa had left work and raced to Hidden Valley. She went to her parents' house first, expecting to stay there, hoping to make amends with her father, but he didn't want her there. He asked her to stay at Aunt Renee's house, which she did. Tonight, though, she would stay at her family home, and he wouldn't be there to turn her away.

Why did he have to shun her and treat her like the bad girl? Sara did things equally as bad—or worse—she just never got caught.

Her father's disappointment built a wall between them, bricks laid in place with each harsh word, each disapproving glare. His behavior seemed warm and caring toward Sara, and he treated Ramey like she was part of the family, but not Jenessa, never her, not since she was seventeen.

For heaven's sake, it was just one mistake—why couldn't he have forgiven me?

No longer able to contain the tears, they stormed down her cheeks.

~*~

Jenessa breathed deeply and dried her tears, but her mind continued to race over the events of the past, including the few years she'd spent in Hidden Valley. As she passed the city-limits sign coming into town, a siren blared behind her. She glanced up into her rearview mirror and noticed a police car following her closely with its blue-and-red lights flashing.

She pulled her car over to the side of the road. Had she been so deep in thought that she hadn't noticed the drop in speed limit or how fast she was going?

Pushing the button in the door, she rolled the two front windows down, feeling the summer heat pour in from outside. She turned the engine off and rummaged through the glove compartment for her insurance and registration, fished her license out of her wallet, and waited for the officer.

"License, registration, and insurance, ma'am," a deep male voice said.

She handed them all over to him, too embarrassed to make eye contact.

"Your license says Jenessa Jones."

"That's right," she replied, looking up at him, shading her eyes with her hand. The bright sun was just over his shoulder, making it hard to make out his face.

The tall officer crouched down beside the car so his head was at window level. "I used to know a Jenessa Jones in high school. Could that be you?"

Jenessa looked over at the man as he pulled his sunglasses off. He did look vaguely familiar, but she hadn't been in high school for a long time, and teenagers have a tendency to change as they grow up. Surely she would have remembered someone as handsome as this guy if they had gone to school together.

"I'm sorry, it's been a lot of years since I've seen anyone from high school. You do look familiar, though," she said, more to be polite than anything else. "What's your name?"

"Are you kidding? It's me, Michael Baxter."

"Michael?" She hoped her surprise didn't show. He didn't look like this in high school. They had been friends, both of them working on the school newspaper, but back then he was gangly and awkward with braces and pimples all over his face. He wasn't as tall or as well built as he was now, that's for sure, not to mention the clear skin and straight teeth. "I'm sorry I didn't recognize you, you've changed so much."

"Well, you haven't. Pretty as ever."

"Not fair, you got to look at my driver's license."

"Fair enough, but I think I still would have recognized you. Those green eyes are hard to forget."

Was he flirting with her?

"What's it been? Ten or twelve years?" he asked.

"Twelve."

"What are you doing back in town?"

"My dad just died." The words caught in her throat.

"Oh, man, I'm sorry to hear that. He seemed like a nice guy. Attorney in town, right?"

"Yes, he was. Thanks for saying that, but I really need to get going. Are you going to give me a ticket?"

"Since it's you, Jen, and you seem to have a pretty good reason for not watching your speedometer, I'll let you off with a warning." His gaze met hers and lingered for a moment. "I'd love to catch up while you're in town. Maybe I'll see you around." He handed back her license and other items.

She accepted them and nodded. "Yeah, maybe."

He put a hand on the door, pulled himself up and walked back to his car. She watched him in her side mirror. That was really her old high school friend Michael Baxter? She rolled her windows up and turned on the air conditioner full blast, wondering what he'd been doing with himself for all these years. College no doubt, and obviously he became a policeman at some point.

The heaviness of regret settled on her, thinking about how she'd lost contact with all of her friends from high school, all except Ramey. Since she couldn't change what had happened and had no reason to return to Sacramento now, it was best not to replay the past over and over in her mind. Her future, whatever it would be, lay in the town straight ahead of her. Hidden Valley would be home for now, and the thought that she might run into Michael again sometime spread a hopeful smile across her face.

As promised, Jenessa phoned Aunt Renee to let her know she was almost there. But before heading to her aunt's house she decided to stop by The Sweet Spot, a popular bakery and café, to see if Ramey and Sara might still be there.

Ramey and Jenessa's mother had opened The Sweet Spot six years ago. Her mother had gone to culinary school while her dad had begun his law practice in San Francisco, before they started having babies. Her mother loved to bake and became an expert pastry chef. She never worked for anyone else, but she would whip up the most delicious treats for her husband's clients, filling gift baskets with delectable goodies or making a fabulous cake for a partner's birthday. Often people from the firm would ask her to make something spectacular for one of their client parties, which she loved doing.

As Ramey spent more and more time at the Jones's house, Jenessa's mother began teaching her about pastries, cakes, breads, and cookies. Jenessa and Sara never seemed that interested in baking, so her mother was thrilled to share her passion with Ramey.

After Ramey graduated from high school, and her alcoholic mother ran off with her latest boyfriend, she and Jenessa's mother spent more and more time in the kitchen. Eventually, they came up with the idea of opening a bakery together.

Her dad had tried his best to discourage them. He wasn't pleased that his wife wanted to work, afraid the community would get the idea he wasn't able to support his family—at least that's what her mother had told her. Eventually, he gave in to their pleadings and The Sweet Spot Bakery and Café was born.

As Jenessa drove into town, she eyed the quaint stores and shops that lined Main Street. Sure, there was a Costco and a Wal-Mart out by the freeway, not far from the university, but downtown Hidden Valley was as pristine and charming as she remembered it. The Sweet Spot sat on a corner with small tables and chairs arranged outside under the pink-and-white striped awning with the name printed in black script across it.

Jenessa pulled into a diagonal parking spot in front of the shop and went inside.

"Oh, my gosh, Jenessa!" Ramey exclaimed with a broad smile, her blue eyes wide and her red curls bouncing around her neck. She came around from behind the counter and threw her arms around her friend. "I'm so glad to see you."

Ramey stood a couple of inches taller than Jenessa's slender five-foot-five-inch frame and had a good twenty pounds on her.

Jenessa returned the hug. She had been so lonesome in the big city, trying to make it on her own, that she almost didn't want to let go.

"Isn't it the worst thing in the world? Your dad passing away?" Ramey gushed, her voice cracking with sadness. "I'm so, so sorry."

"Thank you, Ramey." Jenessa patted her friend's back. He had been like a father to Ramey, as well. "I know he thought of you as part of our family."

"Aww." Ramey released Jenessa and wiped a few tears from under her eyes, then took a deep breath. "Well, we were just about to close for the day. Sara has already gone over to Aunt Renee's. They're expecting you."

Sara had been doing the books for her mom and Ramey part-time after they opened the business, but since her mother's passing, she had left her full-time job to take a more active role in running the place.

"I was headed there next," Jenessa replied.

Like Jenessa, Sara had gone to college after high school, but she was considerably more interested in boys and partying than she was in getting an education. So, she'd decided after two years she'd had enough. She got her Associates Degree in Business and called it good. She had worked as a bank teller and then became the bookkeeper for a general contractor in the area. But since her mother's death, The Sweet Spot had become her main focus.

"Why don't you start on over and I'll meet you all as soon as I'm done here." Ramey lowered her voice. "I guess I should have closed the minute we got word, but since I'm not *really* family, I thought I'd give them some time alone."

"You're just like family." Jenessa draped an arm around her friend again.

The little bells jingled as the front door opened and Ramey looked past Jenessa to see the next customer. "Sorry, but we're about to close."

"I just wanted a coffee to go."

I know that voice. Jenessa stiffened and her heartbeat quickened. Hoping she was wrong, she slowly turned around.

Standing before her was a tall, thirty-year-old man with wavy blond hair and piercing blue eyes.

"Jenessa?"

She swallowed down the lump that had risen into her throat, seeing that his broad shoulders and engaging smile were just as she had remembered them.

CHAPTER 2

"LOGAN."

It had been a long time since Jenessa had seen her old boyfriend and he had grown into quite a handsome man.

He spread his arms out and stepped toward her.

She let him give her a quick hug, wondering if he could feel her stiffness. She remembered the tears she had spilled on the drive down and hoped her makeup wasn't smeared all down her face. It had been years since she had seen him, and this was not the way she wanted to run into her ex again.

"I heard about your dad and I'm so sorry," Logan said.

"You already heard?" Ramey asked.

"He was my father's attorney," he replied, his brilliant blue eyes still on Jenessa. "My dad phoned me a little while ago about it. I wondered if you'd be back in town."

"You didn't think I'd come for my dad's funeral?" Jenessa snapped.

"Well, I know you two didn't exactly get along."

"No thanks to you," she huffed.

"You know, Ramey," Logan raised his gaze to the redhead, "I think I'll take a rain check on that coffee." He backed toward the door, shifting his attention again to Jenessa. "I am truly sorry about your dad." He turned and stepped outside.

Jenessa watched through the large storefront windows as he walked down the street and out of sight. That wasn't the way she had envisioned running into her old flame. She had played the scene repeatedly in her mind over the years—what she would say, what he would say, what she would be wearing and looking fabulous in. Not that she wanted him back. Rather, she wanted him to want *her* back, to feel some of the pain he had caused her back then.

It all seemed so silly now. They had been high school sweethearts, little more than children at the time. She shook her head at the thought. He had obviously moved on, probably dated a long string of gorgeous coeds in college and now had some other lovely creature in his life.

"What was that about?" Ramey arched an eyebrow at her.

Jenessa turned away from the window. "I don't know. I didn't think I'd have that reaction the first time I ran into him. Just hearing his voice somehow dredged up our dirty past."

"After all this time?"

"Yeah. Crazy, huh." Jenessa grimaced.

"Well, I'm sure he'll forget about it. Things will be better the next time you see him."

She peered up into Ramey's smiling eyes. Her friend was always the optimist. "Maybe."

Ramey walked back behind the counter. "I need to close up. Why don't you head over to Aunt Renee's and let her know I'm right behind you."

Jenessa loved her aunt Renee. With her mother gone, Aunt Renee had tried to step in as the buffer between Jenessa and her father whenever she could. But her aunt was not all sugar, she could sometimes be rather spicy and a bit pushy, believing she always knew what was best for everyone, and she wasn't shy about letting them know.

Jenessa moved to the door. "Okay, see you over there."

~*~

Jenessa pulled into the long driveway in front of Aunt Renee's stately home on Monte Vista Drive, a neighborhood overflowing with large and expensive homes built in a bygone era. She rolled her windows down, and her little car sputtered a few times after she turned the engine off. Parked in the shade of the tall trees that divided the properties, she hoped there was nothing among the boxed possessions in her old Toyota that would melt in the sizzling July heat.

She crossed the front lawn and stood before the two-story red brick Georgian with its crisp white trim and black shutters. Almost as soon as she pushed the doorbell, the wide black door swung open.

Her sister flung her arms around Jenessa and sobbed on her shoulder. "I'd almost given up on you," Sara said. "What took you so long?"

"I'm happy to see you too," Jenessa responded.

"Come inside, girls," she could hear their aunt calling from somewhere inside the house. "You're letting all the heat in."

Sara stepped aside to let Jenessa in and followed her down the wide hallway. Passing the grand staircase, they continued down the hall with its dark, polished hardwood floors, an array of family photos and artwork strategically hung on both sides. Aunt Renee sat on a barstool at the breakfast bar with a slab granite countertop that enclosed half of the expansive, newly renovated kitchen.

As the girls approached, Aunt Renee slid off the stool and opened her arms to Jenessa, pulling her into a firm embrace. Jenessa noticed Aunt Renee's lower mascara was smudged a little and her pale green eyes were rimmed with red.

"I can't believe he's gone," her aunt said in little more than a whisper. She released Jenessa and dabbed at the side of her eyes with a white handkerchief.

"I didn't know he had anything wrong with his heart. He seemed so healthy to me." Although, Jenessa had to admit, she hadn't seen the man for quite some time.

"He had a pretty stressful job," Sara said, "working for that Grey Alexander. Seems like Daddy was always having to clean up his messes."

Daddy? Jenessa hadn't called him that since she was a kid, but then, he and Sara had a different relationship than she'd had with her father. A twinge of jealousy pricked her heart.

"It was a long drive," Jenessa said. "Mind if I freshen up?"

"Sure, sweetie, you know your way to the powder room." Aunt Renee delicately blew her nose.

Jenessa closed the door to the half-bath and stood before the mirror. She had spilled her tears for her father on the drive down and no more threatened to come at the moment. She wondered if Ramey, Sara, and Aunt Renee might think she didn't care—there was certainly no shortage of tears between the three of them. Yes, she mourned her father's passing, but she also grieved for what could have been between them. At the moment, she simply felt numb.

After drawing in a long breath, she exhaled slowly, feeling some of her stress leaving with the air as it passed through her lips. She ran her fingers through her hair, wiped clean the bit of mascara that had bled under her eyes, and applied a fresh coat of lip gloss. The fading redness in the whites of her eyes made the green more intense, particularly against her dark hair.

As she stared at herself in the mirror, she thought about her unexpected run-in with Logan, but she quickly pushed him out of her thoughts. There was grieving to be done, funeral plans to be made, and decisions to be mulled over for what she would do with her future. Now was not the time to lament over lost love.

By the time she emerged from the powder room, Ramey had arrived. She and Sara were seated on the floral sofas in the great room with Aunt Renee, talking quietly, surrounded by a wall of french doors and whitepaned windows that overlooked the garden and pool area. The room had been added to the rear of the old house, off the new kitchen and breakfast area, in the latest remodeling project, Jenessa assumed.

Ramey raised her head in Jenessa's direction as she walked in. "If you're hungry, I brought some muffins and bagels that didn't sell today. They're still fresh."

"Thanks." Jenessa grabbed a plump cinnamon bagel out of the paper bakery bag and joined the others. She kicked off her flip-flops and tucked her feet under her as she dropped down onto a sage-green overstuffed chair nestled next to one of the sofas. "Did anyone see Dad's body?"

"I did," Aunt Renee replied. "Since he was already gone when the paramedics arrived, they took his body to the morgue. The medical examiner recognized him and knew I was David's sister—his wife is on a couple of charities with me—so he phoned me."

"What do we do now?" Sara asked, her eyes moist and red from crying.

"Does anyone know what Dad wanted, in terms of a funeral or cremation?" Jenessa tore off a piece of marbled bagel and stuck it in her mouth.

"We hadn't talked about it," Aunt Renee said. "I assume he wrote his last wishes down somewhere. Attorneys are like that, you know."

Jenessa swallowed and cleared her throat. "I'll look through his office at the house."

"Are you staying there?" Sara asked.

"That was the plan."

"I thought you might want to stay here," Aunt Renee offered. "Are you sure you want to be in that big old house all alone?"

"I think it'll do me good to go through his things. I'll see if I can find his Will and his burial instructions."

"How long can you stay, Jenessa?" Ramey asked.

"As long as I need to."

"What about your job?" Sara asked. "Won't they expect you back after a few days?"

Jenessa hesitated. She hadn't wanted to tell anyone, but now was as good a time as any. "Not really. I got laid off a few weeks back. I've been job hunting, but no luck yet."

"So the timing is perfect," Aunt Renee said. "I hope you'll stay in Hidden Valley for a long time, hon. We've missed you. Haven't we girls?"

Ramey quickly agreed. Sara shrugged.

"And speaking of perfect timing," Ramey leaned over and patted Jenessa's knee, "just last week I heard that the Hidden Valley Herald is looking for a reporter. Maybe you should go down and apply."

She did need a job. Even though, career-wise, taking a position at a small-town paper would be a step backward from the Sacramento job, her mother always told her that beggars can't be choosers.

"Maybe I should wait a few days, until we work out the funeral arrangements and all." Jenessa had hoped to settle in and get used to the small-town life again before going out and trying to find another job.

"I wouldn't put it off," Aunt Renee countered. "The job could be gone by then. If you're out of work, you need to strike while the iron's hot."

Beggars can't be choosers? Strike while the iron's hot? Where did the older generation come up with all these sayings?

Jenessa pulled another piece of bagel off and chewed on it. She really couldn't afford to be choosy. Earlier that morning she had been willing to clean toilets for cash. How bad could a small-town newspaper be?

It would put some money in her bank account, which was in dire need of an infusion, and maybe she could finally fix that bucket of bolts she drove. With her family home empty now, she had a place to live rent-free, at least for a while. This job, if they hired her, would give her time to think about what she might do with the rest of her life.

With all eyes on her, eagerly awaiting her answer, she relented. "All right, I'll go down and apply tomorrow."

"And you won't have to worry about running into Logan again," Ramey said. "He works at his father's real estate office, not the newspaper."

Aunt Renee's eyes lit up. "Run into Logan again?"

"Tell us more," Sara chimed in, sounding more surprised than interested. "When did you see Logan?"

"It was nothing, really." Jenessa didn't want to discuss Logan with them, or with anyone for that matter. "He stopped by The Sweet Spot as Ramey was closing up and then he left."

"Just like that?" Sara sounded like she didn't believe her sister.

Ramey leaned forward. "It was more like Jenessa ran him off."

"Oh, dear girl," Aunt Renee sighed. "You can't stay in this town and not run into Logan Alexander. You'd better make peace with him or you'll surely make yourself miserable."

Her aunt was right, but she didn't want to talk about it. Her initial reaction to running into Logan was so visceral that it knocked her off balance, emotionally. She hadn't meant to bite his head off. That wasn't how their first meeting was supposed to go, at least not in the hundred times she had replayed it in her mind during the first few years following their break up.

After a while she had managed to think of him less and less, until the last couple of years she hadn't thought of him at all—until today. She'd have to figure out a way to be in that man's presence without going ballistic.

"Can we *pu-leeze* change the subject?" Jenessa begged, popping the last of the bagel into her mouth.

~*~

As the afternoon flowed into the early evening, Aunt Renee ordered take-out from a local restaurant that specialized in fresh and organic food, requesting that they deliver the meals, which was not their usual custom. But Renee Giraldy could be convincing, and after promising a sizeable tip, her doorbell soon rang with her delivery.

Sara and Ramey unpacked the food and set plates and glasses out on the casual dining table between the kitchen and the great room. As Aunt Renee filled a crystal pitcher with water and ice, Jenessa grabbed the napkins and utensils and set the table. Each did their part and dinner came together like clockwork.

Jenessa enjoyed the meal with her family, something she had not done in a very long time. Even though it was not under the best of circumstances, it felt warm and comfortable—a far cry from the years of eating frozen meals out of the microwave, alone in her apartment, sometimes consuming them over the kitchen sink or grabbing bites while working on a story on her laptop.

She had concentrated on her education, and then on her work. She hadn't taken the time to make many friends in Sacramento, even among her co-workers at the newspaper, focusing more on her job as an investigative reporter. Working her way up from covering weddings and social events, she had proven her ability to write and to dig for the truth while producing compelling human-interest stories.

And as pretty as she was, Jenessa had shied away from getting too deeply involved in romantic relationships—not in college and not after. She had dated a number of men over the years, but as soon as she noticed they were getting serious, she found some way to demolish the relationship.

She had given her heart to one man, Logan Alexander, and it had turned into a disaster. For her own emotional protection, whether purposely or subconsciously, she protected herself from going through anything like that again.

When she was seventeen, Jenessa had loved Logan so completely, so intensely, she'd thought she might burn up and disappear in a cloud of smoke. And he had loved her, or at least he'd said he did. But he broke her heart and ruined her life, and she didn't ever want to feel that way again.

Coming home to Hidden Valley, would she finally be ready to open her heart to another man?

~*~

Dinner was almost over. Aunt Renee brought another pitcher of ice water to the table and offered to pour.

"No more for me," Jenessa said. She finished her Caesar salad with grilled chicken and sourdough rolls and couldn't remember when anything had tasted so good. "I should get going pretty soon. I want to go through Dad's desk and his filing cabinet before I go to bed. Maybe I can find his funeral and burial instructions."

Sara and Ramey decided they would stay over at Aunt Renee's so none of them would have to be alone that night.

Ramey was single, having not married yet. Actually, she had hardly dated, but she remained hopeful and optimistic. Jenessa always thought what Ramey lacked in beauty she made up for in sweetness and charm.

At the moment, Sara was single too. She was usually kind, always beautiful and carefree, blessed with dark honey-colored hair and familial soft green eyes, looking more like Aunt Renee than she did her own mother. She was a little shorter than Jenessa, with a slim, petite build.

Sara had married at twenty-one and, much to her parents' dismay, she was divorced by twenty-three. In the last couple of years, she'd had a string of boyfriends, but as far as Jenessa knew, none of them were serious.

Jenessa stood. "I think I should be going." She was looking forward to staying the night, alone, at her parents' home. She didn't mind the solitude—she was used to it. In fact, she was a little excited to get busy digging through her Dad's office, hoping to find more than just his final wishes.

After saying her good-byes to the girls and giving hugs all around, she left her aunt's home and drove her bucket of bolts to her parents' house. It was located a couple of blocks from the high school, in a neighborhood of well-kept, upscale, older homes. Although it didn't rival the grandeur of Aunt Renee's neighborhood, it was beautiful nonetheless.

As Jenessa drove past her old school, she swore she saw a vision of herself with Logan, sitting on the front steps, holding hands. He was wearing his letterman jacket as the football team's star quarterback. The big fish in a small pond.

The school had stood in that spot since the nineteen forties. It was two stories of faded red brick with ornate detailing and beige stonework arching over the main entrance, and it sat perched atop several rows of stone steps. There were broad lawns out front, with tall evergreen trees, and in the center of the main walkway to the heavy wooden front doors there was a circular fountain, with thick masonry for seating.

Her family had moved to Hidden Valley at the beginning of her sophomore year, which felt like a lifetime ago now. Although she had noticed Logan not long after changing to her new school—he was hard to miss—they hadn't begun dating until the fall of her junior year. He was a grade ahead of her in school and would be graduating, then heading off to college on a football scholarship.

She had been busy working on the school newspaper, realizing early on how much she enjoyed writing and pursuing a story. It was that year that she decided to major in journalism when she went to college.

In the spring, he asked her to the prom. It was like a fairytale. Her mother had taken her to the city a few weeks before the dance and they had shopped for just the right gown, a strapless number, pale pink and flowing. Mom had paid for Jenessa to have her hair done, swept up with curls cascading down the back and a few wispy tendrils falling loosely around her face. Logan showed up to her house, handsomely dressed in a black tuxedo and bow tie with a gorgeous corsage of deep pink roses for her wrist.

Her mother had the camera out and was all smiles as she excitedly insisted on several photos of the couple before she would let them leave. Jenessa remembered her father had stood in the background, watching quietly.

The memory dissolved as she reached her old home and pulled into the driveway. The house was English Tudor style and had been built not long after the high school. Before her parents acquired it, the previous owners had done a total updating of the kitchen and bathrooms, even going as far as having all of the hardwood floors beautifully refinished.

She recalled the day they'd moved in, her father smugly commenting that it was a fitting home for a successful attorney. That phrase always stuck with her— *a fitting home*.

After turning her key in the lock, she pushed the quaint arched-top door open. It was midsummer, so the sun would not be setting for another hour or so and she was glad for the light that streamed in the windows, not to mention thankful the air conditioning was on.

Jenessa dragged her suitcase and carry-on bag up the stairs to her old bedroom. It was just the way she had left it the last time she was there, except for the layer of dust. When her mother was alive, she dusted and vacuumed and put fresh sheets on the bed when her daughter was coming home for a visit. It was clear no one had set foot in this room since her death.

After retrieving a clean set of sheets from the hall linen closet, Jenessa set about making up the bed. As for the dusting and vacuuming, she decided she'd leave them for the morning. She was anxious to get to her father's office downstairs and start going through his papers. The thought of it brought a surprising rush of tears.

She slunk down onto her bed and wiped them away with her fingers. Her dad was gone. The finality of it saddened her. There would be no more confrontations, no more cold shoulders, and no more chances to make amends.

The sun had almost set by the time she came downstairs. She flicked on a few lights as she meandered through the house, coming to rest at her father's large antique desk. An eerie sensation rippled over her, like she was sitting there without his permission and somehow he would know.

Jenessa shuddered and shook off the feeling. She pulled out one of the deep side drawers and rummaged through it, peering into the folders and hanging files. Then she searched the second drawer. Nothing of value there.

She tugged on the center lap drawer, but it was locked. She glanced around. Where was the key?

It hadn't occurred to her before, but she wondered now where his personal effects were—his clothes, his wallet, his keys. Was his car still parked in the lot next to his law office?

She made a notation on a yellow sticky note to find out about these things first thing in the morning. Perhaps Aunt Renee had recovered them when she went down to the coroner's office.

There were several small, framed photos set on the corner of his desk. One had the entire family, before they'd relocated to Hidden Valley. The other two were individual school pictures of her and her sister after their move. She was a little surprised to see her picture there among the others. Had he really wanted to see her face every day?

She half-expected to see Ramey's photo on his desk as well, but no.

Next, she turned her attention to the four-drawer file cabinet that sat in the corner, to the right of the large window that held a view of the manicured backyard. She painstakingly went through the top two drawers, file by file, page by page, but no luck.

It was getting late and she was ready to turn in for the night. Exhausted, Jenessa dropped down into her father's executive chair again and her gaze floated around the room. She leaned back against the black leather and picked up the faint scent of his aftershave. Then, she ran her hands over his leather desk blotter. He had spent so many hours in this room and she sensed his presence.

Tears moistened her eyes once more, then trickled down her cheeks. She would never see his face again, or have the opportunity to make right what had gone so terribly wrong. With her head in her hands she sat in his office and sobbed.

When no more tears came, she flicked the desk lamp off and walked out. After turning off all the lights in the house, except in the central hallway, she slowly climbed the stairs to her room. Tomorrow she would tackle the other two drawers in the office, but first she had to apply for the reporter job and check on her father's personal effects.

After stripping out of her clothes and tugging a short nightgown over her head, she pulled off her watch and gold hoop earrings, opening the top drawer of her dresser to store them. Something scraped along the drawer as she opened it.

That's odd. Sticking her hand into the far back and upper part of the drawer, her fingers touched what felt like a stiff piece of paper. She worked it loose, trying not to rip it, and pulled it out.

A knot grew in her throat as she turned it over and saw what it was. She could hardly swallow. The hidden paper was a picture of her and Logan on prom night, one of the photos her mother had taken. She thought she had destroyed those photos, along with anything else that reminded her of him.

How long had that picture been wedged at the back of that drawer? She threw the photo back in the drawer and slammed it shut. She should have thrown it in the trash, but it had survived this many years, one more day wouldn't matter.

She pulled the covers back, clicked off the lamp, and climbed in bed. Exhaling a long breath, she laid back against her pillow. Closing her eyes, she hoped for sleep.

Why did she have to find that photo of Logan right before she went to bed? All it did was get her blood boiling. She pulled the blankets over her head and let out a long, loud sigh.

She had tried for the last twelve years to forget that pompous, self-centered, sorry-excuse-for-a-man. Now, she would probably dream about him.

CHAPTER 3

THE BRIGHT MORNING SUN streaming in through the bedroom window woke Jenessa with a start as she opened her eyes and got her bearings. She rolled over and looked at the clock, deciding she'd better get up. She could hear her father's voice in her head, telling her there was too much to do to laze around after seven o'clock.

She had been right last night. Seeing the old prom photo of her and Logan had caused her to toss and turn for hours, replaying in her mind the good times, and the bad. True to life, her dreams of Logan had always ended with the bad.

Sliding her legs over the side of the bed, she stumbled down the stairs and into the kitchen. Still groggy and bleary-eyed, Jenessa managed to make herself a pot of coffee. She would need it to look alert when she approached the managing editor of the town's newspaper.

Rather than call him, because it would be too easy for him to brush her off, she decided she'd show up in person, a friendly smile on her face and her resume in her hand. She would sell him on her virtues and why they needed to hire her.

Once she got her first cup of the day, she wandered into her father's office. She paused again at the photos. Had he really wanted her picture on his desk, or had her mother framed all the photos and stuck them in an orderly fashion, facing him from the corner of his desk, trying to remind him he had *two* daughters? She guessed it was more likely the latter.

There were two file drawers still to go through in the hopes of discovering his burial wishes. They needed to find out soon because the coroner's office would want to know where to send the body, and then there were arrangements to be made. It wasn't like when her mother died. Her mother had made it clear to her husband and her daughters what she wanted when she died—to be buried in the town cemetery under a big elm tree that would give shade to her family when they came to visit her.

Midway through her task, at quarter to eight, Jenessa received a call from her aunt.

"Any luck?" Aunt Renee asked.

"Not yet. I've still got one more drawer to go through. Then there's the lap drawer. It's locked and I don't know where the key is. Do you?"

"No, haven't a clue, hon."

"Sorry, Aunt Renee, but I may have to bust into it."

"Oh, sweet girl, no! That desk is an antique. Why don't we check with your dad's attorney? I'm certain he had someone draw up his Will."

"I haven't found anything yet, but knowing my father, I'm sure he would have too. Probably one of the lawyers in his firm."

"Do you want me to call and talk to his secretary?" Aunt Renee offered. "She probably knows."

"I'm headed down to the newspaper later this morning to apply for that job. Why don't I drop by the office and see what I can dig up in person."

"All right, hon. Come by after you're done. Sara and I will be here. We'll want to hear all about your interview."

"Where's Ramey?"

"She's gone, down to The Sweet Spot. She's always there before five, baking and opening up the shop. Sara's not going in today, though. She's staying here with me."

Stopping at The Sweet Spot to see Ramey sounded good, not to mention a delicious cup of coffee and a fresh cinnamon roll. "I've got to go and get ready. I'll let you know if I find out anything."

~*~

After slipping into a black pencil skirt and white silk top, Jenessa headed down to The Sweet Spot. Her mouth watered just thinking about Ramey's decadent cinnamon rolls.

She found a place to park near the café and breezed through the door. An older woman, with her dark hair pulled back into a bun, stood behind the counter with Ramey, waiting on several customers.

When Ramey caught sight of Jenessa, she smiled broadly and her eyes lit up. "Hey, you!" Her face reflected the joy at seeing her old friend again. "Be with you in a sec."

Jenessa took her place in line and waited her turn, watching as the two women expertly served their customers.

"I'm glad you stopped in. What can I get for you?" Ramey asked when Jenessa got to the front of the line.

"Busy place." Jenessa glanced around the small shop.

"Yes, it is—thankfully."

"Can I get a mocha-cappuccino and a cinnamon roll?"

"Absolutely." Ramey leaned forward and lowered her voice. "If you can wait for a bit, the crowd'll die down and we can talk."

"Sure, I'll grab a table if there's one free."

Ramey gestured to the right. "Over in the corner. Grab it and I'll bring your order out." Then her gaze went to the next person in line. "Good morning, Officer."

Officer? Jenessa whirled around with a smile, wondering if Ramey was greeting their old friend, Michael. Hope dissolved when she saw it was a middle-aged uniformed patrolman she didn't recognize. He met her gaze and her cheeks warmed. "I'll just go sit down now."

As she stepped away, Michael walked through the door. "Jenessa?"

"Michael." Before she could help it, a grin spread across her face. "Nice to see you again. I was just about to grab a table. Would you like to join me?"

"Can't. My partner and I are only here to pick up some coffee and—"

"Donuts?" She chuckled, arching a brow at him.

"Stereotyping us cops?" He grinned back at her. "Actually, coffee and a breakfast cookie."

"Uh-huh." She wasn't convinced.

"They're amazing—healthy too. You should try one."

"I know. My mom used to make them for us when we were growing up."

"Oh, I forgot." He looked a little embarrassed. "Your mom used to run this place."

She nodded. "She and Ramey."

"By the way," he began, "I wanted to offer my condolences again. Your father was a good man."

"Thank you. Yes he was."

"After the funeral and all," Michael continued, "if you're sticking around town for a while, why don't we get together? Have dinner or something. I'd love to catch up."

"Hey, Baxter!" his partner called from the doorway.

Michael's gaze shifted to the other officer.

"I've got the stuff," his partner said. "Now, we've got to get going."

Michael looked back at Jenessa and raised his eyebrows, apparently waiting for an answer.

"Yeah, sure. I'd like that," she said. "Give me a call."

He smiled and gave a casual wave as he strolled out the door.

Through the window, she watched her old friend and his partner climb into their cruiser. *Shoot, I never gave him my phone number!*

"Oh well." Jenessa shrugged, hoping to run into him again as she watched as them drive away. She took a seat at the small table in the corner and waited for Ramey.

"Here we are." Ramey set the coffee and cinnamon roll down in front of her, then sank down on the chair opposite Jenessa. "Did you talk to Aunt Renee this morning?"

"Yes, she phoned me." Jenessa took a small sip of the hot coffee. She explained that she hadn't found her father's burial instructions yet and she was headed to his office, after stopping in at the newspaper to inquire about the reporter position.

"Charles McAllister is the person you want to see at the paper," Ramey said. "He was in here last week talking about the position being open, asking if I knew anyone who might be interested. I didn't at the time, but now..." She gestured toward Jenessa.

"Thanks for the tip. After I finish this scrumptious cinnamon roll, I'll head over there."

"Well, I'd better get back to work," Ramey said. "I probably shouldn't have come in today, maybe stayed with Sara and Aunt Renee, but I needed to keep busy. Besides, somebody had to do the baking this morning and help Rosie with the morning rush." Ramey smiled wistfully, then stood. "I'll leave you to your breakfast."

~*~

The bright summer sunlight bounced off the sidewalk as Jenessa stood outside of the newspaper office, smoothing her fitted skirt and running her hand lightly over her hair. She pulled in a quick breath and plastered a big smile on her face before pushing the glass door open. Wanting to dazzle Mr. McAllister with her experience and her wit, she hoped he couldn't smell the scent of desperation on her. She needed this job, badly.

She waltzed into the building and up to the receptionist's desk. "I'd like to see Mr. Charles McAllister, please."

"Do you have an appointment?" The gray-haired woman peered over the top of her glasses.

"No, sorry. I'm here about the reporter job."

"I see." The woman raised a wrinkled finger, signaling for her to wait a moment. She picked up the phone receiver and punched a few buttons on the console. "What is your name, dear?"

"Jenessa Jones."

The elderly receptionist turned her attention back to the phone. "There's a young lady here to see you about the reporter job. Says her name is Jenessa Jones." The receptionist paused, listening to the response on the other end of the line. "All right."

She slowly hung up the receiver and brought her gaze back to Jenessa. "Please, have a seat and Mr. McAllister will be out in a few minutes." The woman pointed toward a small cluster of chairs against the opposite wall.

Jenessa did her best to smile sweetly at the woman, wondering how long she had been with the newspaper—from its opening, perhaps. "Thank you."

She took a seat, and a few minutes turned into thirty before Charles McAllister emerged from his office and strolled up the hallway to the reception area. He was a tall, average-looking man, late thirties maybe, with thick, medium-brown hair and hazel eyes. "Ms. Jones?" he asked.

Jenessa stood and took his extended hand.

"Charles McAllister," he said, smiling and giving her hand a light shake. "I heard you're here about the reporter job?"

"Yes. Do you have a few minutes?" She offered him her resume.

Taking it, he did a cursory review of it. "Sure, why don't you come back to my office?" He turned and began to walk away. "Alice, hold my calls, please."

Jenessa followed him, close behind, down a hall lined with small offices. There was a large door at the end of the hall, which she assumed led to the printing area. Mr. McAllister stopped at the doorway to his office and ushered her in.

"Have a seat," he said, following her in, leaving the door ajar. He took his place behind a large desk that was covered with piles of paperwork, files, and stacking wire trays. He looked down at her resume again. "I thought I might hear from you today."

"You did?" That was odd. "How did you—"

"Your aunt. She phoned me first thing this morning, said you'd be coming in and I'd be a fool not to hire you."

"You know my aunt?"

"Everybody who's anybody in this town knows your aunt."

"Oh, I'm so sorry. I have to apologize for her—" Jenessa's cheeks flushed hot. She was more than a little embarrassed that her aunt had stuck her nose in the middle of things, but at this point, any extra help should be appreciated.

"No, don't be silly," he said with a slight wave of his hand. "We need someone, and, according to Mrs. Giraldy, you're a hard worker with lots of in-depth experience at a large newspaper."

"Yes, that's true, but don't forget I was once the assistant editor of the Hidden Valley High School paper."

He looked at her oddly, then laughed. "I see you have a sense of humor, too. That'll come in handy."

Jenessa wasn't sure what to make of that last statement. "Sorry?"

"You'll have your hands full with a myriad of stories. Of course you'll cover the police beat, although it's not like what you've been used to in Sacramento. Yes, there has been a slight increase of crime in Hidden Valley, with the times being what they are, but it isn't as glamorous as the big city stuff you're used to. You'll mostly be covering weddings and social events, human-interest stories—things like that."

"If you don't mind my asking, who's been handling those things up until now?"

"Priscilla Mosely, but she's pregnant and the baby's due next month. As far as I know, she isn't planning to come back. I've been trying to take up the slack where I can, because she hasn't been able to work as many hours as she used to, but as you can see," he gestured with a broad sweep of his hand over his desk, "I have my own work to do. We've been looking for someone for the past couple of months, but we've had no takers. The pay isn't that great and the hours can be long."

"The long hours I'm used to. The pay, well, I'll adjust." Her mother's words, *beggars can't be choosers*, rang again in her ears.

"So, when can you start?"

Did he just offer me the job?

Jenessa leaned forward in her chair. "I don't know if you heard, but my father died yesterday."

"I did hear about that, David Jones, the attorney, right?"

"Yes." She sat back and loosely crossed her arms. "I wouldn't even have come in to see you today, with my father's passing and all the funeral arrangements to be made, but Aunt Renee urged me not to wait, in case the job got snapped up, right out from under me." Apparently it could have waited.

"Let me say that I am sorry for your loss, Miss Jones. I didn't know him personally, but your dad had a good reputation in town."

"Thank you for that. And please, call me Jenessa, especially if we're going to be working together."

"Jenessa, it is." His large black leather chair squeaked as he leaned back in it. "So, when do you think you can begin?"

"Let's see, today is Tuesday..." She worked through what had to be done, deciding that the funeral would likely be Friday or Saturday. "I'm guessing by next Monday."

"All right, but if you find your schedule frees up any sooner than that, please let me know. The news doesn't wait."

Exhilarated, Jenessa almost danced out of the newspaper offices. She got the job! *Finally, some income.*

Though she was grateful for her aunt's meddling—this time—she hoped it wasn't a harbinger of things to come.

~*~

Jenessa strolled a couple of blocks over to her father's law offices. She entered the grand foyer, admiring the polished, gray marble floors and ornate mahogany walls, and then took the elevator to the second level of the old two-story office building. She stepped off and was greeted by an attractive young woman, likely not long out of high school, seated behind the glistening granite reception counter. The names Jones and McCaffrey were emblazoned in bronze on the rich wood-paneled wall behind her.

"May I help you?" the young blonde inquired.

Jenessa confidently strode up to the counter. "Yes, I'm Jenessa Jones, David Jones's daughter."

"Oh, Miss Jones, I am so sorry about your dad. He was such a nice man. I was here when they—"

"Thank you," Jenessa interrupted. "Do you think I could speak with Mr. McCaffrey for a few minutes?"

"Sure. Let me see if he's available." She placed a phone call to his office, then turned her attention back to Jenessa as the main phone began to ring. "Yes, he can see you. Just down the hall and to the right." The young woman snatched up the phone again. "Jones and McCaffrey, how may I direct your call?"

Jenessa followed the woman's instructions and knocked on Mr. McCaffrey's door. She hadn't been to this place in quite a few years, but she remembered attending an open house launch party when the two men first went into business together and moved into these offices.

"Come in," she heard a deep male voice say. She opened the door and Mr. McCaffrey shot out of his chair, stepping toward her with his hand extended.

Dressed in a well-tailored suit, Ian McCaffrey was a bit older than her father, his hair mostly gray, but he appeared to be in good health and he had a strong grip.

"So good to see you again, Jenessa. I wish it was under better circumstances." His voice was warm and sounded sincere. "Here, have a seat." He nodded toward the two club chairs sitting opposite his desk before returning to his seat.

They sat and exchanged pleasantries and small talk for a few minutes before diving into the real reason she was there.

"I've searched Dad's home office for his burial instructions, but I haven't been able to find any. Would you know anything about that?"

"We have his Will here and there might be something in the file with it." He pushed the intercom button on his desk phone. "Kathleen, can you bring me the file for David Jones's estate plan?"

"Right away," the female voice answered over the speaker.

"Do you have any idea when the funeral might be?" he asked.

"Not yet. We'd like to find out what his wishes were before we give the coroner directions on where to release the body. That's why I'm here."

"By *we* I'm assuming you mean you and your sister?"

"Yes, and Aunt Renee."

"Ah, yes." His eyes lit up and a mischievous smile curled on his lips. "Renee Giraldy."

Jenessa wasn't sure what he meant by that. Had he had some kind of personal connection with her in the past? It wouldn't surprise her if he had.

"My guess is that the funeral will be Friday or Saturday," she said. "I'll let you know."

"How long are you staying in town?"

"Actually, I'm moving back. I got a job at the Hidden Valley Herald, and I'll be staying at my folks' house for a while."

His assistant knocked lightly, then entered with a folder that she handed to her boss.

"Thank you, Kathleen."

She walked out and quietly closed the door behind her.

He opened the folder on his massive cherry desk and stuck his glasses on. "Let's see." He flipped through a few pages and pulled out a document. "It says here he wants to be buried beside his wife. Apparently, he had already purchased the plot when he buried your mother."

Under the big elm tree.

He handed her the sheet of paper and she scanned over it. Everything was detailed from the coffin model to the church where her dad wanted the funeral service held, listing the pastor he had chosen to preside and the music he wished to be played. That had been her father, disciplined and orderly, carefully orchestrating his perfect, neat little life—including what would happen at the end of it.

"So considerate of him to think of everything," she said, her voice sounding a bit sarcastic. She hadn't meant for it to betray her underlying feelings.

Mr. McCaffrey frowned quizzically. "I know he didn't want you girls to be burdened with it," he said. "Oh, and by the way, his car is still in the parking lot."

"I thought it might be. As soon as I get the keys from the coroner's office, I'll come by and pick it up." She folded the paper and tucked it in her purse. "Is there anything else I should know?"

"Like what?"

"His finances. How can I find out if he's current on the house payments and car payments? You know, that sort of thing."

"Both the house and car are paid for, so no worries there. He was very disciplined—he hated owing anyone anything."

~*~

Once Jenessa left the law offices, she drove over to her aunt's house to share what she'd learned and to spend some time with her family. Sitting around the breakfast table, Sara and Aunt Renee were anxious to get the ball rolling on the arrangements.

Jenessa took a seat beside her aunt. After she explained what she had found out, Aunt Renee's shoulders dropped and her face seemed to relax, obviously relieved that her brother had left what was tantamount to step-by-step instructions.

"You haven't mentioned a word about your job interview, dear," Aunt Renee noted. "How did it go?"

"It went terrifically," she beamed. "I start on Monday."

"Oh, Jenessa, I knew you could do it," Aunt Renee gushed.

Jenessa rested a hand on her aunt's forearm. "You didn't warn me you were going to call ahead and lay the groundwork for me."

"I knew you'd tell me not to, and I wanted to help."

"I appreciate it, really," she said, pulling her hand back. "But I would like to think I could have gotten the job on my own."

"Of course you could have, dear, but there's nothing wrong with a little nudge from the right person. Nepotism goes a long way in this town."

"What do you mean?" Jenessa asked.

"You don't think Logan Alexander would be doing as well as he is without his father opening doors for him, do you?"

Jenessa thought about Grey Alexander, unquestionably the most powerful man in this town.

Besides having been the mayor not long ago, he was the president of one of the town's banks, as well as owning a real estate company, a mortgage company, and the Hidden Valley Herald. He had become her father's biggest client shortly after they moved to town, and now he was her employer. That last fact caught in her throat and made her cough.

"Are you okay, dear?"

Jenessa swallowed hard and crossed her arms. "I'm trying not to think of Logan Alexander—if I can help it."

"I'll bet." Sara rolled her eyes, her voice bordering on accusatory.

Jenessa fixed her eyes on her sister. "What does that mean?"

"I know you chatted with him at the café yesterday. Spark any old feelings?" Sara pressed, narrowing her eyes.

What was Sara's attitude about? Regardless, Jenessa wasn't about to admit what running into that man had sparked in her. "Logan and I are old news. Just leave it at that." Jenessa raised her eyebrows and cocked her head, hoping Sara would catch the hint.

Lifting her wrist, Jenessa peeked at her watch. "We should head down to the coroner's office and pick up Dad's effects before it gets too late."

"I'll drive," Sara snapped. "I don't trust that rattle-trap you're driving."

Jenessa shot her sister a sideways frown. Sara was right, of course, but that was her rattle-trap, thank you very much. Not wanting to argue, Jenessa shifted her attention to her aunt. "Dad's keys should be among his personal effects, don't you think?"

"Should be," Aunt Renee replied. "Why?"

"Because his car needs to be picked up from the office. Plus, I'm hoping the key to the lap drawer of his desk at home will be on his key ring."

"Why don't you girls go take care of that, and I'll call the funeral home to start making the arrangements," Aunt Renee suggested. "I think I'll feel better getting the plans nailed down."

"Okay," Jenessa agreed, "and I'll write the obituary when I get back and send it in to the newspaper. By then maybe you'll have an idea of when and where the funeral will be and I can include it."

The girls waved good-bye as they stepped out the front door.

~*~

As suspected, their father's keys were among the personal effects the girls picked up from the coroner's office. After they retrieved everything, Sara drove to the parking lot of their father's office and Jenessa climbed out.

"I'm going to take Dad's car home and hang around there for a while. I have another drawer I want to go through. I'll see you and Aunt Renee for dinner."

"Fine," Sara retorted and drove off.

What is her problem?

As Jenessa watched her sister speed away, it suddenly occurred to her that she didn't know what her father drove, except that by the insignia on the key fob it was a Mercedes. Sara had mentioned he had bought a new car a few months after their mom's death, but Jenessa hadn't been home since the funeral.

Standing in the middle of the parking lot, surveying the various vehicles, she noticed there were several different models of Mercedes parked there. She began pointing the key fob at the different cars, pushing the *unlock* button, hoping for a chirp or flashing lights to tell her which one was his.

On the third try she found success.

"Oh my!" A thrill zinged through her body and lit her up with delight when the dark blue SLK 250 Roadster beeped and its lights flashed. Driving this was definitely a step up from her rattle-trap.

CHAPTER 4

JENESSA RUSHED TO THE SLEEK sports car and her gaze glided slowly over it, admiring the beauty for a prolonged moment. Giddy with anticipation, she opened the car door and let the pent-up heat rush out before sliding behind the wheel.

She stuck the key into the ignition and fired it up. After flipping on the air conditioner full blast, she caressed the luxuriously soft, ivory leather seats as she listened to the finely tuned engine purr.

She shifted into reverse and carefully backed out of the space. Pulling the car out of the lot and onto the street, Jenessa relished every second she spent behind the wheel. As she headed toward home, she had the wild idea of taking the two-seat Roadster for a spin a few miles out of town, up toward Jonas Lake. She wanted to open it up and see what this baby could do.

Before she had the chance to play Mario Andretti, her cell phone began jingling in her purse. She pulled the sports car over and dug it out, but she did not recognize the number. "Hello."

"Jenessa, this is Charles McAllister."

"Hello, Mr. McAllister. What can I do for you?"

"First, call me Charles, since we're going to be working together."

"Okay, Charles. What can I do for you?"

"I know you weren't planning to start work until next Monday, but a pretty big news story just broke and I need someone with experience to dig into it. I was wondering if you'd want to start work early and take it on."

A big news story? In sleepy Hidden Valley? "Yeah, sure, I don't mind. There's not much to do until the funeral. Aunt Renee is handling most of the details. What's the story?"

"A body was found up by Jonas Lake."

"A body?"

"Well, remains actually. My contact in the police department gave me the heads-up and I'd like to send you up there to investigate."

"Did your contact say how the remains were discovered?"

"Seems a new cabin is going up, just at the foundation stage. The owners and their dogs were walking around the place, checking on the work, and the dogs started digging. It appears, from what the police have found so far, when the contractor broke ground for the foundation, he must have partially unearthed the remains."

"I'll head out there right now." Worked for her. Now she had a legitimate reason to head up to the lake. "What's the address?"

She jotted down the information on a small notepad she kept in her purse. She was always prepared—you could take the job away from the reporter, but you couldn't take the reporter away from the job. "I'll report back to you this afternoon on what I discover."

"Terrific. Thanks for stepping up. I'll wait to hear back from you."

Excited for the thrill of the drive and the breaking news assignment, she was already going more than twenty miles per hour over the speed limit before she hit the city limits. Still a half mile or so from crossing the line, she heard a siren blaring behind her. She glanced up into the rearview mirror and saw the dreaded blue-and-red flashing lights.

She took her foot off the gas, shifted down, and rolled to a stop at the side of the road. Feeling around inside her purse, she pulled out her wallet, ready to hand over her driver's license. She had gotten out of a ticket the day before, but it was doubtful she'd be able to wrangle her way out of this one.

The expected knock on her window came and she pushed the button to lower the glass.

"Do you know how fast you were going, ma'am?" The officer flipped open his ticket book.

"Michael?" She looked up at him, pulling her sunglasses off and shading her eyes with her hand.

"Jenessa?" He sounded as surprised as she felt. Squatting down to the level of her low sports car, he took off his sunglasses too and stuck them in his shirt pocket. "We have to stop meeting like this."

He pulled himself up to his feet again, took a step back, and admired her automobile. "New ride?"

"My dad's."

"I thought I'd seen it around town, only it wasn't flying down the street. Where were you going in such a hurry?"

"To the lake. I have to cover a breaking story."

"Oh, the bones some dogs dug up? I heard about that. So, you're a reporter?"

"Yes, I am." They hadn't had an opportunity yet to catch up. Even at that, she was a bit surprised that he really knew nothing about her. She assumed Ramey or Sara would have kept him updated, but apparently that wasn't the case. "And yes, that's the story. So, as you can see, I really need to get going." She hoped he'd let her out of a ticket—again.

"I thought you were taking a break from work this week because of the funeral."

She hadn't told him she'd been laid off from her previous job and had accepted a position with the local paper. Now didn't seem the right time to go into it. She offered a shrug. "The news never stops."

"You'll need to slow down, Jen, breaking news or not."

"The car got away from me, I guess. There's something very freeing and exhilarating about driving a fast car."

"Something very dangerous, too. I don't remember you being such a risk taker."

"People change."

58

"Ain't that the truth," he said with a smirk.

What exactly did he mean by that? Was he thinking back to something, or someone, in his own life?

"I'll let you off with a warning again, but this will have to be the last time."

"I appreciate that, Officer." She gave him a mock salute. "It won't happen again." She grinned.

"You have a nice afternoon, ma'am." He tipped his hat and walked back to his car, tossing a final comment over his shoulder. "And don't forget about that dinner you promised me."

She watched him in the side mirror as he climbed into his cruiser. Dinner would be nice, and catching up with him sounded good, finding out how his life turned out—hopefully better than hers—and why someone hadn't already snatched up a great guy like him.

~*~

Jenessa pulled back onto the street and continued on the road out of town. She kept the car at the speed limit until she was a couple of miles out into the country, heading for the foothills. As the road began to incline, she opened it up, applying more pressure to the gas pedal, feeling the exhilaration of the speed. The powerful engine gave no resistance to the hill and the car clung to the curves like a race car. Before she knew it, the sparkling water of Jonas Lake was coming into view.

She slowed and turned right at the road that led to the lake, golden meadows flanking each side. She remembered this place from when she was a teenager, coming up here with friends.

The road eventually split. She paused, eyeing her choices. She could drive straight ahead to the beach and marina, or she could take the road to the left, leading to the homes and cabins that had been built around the lake.

Jenessa hesitated, feeling short of breath. She had taken the left road only once before—with Logan. He had taken her to his family's lake house one summer day—a day that changed her life forever.

~*~

Sucking in a shuddering gasp of air, Jenessa chose the road that curved off to the left. She could see the rooftops and decks jutting out from several of the lake homes that had been built along the waterfront. She wasn't sure which rooftop belonged to the Alexanders' lake house. It seemed like a lifetime ago when she had been there with Logan.

But she was here about a story, not to dwell in the past. Jenessa picked up the notepad to find the house number. It read seven-fifty-five. She continued down the road.

After passing a few homes, she saw the numbers seven-five-five painted on a two-by-four. Someone had used red spray paint to write the numbers on a scrap piece of wood, and then had driven it into the ground. Although, it seemed rather unnecessary to have the address. The yellow crime scene tape, construction vehicles, and police cars were a clear enough beacon to the scene of the crime.

A space opened up, beyond the other vehicles, and she pulled her dad's car into it. She stuck her notepad and camera into her leather handbag, then slung the bag over her shoulder. She climbed out of the flashy Roadster, making her way to the cordoned-off area, hoping to talk to whoever was in charge.

A burst of exhilaration coursed through her veins. It felt good to be back on the job. She'd missed this.

Pulling her digital camera out of her purse, she stood surveying the property in question. It was mostly an empty piece of land with a few trees that had been cleared to put in the foundation. Glancing around, she froze when she recognized the lake house to the right— she had been there before. It was Logan's.

Her insides twisted. The air suddenly grew heavy around her. She couldn't take her eyes off of the Alexanders' home. Beads of sweat formed on her forehead, and she forced her empty hand to wipe the perspiration away. She ordered herself to look away, but she couldn't.

Jenessa had been unprepared for such a visceral reaction. It had been so many years ago when she had been there. Why did the memory of that day feel so fresh, like it was only a few days ago?

In reality, it had been twelve years. When she was a young and naïve seventeen-year-old, Logan had brought her here, just the two of them. They'd spent the afternoon on the lake, and on the beach. It had been a perfect day. As evening came, they'd made dinner together at the lake house, Logan grilling burgers on the deck that faced the lake, as she'd prepared the condiments.

After dinner they'd had dessert. The freezer had been well stocked with numerous flavors of ice cream and they'd tried a scoop of each one, laughing and sitting on the floor in the living room, feeding each other spoonfuls and kissing between bites.

He'd told her how excited he was to be going off to college in a couple of months, to finally be out on his own. He was going to miss her, he'd said, miss seeing her beautiful face every day, miss kissing her soft lips.

When they'd finished with the ice cream, Logan had reclined on the plush area rug, one hand behind his head. He'd patted the floor next to him, and she'd curled up beside him. They'd talked for a while, laughed, looking up at the ceiling, and at each other.

He had propped himself up on one elbow and leaned over to kiss her. "I love you, Jenessa," he'd said.

She had felt the same, but she had wanted him to be the first to say it. Now that he had, she'd gladly returned the sentiment. "I love you too," she'd whispered.

Then, he'd kissed her again, more deeply than he ever had before, his hand sliding around her waist, pulling her closer. As he'd climbed on top, something had awakened in her, something she had always fought against.

Jenessa had wanted to keep her virginity until marriage, but his passionate kisses and his sensual embrace had been so heady, so ardent, that she'd been unable to think straight. Nothing could exist for her outside of the passion he had stirred deep within her.

She had wanted to push him away, but she'd wanted to keep him close too. She had never felt desire like this before.

"I love you, Jenessa," he'd repeated, his body pressed against hers, kissing a sensitive place below her ear, and she'd come undone.

It was hard for her to believe that had been twelve years ago—from the way her heart was racing right now, she could have sworn it happened just yesterday.

~*~

"Hello. Can I help you?" a male voice said.

His voice broke her trance, and she pulled her gaze away from the Alexanders' lake house and turned to face the man in a police uniform standing beside her, remembering why she was there.

"Hello, Officer. Yes, I'm Jenessa Jones from the Hidden Valley Herald. I'm looking for whoever is in charge here."

"That would be Detective George Provenza." The officer pointed to a man with silver hair, likely early sixties, wearing a button-down shirt and tan slacks, standing and talking with a few other people. "The one in the light blue shirt, gray hair."

She started to duck under the yellow tape when the officer grabbed her arm. "I'm sorry, ma'am, but you can't go in there."

"I need to speak with the detective and take some photos for the newspaper. Do you mind telling him I'm here?"

"All right, but you wait here." He pointed at the ground outside of the cordoned-off area. "I don't think he'll let you snap any pictures, but he might be open to speaking with you."

63

Staying where she was ordered, Jenessa watched the officer dip under the tape and go to talk to the detective. Both men turned, glanced her way, then looked away again to continue their conversation.

The officer returned and told her the detective would give her a statement as soon as he was finished talking to the couple who made the grisly discovery. A few onlookers had approached the tape. The officer, arms straight out to his sides, warned them to back away.

The sound of a large vehicle approaching caught Jenessa's attention and she spun around. It was a sizeable black van with the words *Crime Scene Investigation Unit* painted on it. The officer moved the small crowd to the side and the van parked between them and her.

When the CSI team disembarked from the van and moved toward the scene, Jenessa ducked under the tape with them and used them to shield her from the detective's view. As they moved in unison toward the site of the unearthed remains, on the far side of the foundation set-up, Jenessa leaned in and managed to snap a few photos before the detective noticed her.

"What the hell do you think you're doing, lady?" Provenza hollered.

Jenessa froze and all eyes were suddenly on her.

She sucked in a breath and quickly regained her composure. Turning toward him, she gave him her answer. "My job, Detective. Same as you." She stuck out her hand. "Jenessa Jones, Hidden Valley Herald. My editor sent me here to cover this story. I hear you're the man in charge."

"I am. I thought my officer told you to wait out there," he growled, motioning beyond the tape.

"Yes, sorry about that. But when the CSI van drove up, I thought I'd lose my opportunity if I just stood around and waited."

"Opportunity for what?"

"Well, if this is such a big deal that you needed to call in help from the big city, this place is going to be crawling with out-of-town reporters and news crews. I figured I'd give you the chance to fill me in first, so the real story gets out, not some tale that gets blown out of proportion, making Hidden Valley sound like a hotbed of crime. You wouldn't want that, would you, Detective?"

"No, of course not, but—"

"And I'll make sure everyone knows you're the man in charge—I'll even make sure your name gets spelled right. Provenza—that's with a V and a Z, right?"

"I can't have people roaming around the crime scene, no matter how good a reporter you are, Miss…"

"Jones, Jenessa Jones. I can work with you or I can work without you, but make no mistake, Detective, I will get my story. Your choice." She shrugged.

"But this is a murder scene, Miss Jones, and you're a civilian," he said, poking a finger in her face.

She stood her ground and refused to back down. "I'm the press. I'm fully aware that this is a murder scene, and I won't get in your way. I'm after the story, the truth, Detective."

"Hmm." He paused and eyed her. "I see Charles McAllister has hired himself a bull dog."

"Excuse me?" she asked, not sure if she should be offended or simply confused by the comment.

"A bull dog—you know, a firecracker, a pistol, a feisty woman—someone who'll keep digging, grab hold and won't let go."

"I'll take that as a compliment," she said with a satisfied smile.

"That's how I meant it. I can see I'm not getting rid of you, so as soon as I finish interviewing the people who found the bones, I'll give you a statement. You can look around, but stay out of the CSI unit's way. Deal?"

"Deal." A smile was hinting at her lips but she worked to rein it in, wanting the detective to think it was his idea.

He turned and went back to the couple who owned the property and resumed the questioning. He hadn't said she couldn't take any photos.

~*~

Before long the detective met up with Jenessa and gave her his statement. The couple that called it in owned the property that was under construction. They'd come to check on it early that morning, walking their two Weimaraners. As they'd walked around the framing for the foundation, the dogs began digging furiously at the far back corner and came up with some bones in their mouths.

From the size and shape of the bones, the people realized they could be human. Once they were able to wrestle the bones away from their dogs, they'd phoned the Hidden Valley police to report what they'd found.

When the detective saw what he was dealing with, he called for the state CSI team to examine and retrieve the remains.

The CSI unit extracted all the bones and any other material on and around them.

"Do they know if it was a woman or a man?" Jenessa asked.

"They have a guess, but I don't think I should say until they release their findings," Provenza said.

Jenessa leaned in and kept her voice low. "I heard one of the CSIs refer to the remains as *her*. That leads me to believe they think it was a woman."

"Well, there you have it," he said softly. "But you didn't hear it from me."

She hadn't actually heard anyone say the remains were a *her*, but the bluff worked.

"Any idea how long she's been buried?" she asked.

"They won't know 'til they get her back to their lab."

"If you could let me know as soon as you do, then I can add that fact into my story. Maybe someone will remember something out of the ordinary around that time."

"I can't be giving out that kind of information."

"The townspeople will want to know, Detective."

He glared at her. "I'll think on it."

"Seems like it must have been a shallow grave. Am I right?"

"A few feet down, I'm guessing. Ten or twenty years ago there weren't as many homes here as there are now. That house would have been here," he pointed to the Alexanders' house, "but this house under construction and the next one over would have just been treed woodlands back then. Maybe even the next house after that."

"I know it's early, but any gut feelings about who may have done this?" she asked.

"Not yet. It's way too early. Could have been some random partiers from town who got out of hand and someone ended up dead. Maybe they buried her quick because they were afraid of someone finding out."

Jenessa knew what he meant. Going to the lake often meant beer parties, and sometimes smoking pot, for some of the teens and twenties crowd from Hidden Valley back in the day. Not knowing when this woman died, it was hard to say what was going on. For all she knew it could have happened in the nineteen fifties, although, with the few shreds of clothing still attached, it likely wasn't that long ago.

"Is there anything else you can tell me, Detective?" Jenessa asked.

"I think that's about it for now."

~*~

Jenessa swung the Roadster around and headed for home. She peeked over her shoulder at the Alexanders' lake house as she cruised past it. She instantly wished she had kept her eyes straight ahead. Her pulse quickened and her throat tightened.

She couldn't help but think of Logan—and that night. A light layer of perspiration formed on her skin at the thought, and tiny chill bumps covered her arms as the cold air from the air conditioner hit her.

CHAPTER 5

ONCE OUT ON THE MAIN ROAD, she laid her foot heavy on the pedal, trying to escape the painful memories of what began in that lake house that ill-fated night. She flew around the curves, leaning into the centrifugal force. At times, the tires squealed, trying to stay on the road. Rather than feeling free, now she felt bound, constricted, the sequence of events playing over in her rattled mind.

Six weeks after the passionate night at the lake house, Jenessa had discovered she was pregnant. Opposite of everything she had heard as a teenager, it truly did only take one time—that one night when she'd given herself to Logan. He was leaving for college in a few weeks and she had planned to return to high school for her senior year. But not after that night—everything changed—at least for her.

The first person she had told was her best friend Ramey. Sweet and tender-hearted, Ramey had cried with

Jenessa and lamented over what would happen next, to her and to the baby.

Then Jenessa had told Logan. He had picked her up at her house that evening, and they were on their way to the movies. He pulled his car into a parking space and turned the engine off.

She put her hand on his arm as he reached for the door handle. "Wait, Logan." He turned back and looked at her. "I have something I need to tell you."

"What is it?" A slight frown furrowed his brow as he settled back into his seat.

She paused, searching for the right words to lessen the shock, but none would come, so she just said it. "I'm pregnant."

"Pregnant? But how? We only did it that one time."

"I know that, but yet I am." She held her breath, searched his face, waiting for his response. Did he love her as much as she loved him?

He stared at her in silence for a long time, then finally spoke. "We can't keep it."

She shifted in her seat to face him straight on. "We're not talking about a puppy, Logan." Surely he didn't mean abortion.

"Of course, I know that, but I'm leaving for the university in a few weeks, I have football practice starting. And you still have another year left of high school before you go off to college. We can't get stuck raising a baby. You can't think that—"

Tears filled her eyes as he spoke. Desperation shook her and she grasped his hand. "Maybe we could—"

He pulled away from her. "Oh, my God, you do."

"Just listen to me, Logan. We could get married. I'll get my GED and go to school with you. Colleges have housing for married students, we could stay there until the baby was old enough for daycare. Then I could start taking courses. It could work."

"No, it couldn't." His features twisted in anguish for a brief moment, then he laid his head back against the headrest and expelled a rush of air. His expression softened a little as he leaned toward her and spoke. "We can't get married—that's out of the question—we're just kids ourselves." His lips were strained as he spoke. "Our whole lives are ahead of us, Jenessa. I think abortion is the best answer."

There it was. That was exactly what he meant. "I'm not going to kill our baby because it's the easiest thing to do," she snapped.

"Then have the thing and put it up for adoption," he shot back. "Keeping it will only ruin our lives."

"The thing?" she questioned, her eyes growing wide with anger.

"I didn't mean it like that." He shook his head and dropped his chin with exasperation. Then his gaze met hers again and he took her by the arm. "Whether it's a boy or a girl doesn't matter, it's just a little blob right now, so get rid of it."

"Don't be ridiculous, Logan. It's not a blob, it's a baby—our baby." She yanked away from his grip. She could no longer hold back the tears and they spilled down her cheeks.

As much as either of them hated the thought of telling their folks, they agreed they had to. Their parents were friends, sort of. Actually, Logan's father was her

71

dad's biggest client and they traveled in some of the same social circles.

Fearful and nervous, Jenessa and Logan gathered their parents together in one room, at the Alexanders' palatial home, and broke the news to all of them at once. Logan's father and stepmother were furious, Jenessa's parents were mortified.

Not that any of the adults asked the teenagers' opinions, but Jenessa made it clear she wanted to keep the baby and suggested they get married. Logan said he wanted her to have an abortion so they could both get on with their lives. In the end, the parents decided it would be best if Jenessa went to live outside of Hidden Valley, have the baby, and put it up for adoption.

It was easier for them to call the baby *it* so there would be no emotional attachment, they claimed. But no matter what they called her baby, Jenessa knew she would forever have an emotional attachment to the child.

That night, Grey Alexander had offered to pay all of Jenessa's medical expenses. There was something powerful and dark in the man's eyes that always made her uncomfortable in his presence, but this particular night it was exponentially worse. Something in her heart told her maybe it was a good thing she wasn't going to be part of his family.

Her father had stood up to Mr. Alexander and insisted on paying his half, fulfilling his paternal obligation. They were both at fault, he had reasoned, Jenessa and Logan, and the financial burden should be shared equally.

So the final decision was made. For the sake of all concerned, the parents had said, Jenessa would be sent to her grandmother's home in Santa Rosa until the baby was born and given up for adoption, and Logan would go off to college to play football, as planned.

From that day on, Jenessa's father never treated her the same.

~*~

The drive home from the crime scene at Jonas Lake was a blur. Before she realized it, Jenessa found herself pulling into the driveway of her parents' home. She went inside and changed into shorts and a tank top, excited to get started writing her story.

She phoned her boss and told him what she had so far, that she hoped to hear from the detective as to how long the bones had been there, and confirmation that it was a woman's skeleton.

"I was able to snap a few photos, so I'll look through them and see if there's anything we can print," she said.

He asked her to give him all she had so far and he'd run it in the morning newspaper. "The television news will probably be reporting on it tonight, but the article should give a more in-depth story."

"I didn't see any TV news crews there when I left," she reported, "but it would take them at least a couple of hours to drive there from Sacramento or Fresno."

"True."

"They may not even think it's a big enough story to run with, compared to the expense of sending a crew."

"I hope you're right, Jenessa. I'd like the paper to get the scoop on a news story for a change."

"If the remains turn out to be those of a celebrity or linked to someone important, I'm sure they'll be all over it. But that doesn't seem likely."

"Send me what you have by six," McAllister said.

"Will do."

~*~

Jenessa wrote her story, what little she knew, wishing she'd hear back from the detective about the timeline. After reviewing and editing, she still hadn't heard, so she decided to make a preemptive call.

"Detective, this is Jenessa Jones, from the Hidden Valley Herald."

"Hello, Ms. Jones. I'm kind of busy right now. Can I call you back?"

"Just one question—have you heard from the CSI team on how long the bones that were discovered this morning had been buried?"

"They've barely had time to get back to their lab."

"I know. I was just hoping."

"I can tell you this much, at the scene the lead investigator said she suspected between ten and fifteen years. They'll be running a carbon dating test to try to pinpoint it a little more accurately, but that may be as close as they can get. No promises."

"Do you think they'll be able to give us any more details, like age, height, ethnicity? Anything like that?"

"That's a heck of a lot more than just one question," he snapped.

"I need it for my story, Detective. If someone could help identify who this woman was, then it'll help you find out who killed her and buried her. She deserves that much, don't you think?"

"I'd like to tell you more, but I can't release those details just yet."

"Then when?"

"I can't say. My captain wants to play it close to the vest until we know who she was."

"He must have some idea, then." *Who was he trying to protect?*

"I really can't say. I need to go. Good luck."

~*~

Her conversation with the detective left her unsettled. She knew there were times the police withheld certain facts that only a killer would know. Was that it? Did they already find something that could point to the killer?

Maybe her contacts at the Sacramento paper had an in at the state crime lab. She decided to call her old boss, Jack Linear.

"I have a cousin at the lab," he told her, after she'd explained the situation.

"Would she be willing to talk to me?"

"Depends. I'm sure she's not going to break the law or risk losing her job."

"Hey, I'm only trying to find out who the woman was, and more precisely, when she was killed. If she could get me the approximate age, height, race—you know, that kind of thing."

"Maybe she'd do it if you could guarantee her anonymity."

"Absolutely. You know me, I would never divulge my source."

"If she's willing, I'll have her call you. Same number?" Jack asked.

"Yes. Thanks for the help."

Jenessa downloaded the photos from her camera into her computer and pulled them up on her laptop screen. She scanned through them, looking for the best front-page shot. She had been able to take six, from different angles, before the detective stopped her.

From the photos, she could see that a bit of old fabric still remained on the body, and several brass buttons lay in the pelvic cavity, near the waist, looking like they might have come from blue jeans or cut-offs. There was a narrow silver chain around the neck area with something oval hanging from it, probably a necklace of some kind.

In one photo, she picked up something beside the body—a button maybe? Or was it an earring? She opened the picture in her Photoshop software and enlarged it. Still, she couldn't tell what it was, it was too blurry. She sharpened the image, added contrast and took the size down a notch. It was square-ish with a design of some sort on it—but what was it?

Jack Linear's cousin hadn't called her yet. More details would definitely add to the story, but she had no way of contacting the woman herself. All she could do was wait and hope she called.

As the afternoon wore on into evening, time was beginning to run out and she had to get her story in. The Herald wasn't a big-city paper. The printing staff didn't work through the night in Hidden Valley like they did in Sacramento.

Jenessa needed to choose a photo and be done with it for the night. Most of the pictures had an investigator's hand or shoulder, or some other body part, intruding into the shot, so she chose the cleanest, most eye-catching photo and sent it to her editor, along with her story.

She dialed Charles McAllister's number and he answered on the first ring.

"Charles, this is Jenessa. My story is on its way to you."

"Great. I'll be able to get it into the morning paper. I saved a spot on the front page."

"I sent a photo along. I hope you can use it."

"Even better."

"I'm certain there's more to this story, though. I just need more time to uncover it. I'll stay on it."

"I knew having a big-city reporter working for us would be good for this town."

"Sacramento is not exactly the big city."

"Compared to Hidden Valley it is. Not much happens here, so when something like this pops up, our readers will be riveted. When's the next installment?"

"I can't say, but I'll keep you in the loop. This is a homicide investigation and the police are pretty tight-lipped about the details, but I'll keep digging and follow it wherever it leads." Jenessa was vibrating with excitement—it felt good to be back in the saddle again.

"Sounds fantastic, Jenessa. But don't forget—"

"Forget what?"

"I still need you to do the weddings and social events."

~*~

Jenessa went into her father's office to tackle the last drawer of his file cabinet.

After an hour of searching, she shut the cabinet. Nothing.

The desk's lap drawer drew her attention once more. She searched her father's key ring, but only the keys to the car and the house were on it.

Should she break into it? Then she remembered her aunt's pointed admonishment not to damage the valuable antique.

Could she pick the lock? How hard could it be?

She tried a metal nail file, an ice pick, a bobby pin, other keys—but nothing worked. It looked so easy in the movies. She wondered if her friend Michael, as a policeman, might know of any small-time criminals she could hire to pick it.

She could call a locksmith, but what if there was something sensitive in the drawer? With the way gossip flew around that town with lightning speed, she couldn't risk it.

Tomorrow she would call Michael, she decided, but for right now it was time to go to Aunt Renee's for dinner with the family. She liked the sound of that— *dinner with the family.*

She grabbed her purse and hopped into the Roadster. As she drove to her aunt's home, she wondered if anyone would have any objections to her driving this car regularly, as opposed to her old Toyota. It would certainly be a huge improvement, and she wouldn't have to worry every time she tried to start it up if it actually would.

~*~

When she arrived at Aunt Renee's home, Ramey was already there, having left an employee to close up the shop. Jenessa noticed her out on the patio, manning the grill, with the sparkling blue pool in the distance.

After greeting Sara and her aunt, she stepped out through the french doors to say hello to her friend. "What's cooking?" Jenessa pulled the door shut behind her.

"Hey, Jen." Ramey threw an arm around her shoulder and gave her a quick squeeze. "Salmon."

"Looks good."

"I heard you snagged that job today at the newspaper," Ramey said, lifting a Salmon steak with the metal spatula, checking for doneness. "Congratulations. I'm so happy you're sticking around."

"For a while, anyway." Jenessa wondered if she should mention her first assignment, but thought she'd hold off for a bit.

"A long while, I hope." Ramey flashed her a big smile.

"We'll see." Jenessa walked farther out on the patio and looked at the tempting pool. "Want to swim later?"

"Me, in a suit?"

"You're among friends, Ramey."

"Maybe." She flipped the fish on the grill.

Jenessa returned to Ramey's side. "Hey, I was wondering…what's with Michael Baxter?"

"What do you mean?"

"What's his story? What happened to him after high school?"

Ramey grinned. "Interested?"

"No, not really," Jenessa replied, working to keep her voice even and casual. "I mean, well, we were friends in high school and then we lost touch after I left. I've run into him a few times since I got back and I just wondered."

"Hmm." Ramey eyed Jenessa like she wasn't sure that's all it was. "He went into the army after high school, then he went to college back east. He met a girl there and they got married, had a baby, then she left him."

"What?" That wasn't at all what Jenessa had expected to hear.

"Yes, that's what happened. He moved his little family back here to Hidden Valley and one day she up and left him."

"What about the baby?"

"Oh, she left him here with Michael. The boy's about five now."

"He has a son?" Jenessa's hand flew to her chest as a tingling sensation spread across it. The baby she had given up for adoption had been a boy.

"Yeah, little Jake, short for Jacob," Ramey replied.

"I had no idea." Did he look like his daddy? "Jacob Baxter," Jenessa muttered.

"Yeah, pretty sad. Michael's such a nice guy." Ramey had known Michael all her life. They had both been born and raised in Hidden Valley.

"How did he manage with a job and a baby?"

"Well, you know his folks still live here. His mom watched the baby while Michael was at work—still does. I think Jake's going into kindergarten in the fall."

One of the french doors opened and Sara stepped out with a platter. "What are you girls talking about?"

"Nothing special," Jenessa said. "Just catching up." She gave Ramey a wink and walked back inside before Sara could stir something up.

CHAPTER 6

THEY SAT DOWN TO DINNER. The chatter around the table was background noise to Jenessa, her mind was on Michael and his little boy.

"The salmon is delicious, Ramey," Aunt Renee praised. "Isn't it, Jenessa?"

Hearing her name brought her attention back to the table. "What?"

"The salmon." Aunt Renee lifted her forkful of fish. "Delicious, isn't it?"

"Oh, yes. Delicious. Great job, Ramey," Jenessa recovered.

"Special seasoning?" Sara asked.

"Your mom's recipe," Ramey replied. "The risotto is hers too."

"I'm glad you learned to cook from her, because her recipes were wasted on my sister and me," Sara said.

Jenessa had to agree. Their interests always seemed to lie elsewhere. "Maybe now that we're grown up you can teach us a few things, Ramey."

"Men are always impressed by a good meal, girls," Aunt Renee noted. "I can't believe I've got three lovely single ladies right here and not a man in sight for any of you." She grimaced and shook her head.

"Okay, moving on to another subject," Jenessa cut in, glancing around the table. "Would any of you object to my driving Dad's car for a while? My old Toyota is on its last leg, and I, frankly, don't have the money to repair it right now."

"I wonder who he left it to in his Will," Sara said, taking a bite of risotto.

The last thing Jenessa wanted was to battle her sister over the car. "Until we find that out, do you mind if I drive it? I need a reliable vehicle for my new job."

"As long as you don't bang it up," Sara warned. "Maybe Daddy left it to me."

"Maybe not," Jenessa countered.

Sara frowned. "Then we may want to sell it and split the proceeds after we sort out Daddy's estate. The house too."

"The house?" Jenessa's voice rose. "You want to sell our house?" She was finally beginning to feel at home somewhere, feeling part of a family again, and now her sister was talking about getting rid of her home.

"It's far too big for just one person to live in," Sara replied, wagging her fork at Jenessa. Sara lived in a cozy two-bedroom cottage a few blocks from her folks' house, one that her aunt had helped her decorate.

"Not if one of you girls got married and started a family." Aunt Renee peered at Sara and Jenessa with hopefulness in her eyes. "It would be a perfect house for one of you."

"I vote we table this discussion until another time," Jenessa said. "All in favor say aye."

"Aye," the three younger women shouted.

Aunt Renee's expression deflated. "All right, girls. I know when I'm outnumbered."

Jenessa turned to her aunt. "I brought my laptop to get busy on Dad's obituary after dinner. Do you have the details of the service yet?"

Aunt Renee told her it would be on Friday at ten am at the Monte Vista Chapel down the road. From their father's written instructions, that's where he had wanted it held.

"After we clear the plates, I'll work on the obit," Jenessa said. "Then maybe we can go for a swim."

"Did you bring your suit?" Ramey asked, looking a little squeamish, as if she was hoping for a way not to participate.

"Don't worry, dear, I've got a whole box full upstairs," Aunt Renee said, "bikinis, one-pieces, all different sizes. Towels too."

"I figured you would." Jenessa grinned at Ramey.

~*~

After submitting the obituary to the newspaper by email, the girls spent some time swimming and playing in the pool, while their aunt reclined on a chaise, under a big blue umbrella on the patio, sipping an iced tea. If it hadn't been for the fact that her father had just died suddenly the day before, Jenessa would have considered this one of the happiest evenings she had spent in a long time. A sad commentary on her life thus far.

Around nine o'clock, as the sun was setting behind the western hills and the landscape lights were beginning to flicker on, Jenessa announced she was calling it a night. She came up the steps of the pool, out of the water, and grabbed her towel, twisting it around her waist like a sarong.

"Be right back," she told the others.

After changing out of her bikini and back into her clothes, Jenessa reappeared on the patio. Ramey and Sara had climbed out of the pool as well and were drying off. Jenessa said her good-byes to them, bent down and kissed her aunt on the cheek, and wished them all a good night.

"I'll see you two for breakfast," Jenessa said, pointing at her sister and Ramey, knowing at least one of them would be at The Sweet Spot bright and early. "Save a cinnamon roll for me."

"Take care of that car," Sara ordered.

Jenessa stuck her hand in the air and gave them a casual wave as she walked out the side gate.

Driving the Roadster home was a pleasure. She rolled the windows down, enjoying the pleasant night breeze flowing through her hair. Sleek and powerful, responding to her slightest movement, the car felt like it was made for her. With little objection from her family, she decided she'd consider this baby hers, at least for now.

Once she got home and was alone in her room, she thought back over the day—especially the drive out to the lake. Maybe it hadn't been such a good idea. It had dredged up old memories she had worked so hard to push down. If only she could avoid the lake, but with the story she was investigating, that was simply not possible.

She pulled the top dresser drawer open to grab her pajamas, and there was that stinking prom photo she had shoved in there the night before, a symbol of her misbegotten romance with Logan, the beginning of the end of life as she knew it. She picked up the distressing photo and ripped it in half, then tossed it into the waste basket next to the dresser.

There would be no dreaming of what might have been between them. There was only the stark reality of what was. Her father's sudden death was ironically giving her a second chance at a happy life, and she wasn't going to screw it up again by fantasizing about Logan Alexander.

Now, Michael Baxter was another story. Surprised by what Ramey had said about him, it piqued her interest to know more.

Maybe it was time Jenessa took him up on his offer to have dinner together.

~*~

The next morning, Jenessa woke to the sound of her phone ringing on the nightstand. She rolled over and checked the clock sitting beside it. It read seven thirty-five.

"Hello," she answered groggily.

"Jenessa? Jenessa Jones?" a man's voice asked.

"Yes."

"Sorry, did I wake you?"

She drew in a deep breath and tried to force her eyes to stay open. "First conversation of the day," she grumbled. "Who is this?"

"This is Charles."

"Charles?"

"Yes, McAllister. Are you sure I didn't wake you?"

"No, not at all." She rolled over on her side.

"I wanted to let you know we got the obit you emailed to us last night. It'll be in tomorrow's paper."

"Thank you."

"I see the funeral is Friday morning."

"Yes, that's right." She pulled herself up into a sitting position and pushed her mop of hair off her face.

"This might be kind of tacky, and please tell me if you don't want to do it, but would you mind doing a short story on your dad and the funeral? We're a bit short-handed, as you know, and your father was pretty well-known in the community. You'll already be there and—"

"Sure, I'd be happy to," she replied flatly. She covered her mouth as she yawned. What else could she say? This man had been kind enough to hire her. And he was right—she would already be there. "Anything else?"

"We got your story out in this morning's paper, and I'm already getting buzz about it."

"What kind of buzz?"

"Phone calls, emails, people talking about the story at The Sweet Spot this morning when I stopped in for my morning coffee—you know, *buzz*."

~*~

By the time Jenessa made it down to The Sweet Spot, the early morning crowd had thinned out. She zipped the sports car into a diagonal space right in front of the shop. Her stomach growled at the thought of the waiting cinnamon roll.

She reached for the café's door handle at the same time another hand gripped it. Surprised, she looked up. The hand belonged to Logan.

~*~

"Good morning, Jenessa." Logan smiled at her, a twinkle in his deep blue eyes.

She snapped her hand back like she had been bitten by a snake. Why did he have to be at The Sweet Spot at the exact same time as she was?

He was handsome in his light stone Dockers and polo shirt, an azure blue, like the color of the sea surrounding the Greek Islands. She'd heard he was working at his father's real estate company, and she supposed this was the summer attire for a successful Realtor.

"Morning." She didn't care how good he looked, she was determined to keep her guard up around him.

He pulled the door open and gestured for her to go in. "You first."

She sauntered past him, afraid he'd be standing behind her to get his coffee. So rather than taking her place in line, she went to the bakery case and looked over the cookies, cakes, and other delectables sitting inside it, pretending to be trying to make up her mind.

"Large coffee, two creams, two sugars," he said to the older woman behind the counter.

She felt the heat of his eyes on her. Or was it her imagination?

"Jenessa, would you like anything? My treat," he offered.

Apparently, it wasn't her imagination. She kept her eyes glued to the goodies in front of her. Those mesmerizing blue eyes were not going to draw her in. "No, I'm waiting for Ramey—but thanks."

"That'll be four dollars and thirty-one cents," the clerk said.

He handed her some cash. "How long are you in town for?"

She did not answer.

"Jenessa?" he asked.

"Oh, sorry. Were you talking to me?" She forced herself to look in his general direction, willing herself to avoid his captivating smile.

"Yes, I was."

"Awhile." Then she looked at the woman behind the counter. "Rosie, do think Ramey will be much longer?"

"After I get this gentleman his coffee, I'll let her know you're here."

Logan held his tongue until the woman handed him his cup of coffee and disappeared into the back room. "Listen, I can see you don't want to talk to me, but come on. It's been twelve years. We've both grown up. We're not the kids we were back then."

He paused and she assumed he was waiting for a response, but she gave him none.

"I heard you're staying in town and you took a job at the paper."

Her head spun in his direction and her eyes narrowed. "How did you know that?"

"My father owns the paper, remember?" Logan raised his brows at her for a moment, then the corners of his lips curved up into a mischievous smile. "Besides, in this town, everyone knows everyone else's business. There's nothing that old bitty Alice likes better than spreading news."

"Then why did you ask me how long I would be in town?"

"I wanted to give you the opportunity to tell me yourself."

She wanted to tear her eyes away but was struggling to do so. *Why did he have to grow into such a good-looking man?* His blond waves were beckoning to her, but she would not be drawn into his web again. "Well, now you know." Her cheeks grew hot as her gaze returned to the bakery case.

"Let me take you to lunch this afternoon. We can catch up."

"Sorry, she's having lunch with me," Ramey said, arriving just in time to save her from herself.

"Yes," Jenessa said, not looking up, "sorry."

"Another time, then." He took his coffee and walked out.

"Thanks for rescuing me," Jenessa said with a weak smile.

"Any time. Here's your cinnamon roll." She handed it over the counter on a small plate, covered with plastic wrap. "I had to stick it in the back or there wouldn't have been any left for you. Go sit down and I'll bring you a cup of coffee."

Jenessa took her roll and grabbed a table by the window.

The bells jingled as the door opened again and the sweet sound of a child's laughter preceded the two coming in. "Jake," Ramey called out. "What an awesome surprise!"

Michael was right behind the boy. "We just came from the doctor's office, and I promised Jake one of your famous chocolate cupcakes afterward."

"Oh no. What's wrong?" Ramey asked, looking sincerely worried.

"Nothing bad, just a checkup before school starts," Michael explained and Ramey's expression relaxed.

"I'm going to be in kindergarten," Jake added.

"Good morning, Michael," Jenessa said from where she was seated, not far from him. She rose and strolled over. "Who is this handsome fellow?"

"This is my son, Jake." Michael smiled proudly. "Jake, this is Jenessa Jones. She's an old friend of mine from high school. Can you shake her hand?"

The boy stuck out his little hand. "Nice to meet you," he said stiffly, as if he'd been practicing.

She took his hand and shook it, surprised by the firm grip for such a little guy.

He looked up at his father. "She doesn't look that old, Dad."

Michael covered his mouth to stifle a laugh and dropped down to one knee beside the boy. Jenessa and Ramey looked away to cover their giggles.

"Old friend as in we were friends a long time ago," Michael explained.

"Oh," Jake replied, not at all embarrassed by the gaff.

Ramey quickly grabbed a chocolate cupcake out of the case and handed it over the counter. "Here you go, Jake."

A devilish grin spread across the boy's face as he took the cupcake. His eyes grew wide with anticipation as he opened his mouth to take a bite.

"What do you say?" his dad asked.

Jake managed to squeak out a "thank you" before chomping into the frosted treat.

He looked just like his dad. Had her own son grown up to look like Logan?

"Can I get a couple of napkins, Ramey?" Michael asked.

She grabbed a few and held them out.

"Thanks." He took them just in time, for the boy had already devoured the cupcake and wore almost half the frosting on his face and he was wiping the icing from his hand onto his shirt.

Michael patiently cleaned the chocolate from around the little boy's mouth and cheeks as he squirmed a bit.

"You look like you enjoyed that cupcake, Jake," Jenessa said.

He nodded enthusiastically.

Michael stood, taking Jake's hand. "I'd better get him home and out of these clothes." He paused and looked over at Jenessa. "Today's my day off. How about we have lunch together and do some catching up?"

"Jake, too?" she asked.

"No, just us. My mom can watch him." Michael ruffled his fingers through Jake's hair.

A little sting of disappointment took her by surprise. "All right."

"Let's say Antonio's, at noon," he suggested.

"Sounds nice."

~*~

After breakfast, Jenessa went home to do more research on her story of the gruesome discovery near Jonas Lake. She poured through public records and found who had owned the property prior to the new owners, all the way back twenty years. Without knowing exactly how long ago the woman had been buried there, she needed to cover all her bases.

The Alexanders had owned their lake house for over twenty years—that much she knew—but she needed to discover the identity of the other property owners in the vicinity, going way back, so she kept digging.

She phoned Detective Provenza and asked if he had researched old missing persons reports in the area. He said he had, anyone that had been reported missing from five to twenty-five years ago, female, matching the height and relative age of the victim, but none of them fit her description.

"So you have those details—the height and approximate age of the woman?" she asked. "Would you mind sharing?"

"I don't think I'd better. You're not law enforcement."

"That's true, but I am on your side. If I can help you figure out who this woman was, then you have a better shot at solving this case. Don't you agree?"

"Or a better shot of getting my butt in a ringer."

She chose to ignore that last comment. Instead, she pressed on. "Don't shut me out, Detective, use me. Then, when we find her killer, you'll be the town's hero."

The line was silent for a moment as he seemed to be mulling over his decision. "The town's hero, you say." He huffed. "Oh, all right." His voice lowered and it sounded as if he was cupping his hand around the phone. "She was five-five to five-seven and roughly in her mid-thirties to early forties, but you didn't hear that from me. That's all I can give you."

"I noticed there was something that looked like a necklace in one of the photos I took."

"You took photos?" He sounded angry. "I knew I shouldn't have let you stay at the scene."

"In the end, you'll be glad you did." Or at least she hoped he would be. "Getting back to the photo, there was something that looked like a necklace maybe. Do you have any idea what that was?"

"I've already said too much." He hung up.

She got the uneasy feeling that he was hiding something—but what?

CHAPTER 7

NOON ROLLED AROUND and she pulled up in front of Antonio's Italian Ristorante, just a few blocks from The Sweet Spot Café. She recalled having gone there a few times as a teenager—one of those times was on a date with Logan.

When she walked into the quaint restaurant, Michael was already seated at a table in the middle of the room, dressed in a button-down shirt with a tiny blue-and-white check pattern, and his sleeves were rolled up at the cuffs. Each of the tables in the restaurant were covered with a red-and-white checkered tablecloth and an old dripping candle in the center, just as they had been when she was a girl.

He stood and waved her over, exposing his untucked shirt hanging down over his dark blue jeans. His broad grin told he was delighted to see her.

"Hello," she said, smiling up at him, then glancing around the familiar room. "Waiting long?"

"Not at all."

They exchanged pleasantries, placed their lunch orders, and chatted while they waited for their food.

The waiter brought their pasta dishes and wished them *buon appetito* as he left.

"So, tell me, Michael, what have you been doing with yourself since high school?" She pulled a slice of Italian bread from the basket and began buttering it.

"I joined the army, at my dad's suggestion. He said it would make a man out of me. I guess he thought I was pretty wimpy back then." Michael stuck a small meatball in his mouth.

"Oh, you were not."

"Well, yeah, kinda." He swallowed. "Once I was in, I decided to become a Ranger."

"That's pretty grueling training, isn't it?"

He nodded. "But it certainly did make a man out of me." He grinned at her, flexing his arms and chest.

She laughed a little. "Yes, it certainly did. I hardly recognized you the other day, the first time you pulled me over. You're not the Michael I knew in high school."

"I'm still the same old Michael on the inside, just stronger."

She smiled at the thought. "So what did you do after the army?"

"So many questions." The corner of his mouth tugged up into a crooked smile.

"You're the one who said you wanted to catch up." Jenessa studied his face, watching as he considered his response. His brown eyes were warm and kind, the color of chocolate, and his angular cheekbones and square jaw exuded a quiet strength. "Besides, I'm an investigative reporter. Questions are my life...so spill."

"Okay." He raised both hands in surrender. "After my stint in the army, I went to college back east on my GI bill. That's where I met Josie, Jake's mother. We got married when I was a senior and she was a sophomore. She got pregnant right away—which wasn't the plan—and she ended up dropping out of school when Jake was born. Then, after I graduated, we moved back here. I applied to the police academy and was accepted." He twirled some spaghetti onto his fork.

"As I recall, your dad was a cop, right?"

He nodded. "Retired now."

"So, I'm assuming Josie is no longer in the picture." Jenessa raised her brows to him, wanting to be sensitive to the situation.

"What makes you say that?"

"Well, one, you're here with me, and also Ramey mentioned something about your being a single dad."

"Yeah, I am that. Josie hated the small-town life. She wanted the big city and a big career. In college, her major had been drama, so she packed up and left one day, when Jake was two, and moved to Southern California to try her hand at acting."

"How does a woman just walk away from her marriage and her child?"

"I guess I didn't know her as well as I thought I did." Michael's gaze pensively drifted toward the bank of windows. "It wasn't all her fault, though. I can be pretty rigid sometimes, and she's more of a free spirit. I think that's what attracted me to her."

"Does she stay in contact?"

"Some. She calls once in a while, sends Jake gifts at Christmas, and comes to see him on his birthdays."

"That has to be hard," Jenessa said.

"Especially on Jake." There was a distinct sadness in his voice.

Was it difficult for Michael too? Although it had been three years since she left, was he still in love with her?

Jenessa became aware of the presence of someone standing beside their table and heard the person clear his throat.

"Hello, Jenessa. Michael."

She recognized the voice and her back stiffened. She slowly lifted her head. "Logan."

"Hey, Logan," Michael said, unaware of the totality of the relationship Logan had had with Jenessa, or the little white lie she had told him earlier that morning.

Logan crossed his arms. "I thought you said you were having lunch with Ramey today."

"Plans change," she replied, taking a sip of water, not wanting to make eye contact with him.

"If you didn't want to have lunch with me, you should have just said so." The atmosphere became uncomfortably awkward.

Her gaze briefly flew in Logan's direction, then back down. "You're right, I should have. I apologize." She looked across the table at Michael, who appeared confused by the exchange.

"Enjoy your lunch." Logan turned and marched to a booth at the far back corner of the restaurant.

"Sorry about that," Jenessa said, glancing down as she straightened the linen napkin on her lap. "I ran into him at The Sweet Spot this morning and he asked me to lunch." She took another sip of water, then stared at the straw as she stirred it around in the glass. "I really didn't want to go. Ramey stepped in and rescued me."

"Whatever happened to the two of you? I remember when I graduated the two of you were going hot and heavy."

"That's a good way to put it." She lifted her gaze and looked Michael in the eye. "I guess you could say my life fell apart after that."

"Fell apart? What happened?" His eyes were filled with sincere interest.

Jenessa's gaze darted around, making sure no one was within earshot of her spilling her guts. She leaned forward and lowered her voice to just above a whisper. "I got pregnant that summer."

Michael leaned toward her and kept his voice low, as well. "By Logan?"

She frowned at him and pulled back, sitting up straight in her chair. "Who else would it be?" Did he think she was sleeping around?

"No, I'm sorry. I didn't mean it that way. I was just surprised is all."

"We only did it once." She crossed her arms on the edge of the table. "I was so naïve at the time, I didn't think you could get pregnant the very first time you had sex. He was headed off to college and I was very…well, let's just leave it at that."

"I'm so sorry, Jen." He reached across the small table and put his hand on her crossed arm. "I didn't know anything about it."

"Do you think we could get out of here?" she asked. "I hate talking about this with *him* sitting in the corner over there."

"Sure, we'll get some to-go boxes. We can finish our lunch in the park."

~*~

Crane Park sat in the middle of town, and its tall old trees provided a canopy of shade. It was often the center of local activities, but today it was almost empty. An elderly couple sat at a wooden picnic table, maybe thirty feet away, and a young mother was pushing her little girl on the swings in the playground area.

Sitting side by side at one of the picnic tables, under an imposingly large elm tree, Jenessa and Michael unpacked their boxes from Antonio's and finished their lunch with plastic utensils.

She went on to explain what happened after she and Logan told their parents about the pregnancy and how she had been sent to live with her grandmother. Michael assured her he had no idea what had happened.

After she'd had the baby, and given up her little boy, she licked her wounds for a while at her grandmother's house, but Gran wouldn't let her mope around for long. She urged Jenessa to get on with her life, so she got her GED and went to college at Sacramento State, earning her degree in Journalism.

"I worked for a small newspaper for a couple of years, but then I was hired by a larger newspaper in Sacramento."

Michael's attention seemed to be riveted to her story. Dare she venture to delve into her strained relationship with her father and all the pain and misery that entailed?

He made the decision for her. "How did your folks react to your getting pregnant?"

"Mom was very upset of course—disappointed mostly. That wasn't the life she wanted for me."

"What about your dad? I know that if I'd gotten a girl pregnant in high school, my father would have tanned my hide, then he would have lectured me every day for the rest of my life."

"My dad built a wall instead."

"A wall?" His eyebrows wrinkled into a quizzical expression.

"Like I wasn't even there. I might as well have been dead to him." She busied her hands with the paper napkin in her lap, mindlessly folding it into a tiny square. Her eyes were lowered as she spoke. "My father rarely said two words to me. He couldn't even stand to look at me."

"You mean at first?"

She raised her tearful gaze to him and threw the folded napkin on the table. "No, I mean until the day he died."

They sat on the bench, neither saying a word, for a prolonged moment. Then Michael draped an arm around her shoulders. "I am so sorry."

Jenessa leaned her head against his broad shoulder and felt safe.

After a minute or two of silence, she finally sat up and ran a finger across her cheek to wipe away a tear that had fallen there. "I miss my mom."

"I remember reading about her car crash when it happened. I was already back in Hidden Valley by then. I assume you were in town for her funeral."

"Of course, but that was the last time I was here."

"I can't even imagine—"

"It was horrible." Jenessa dabbed at her cheeks with a napkin. "My dad blamed me."

"I don't understand. Why would he blame you?"

She explained how Thanksgiving that year had been torturous and she had refused to come home again for Christmas, so her mother drove up to see her. "The wreck happened while she was driving back to Hidden Valley."

"That's crazy, it was an accident."

"Didn't matter. Dad seemed to blame me for everything after I got pregnant. He liked his world all nice and neat—no drama, no embarrassment. The community's perception of him was what he cared about most."

"I didn't know things had gotten so bad between you." His voice was deeper than she remembered it, laced with sincere concern. "It's got to be hard living in your old house again."

"Lot of memories there—good and bad." Her gaze fell to her lap again. "At least it's free rent for now." She gave a half-hearted laugh.

"How long do you think you'll stick around?"

She looked up and an impish smile curled on her lips. "You haven't heard? I got a job at the Hidden Valley Herald. I'm here for a while."

His eyes lit up at the news, and his face gave away his delight before his words did. "I think that's great. It'll be fun to have you back." Before she knew what was happening, both of his arms were around her and he pulled her into an enthusiastic embrace.

"Sorry." As quickly as Michael's arms surrounded her, they dropped to his sides, like he had done something wrong. She wondered if he had sensed her tense up in his arms and draw back.

"I think I've spilled my guts to you enough for one day," she said, trying to cover for the awkward moment. "What about you? What do you see in your future?"

"Well…I didn't want to say anything…" He playfully looked around for dramatic effect, pretending he was searching for someone who might overhear. "I don't want to jinx it, but I've applied for the position of Detective. I got through the assessment, and the board review is coming up tomorrow. So, wish me luck."

It was obvious the move up meant a lot to him. A gleeful smile swept over her face. "I wish you all the luck in the world."

Jenessa was happy for him, hopeful he would get what he wanted. It sounded like he had experienced his own brand of heartache since they had been high school friends.

She didn't want to take advantage of Michael, but she couldn't help but wonder if having a police detective as a good friend might come in handy for her as a reporter. Maybe he'd be more forthcoming than old George Provenza.

~*~

The rest of the day was rather uneventful. Jenessa spent most of her time at Aunt Renee's, lazing around the pool, swimming and reading, unable to stop thinking about Michael and Logan.

Aunt Renee had taken care of finalizing details for the funeral and the luncheon after. The ladies of the church had offered to put on a buffet for all the friends and family after the service, which Renee gladly accepted.

After dinner with her aunt, her sister, and Ramey, Jenessa received a call from Jack Linear's cousin. She wouldn't give her name, but she confirmed the estimated height and age of the victim, reporting that the woman was Caucasian and had given birth to at least one child. One of the members of the lab was trying to reconstruct the face from clay on the skeleton, to get a better idea of what the woman might have looked like. She promised to send a photo to Jenessa when the reconstruction was finished, if she could manage it.

Jenessa asked about the necklace, if it had been with the remains when they reached the lab. The woman confirmed that a chain and locket was there.

"Was there a picture inside?" Jenessa asked, knowing there usually was.

"As a matter of fact, yes—a picture of a little redheaded girl, maybe three or four years old."

"Would it be possible for you to send me a photo of it?"

"I guess it couldn't hurt. I'll snap a picture with my phone while the others are out to lunch tomorrow, then I'll email it to you. Is that soon enough?"

"Sure." Jenessa gave the woman her email address and thanked her for the help.

"I know I'm sticking my neck out a bit, but I want to make sure that woman's killer is found. Too many women just disappear and are never heard from again, and nobody seems to care."

"I couldn't agree more," Jenessa said. "You're doing a heroic thing."

"I don't know about that," the woman replied. "But if this lady had a child, maybe the one in the locket, that little girl deserves to know her mother didn't abandon her."

Her words sounded like they were hitting close to home. Was this woman speaking from personal experience?

"You're absolutely right," Jenessa agreed. "Oh, by the way, before I let you go, there was another object I saw near the body when I was at the crime scene. It looked like a button or an earring or something—maybe square with a design of some sort on it."

"I don't know anything about that, but I'll let you know if I hear anything."

~*~

Jenessa spent the next morning puttering around the house, getting reacquainted with her old home. She filled a bowl with high-fiber cereal—not her choice, but it was what her father had left in the cupboard. After pouring a splash of milk on the cereal, she took the first bite, realizing the milk had clearly sat in the refrigerator too long. She dumped the contents of the bowl and went to the fridge to see if there was another carton.

Standing before the open refrigerator, she found none and decided she'd better make a run to the grocery store soon. With no more than a few dollars in her wallet, a half-gallon of milk and a couple of bananas were all she could afford.

That would change soon, though, having already begun her new job. But until she got her first paycheck, she'd have to make do with what was in the house, grateful to have a standing offer for breakfast at The Sweet Spot and dinner at Aunt Renee's.

A partial loaf of bread on the counter caught her attention. If it didn't have mold on it, she'd settle for a piece of toast with strawberry jam.

As the toast was browning, she leaned against the counter and thought of Michael, remembering their lunch together and wondering how his board review was going this morning. She had forgotten to ask him if he knew any small-time criminals who could pick the lock on her father's desk.

She was tempted to phone him right then, but no, she should leave him alone on this important day. Maybe she'd call him tonight and ask how the review went before diving into the subject of someone to pick the lock. Until then, she would eat her toast and begin the long process of going through the kitchen drawers, as well as the dressers and the closet in the master bedroom.

She began looking through her father's closet first. His highly polished dress shoes were precisely stationed on the lower cedar shelves, and his sweaters were neatly folded and stacked on the upper ones. The aroma of his aftershave still clung to them, and to his business suits.

Jenessa pulled one of his sweaters off the shelf and brought it to her face. She breathed in his scent, and a rush of tears made the loss of her father become real. Overwhelmed, she slumped down on the padded bench in the center of the closet and cried. Perhaps she should wait and finish this task when her sister and Ramey could come and help her.

~*~

Around noon, Jenessa made a quick trip to the corner market—an interesting adventure in itself. Several people at the little store recognized her and offered her their condolences before launching into questions about why she'd been away so long and what had she been doing in Sacramento.

"Dear girl, what are you going to do with yourself, now that you're back in Hidden Valley?" the elderly female store clerk asked.

Jenessa had known the woman since they moved into town, years ago. She shrugged and kept her gaze on her few grocery items.

"Do you have a young man waiting for you back in Sacramento?" the clerk asked as she bagged the milk and bananas.

Uncomfortable with all the probing questions, Jenessa paid the woman and beat a hasty retreat. "Thanks, Madge." She waved a hand in the air as she dashed out the door.

As she was sticking the carton in the refrigerator, the tone on her laptop pinged that she had a new email. Just as Jack Linear's cousin had promised, she emailed a picture of the locket, remarkably sharp and clear, laid open on a desk, exposing the photo of the young redheaded girl inside. The child looked happy, with a big grin spread across her face, and bright smiling eyes.

Would Aunt Renee possibly recognize the child? Her aunt had lived in Hidden Valley for about thirty years, so it was a real possibility. Jenessa certainly hoped so, for learning the little girl's identity could shed some light on who the dead woman was.

Jenessa had planned to head over to her aunt's house later in the afternoon to help choose some pictures of her dad to display in the foyer of the church before the funeral. As she glanced at the framed photos arranged on the walls of the main hallway of her own home, she pulled a few good ones down to take with her.

Then, when she pulled into her aunt's long driveway, she noticed her old Toyota still sitting there where she had left it a couple of days earlier. It was surprising that her aunt hadn't asked her to remove it.

With more important things on her mind, Jenessa opened her trunk and lifted out the box of photos, with her laptop sitting on top. She strode up the walkway and into the house.

After greeting Aunt Renee in the breakfast nook and going through the obligatory small talk, Jenessa set her laptop down and turned it on. She showed her aunt the photo of the child as it filled the screen, then launched into the question that was forefront in her mind.

Aunt Renee's eyes grew big and her hand flew to her chest. "Why, I think that's Ramey."

CHAPTER 8

"ARE YOU SURE IT'S RAMEY?" Jenessa's gaze jumped between her aunt and the screen. Could it be that simple?

"Yes, I'm pretty sure. Ask her yourself, if you don't believe me."

"You know what this means, don't you?"

A puzzled expression swept over Aunt Renee's face. "No, I don't understand. Where did you get that picture?"

"This locket was found with the remains up at the lake."

"You mean the decaying body you wrote that article about?"

"Yes, that's exactly what I'm talking about. So, this means the dead woman was Ramey's mother."

"Lucy? Oh, dear. Are you certain?"

Jenessa shrugged. "Who else would have Ramey's photo in her locket?"

"True." Aunt Renee nodded, her expression turning serious. "How do we break it to her?"

"We don't."

"What? Why not?"

"At least not yet. Not until we have confirmation from the crime lab."

"Of course, that would be best. It just wouldn't do to tell the girl her mother is dead if you're wrong about all this," Aunt Renee reasoned.

"But if it is Lucy, this means Ramey's mother didn't abandon her for all these years," Jenessa said. "She hasn't come back because she was dead. Maybe I should at least prepare her for the possibility."

"Jenessa Jones, you'll do no such thing." Her aunt put a firm hand on Jenessa's arm, a gesture insisting that she stop. "The woman has been dead for ten or twelve years you said. Another few hours or days won't change anything."

"But I've got to let the detective know what I suspect," Jenessa's words tumbled out, "and I've got to get a story written by deadline if I want it in tomorrow's paper. And—"

"Slow down, dear. The article can wait a day or two. You don't even have confirmation yet."

"I know, but I've got to—"

"No." The woman was adamant. "Tomorrow is the funeral, Jenessa. We need to take that day to honor your dad, my brother. If you put the article out there tomorrow, the town would be all abuzz about your story," Aunt Renee's hand fluttered through the air with a flourish, "gossiping about the disreputable murder victim. Let them have their gossip another day—just not tomorrow."

"What about the cops? I have to let Detective Provenza know right away. Otherwise, I'll be withholding evidence in a murder investigation."

"My dear, the detective can certainly wait a few hours to be notified. It's not like Lucy just died and the trail of the killer might grow cold—that is, if it is Lucy."

Jenessa sank down on a kitchen chair and dropped her purse on the table, rolling her eyes like a teenager. "I forgot what a small town this is." She shook her head. "All right, I'll wait until this evening to call the detective, assuming the old guy hasn't taken his teeth out and gone to bed yet."

"And I had forgotten what a smart mouth you can be, missy," Aunt Renee retorted, raising her eyebrows and wagging her finger at her niece, looking none too pleased.

"Sorry." Jenessa grimaced and shrugged her shoulders.

"All is forgiven. Now help me select the best photos of your father for the service."

~*~

It was nearly six o'clock when Ramey and Sara arrived at Aunt Renee's for supper, after closing The Sweet Spot. It was a scorching July day and a cool crisp salad with sliced grilled chicken on top sounded heavenly.

"Dinner's almost ready," Jenessa called to them as they stepped into the great room area, Sara giving Aunt Renee a quick peck on the cheek.

"Great, I'm starved," Ramey said, plopping her purse on the counter and pulling up a stool. "It looks delicious."

Aunt Renee and Sara moved toward the counter too and watched as Jenessa put the finishing touches on the individual salads.

"If someone will pour drinks, I think we're ready to eat." Jenessa picked up a couple of the salads and carried them to the table. "Sara, can you grab the other two plates?"

"Don't be so bossy," Sara replied.

Something prickled down Jenessa's neck. Couldn't they have a nice supper without an argument? "Sara, can you *pu-leeze* grab the other two plates for me? Is that better?"

"*Humph,*" was all Sara replied before picking up the dishes and taking them to the table.

Before long, they were all seated around the casual dining table, enjoying the cool and tasty meal. Conversation was light, but Jenessa kept making eye contact with her aunt, hoping for a signal that it was time to broach the subject of finding Ramey's mother.

"Charles was in this morning for his usual coffee and energy bar." Ramey poured a little dressing on her salad. "He mentioned how pleased he was with your work."

"Charles?" Jenessa asked. "You mean Charles McAllister?"

"Of course, silly. Who else would I mean?" Ramey chuckled. "He thanked me for sending you to him. He's such a nice man, don't you think, Jenessa?"

"Sure, I suppose."

"Handsome too." Ramey added. "Isn't he?" She glanced around the table, as if she was hoping for everyone's agreement.

"Oh yes, dear, I couldn't agree more." Aunt Renee patted Ramey on the hand. "He's a very nice man, and not at all bad to look at. And single, you know."

Was Aunt Renee trying to set Ramey up with Charles McAllister? He was almost ten years older than her. Although, Ramey did appear open to the possibility.

"Isn't Charles married?" Jenessa asked, remembering him mentioning that he had a son.

"No," Ramey replied. "His wife died of breast cancer about three years ago."

"Yes, that's right. Such a shame," Aunt Renee added. "Calista was a sweet woman."

"And Charlie is the cutest little boy," Ramey remarked.

"Not so little anymore," Sara chimed in. "He's about ten or twelve, isn't he?"

"That's right," Ramey said. "I seem to remember Charles ordering a cake for Charlie's birthday a few months back, but I don't recall which one."

Did Charlie have his father's thick brown hair and hazel eyes, or did he take after his mother? A heaviness settled in her chest as she thought how Charlie was about the same age as the son she had given up, wondering again if her own little boy would look like Logan.

"I wish I had known my dad," Ramey said with an edge of sadness in her voice. "When I was a kid, I used to imagine him coming for me one day." Ramey peered down at her plate as she pushed the last piece of lettuce around on it. "In my dreams he'd take me to live with him in a beautiful castle and he'd buy me presents and throw big birthday parties for me."

The other three shot each other uncomfortable stares, not sure how to respond to that.

"Funny what kids wish for," Ramey said, finally looking up.

Sara ventured a comment first. "Maybe your mom was trying to protect you from your father. What if he wasn't the great guy you hoped he was?"

"He couldn't have been any worse than my mother was," Ramey retorted. "Or any of the boyfriends she brought around."

Jenessa put her hand on Ramey's as it rested on the table. "You never know." She raised her eyes to Aunt Renee, wondering if now was the time to tell Ramey about her mother.

Renee gave her a slight shake of her head, meaning now was not the right time.

~*~

As Jenessa drove back to her house that evening, she called Detective Provenza to fill him in on her discovery.

"Hello," the detective answered, sounding like Jenessa had awakened him.

"I know it's late and I'm sorry, but I thought you'd like to know—"

"Who is this?" he demanded.

"Oh, sorry, Detective, this is Jenessa Jones, from the Hidden Valley Herald. I have something I thought you would want to know."

"Oh, yeah? What is it?" From the sound of his voice, he wasn't convinced she needed to be bothering him at home.

"I believe I've discovered who the remains belong to."

"If the crime scene investigators haven't determined it yet, how the hell do you know who it was?" he growled.

"I believe the victim's name was Lucy St. John. She was Ramey St. John's mother. You know Ramey, don't you?"

"The young redhead that runs that coffee shop on Main Street?"

"Yes, The Sweet Spot."

"Yeah, that's the one. But what makes you think the bones belong to her mother?"

"Wasn't there a locket found with the body?"

"Yeah, but how'd you know that?"

"I saw it. I was at the crime scene, remember?"

"I remember, pain in my—"

"The locket had a picture inside. I have reason to believe the picture was of Ramey when she was a little girl."

"How the heck do you know that?"

"You know I can't reveal my sources, George."

"That's Detective to you, Miss Jones."

"Check it out, Detective." Jenessa paused, but he was not quick to reply. "Like I told you before, if we work together, we can solve this case faster, and you come out looking like the town hero."

"Yeah, I remember you saying that, but I'm not sure I buy it. I'll solve this case with good ol' fashioned police work."

"Of course you will, George, but having a little help can't hurt. I just want to be the first one to break the story when we discover who murdered her."

"You got anything else or can I get back to sleep?" he grumbled.

"Sweet dreams, Detective."

~*~

Friday came and the church was filled with well-wishers by the time the family had been ushered in. Jenessa swore she felt the people's stares burning holes in her back. The townspeople had come to love her mother and her sister, and they respected her father and her aunt.

But Jenessa? She could only assume they saw her as the black sheep of the family, the one who had run off to God-knows-where. *Keep walking.* She tried to shrug off the feeling. The truth was that it was more likely that none of these people even knew who she was.

A middle-aged woman seated at the glossy, black grand piano began to play softly, and a finely-finished mahogany casket was already displayed at the front of the church. The lid was closed, thank goodness, but

Jenessa knew it would be opened soon and she would have to look at the ghastly pale version of her father.

Walking with her family to the front, she recognized a few other people as her gaze wandered back and forth—the mayor, her father's partner, Grey Alexander and his wife, and Logan. Her eyes shifted to the front when she spotted him.

The funeral would begin .momentarily. Jenessa fidgeted as she sat on the first row of the church with her family members, wishing they'd get on with the service. Her toe tapped nervously on the floor, feeling Logan's gaze hot on her back.

A program had been planned, mostly by Aunt Renee, but with some input from the three girls. Music, speakers, the eulogy. Then people would line up to file past the open casket for the viewing of the body and to say their final good-byes.

As she endured the next sixty minutes, Jenessa's mind was a blur of faces and words and thoughts. Ramey had squeezed her hand a few times during the service, leaning over and whispering something in her ear now and then, but Jenessa's mind was so unsettled that her friend's words were indiscernible.

Finally, the pastor stepped down from the podium and opened the top half of the casket, causing Jenessa's insides to twist. She squeezed her eyes tight, breathing in slowly and wringing her hands.

Oh, God! I don't want to see him, not like this.

Instead, she wanted to see the father she had known as a girl, the daddy that gave her horsey rides on his back and made her laugh. The one who took her fishing in the bay and roller skating in Golden Gate Park. They should have never moved to this place.

Warm tears welled in her eyes and spilled down her cheeks. Sara handed her a tissue, and Ramey held her hand.

The pastor motioned for the family to begin the viewing line. When it was Jenessa's turn, she couldn't do it, not really. She allowed her eyes to blur over his face, focusing on the edge of his sleeves, just above his folded hands—it was the best she could do. Her lips formed a soundless *good-bye* as an errant tear slipped down her cheek, onto the fabric of his jacket.

As she followed her sister up the aisle toward the back of the church, Jenessa kept her head down. When she neared the back rows, a hand reached out and softly clasped her fingers for just a moment. She looked up to find Michael, standing tall in a dark blue suit, wearing a somber expression.

One corner of her mouth turned up into a tiny smile as he released her hand and she kept walking.

~*~

Following the funeral service, the ladies of the church prepared a buffet lunch in the church's fellowship hall. Jenessa was relieved not to have to entertain all these people in her dad's home or Aunt Renee's. As people filled their plates with salads and little sandwiches, Jenessa stood by the door and observed.

Ramey had gone to The Sweet Spot early that morning, as was her routine, and baked her father's favorite carrot cupcakes with cream cheese frosting. She had delivered them to the church kitchen before the service and now they were set out on one of the long tables.

"Did you get a cupcake?" Ramey asked, sidling up to Jenessa.

Jenessa kept watching the crowd, not reacting to the question. "Do you think Dad actually knew all these people?"

"In one way or another, sure. Your dad was pretty well-known around here, well-respected too. Why do you ask?"

"I don't know." Jenessa shook her head. "I feel like I hardly knew him at all. These people probably knew him better than his own daughter." She turned and looked Ramey in the eyes. "You knew him better than I did."

"Maybe, but you have to know he loved you. I remember him saying a few times how proud he was that you were working for a big newspaper and you were going places."

"That doesn't sound like Dad." Was Ramey making that up to make her feel better, telling her what she thought she wanted to hear? He had certainly never said anything like that to Jenessa.

"Oh, look. There's Charles McAllister." A bright smile lit up Ramey's face. "He's waving at us." Her attention was quickly drawn away. "I'm going to go talk to him."

Jenessa watched as Ramey crossed the floor to where Charles was standing. Was there something blossoming between them? Ramey was a sweetheart and she deserved a good man.

"Cupcake?"

Jenessa spun in the direction of the male voice. "Michael." She grinned.

He held out a cupcake on a small plastic plate. "They're delicious."

"Maybe later."

"I'll save it for Jake then." He lowered the plate. "Again, I'm so sorry about your dad."

"Thanks. I really do appreciate your coming. It's nice to see a friendly, familiar face." A sudden warmth rushed through her at his nearness, taking her by surprise.

"I just wanted to see how you're holding up before I head back to work." His hand brushed down her arm and she was sure she felt a spark.

"I appreciate that." Jenessa flashed him a little smile. "I wish we could talk more."

"Me too." His deep brown eyes lit up.

"You see, I've dug up some things on this dead body case I'm investigating and I wanted to ask you a few questions." As Jenessa spoke the words, the sparkle in his eyes dimmed.

"Oh, I see. You just want me for inside information, and here I thought you wanted me for my body."

Her cheeks were on fire. "I...I...well, no, I just meant—"

He chuckled. "I'm only kidding, Jenessa."

She gave his arm a sharp jab. "Michael Baxter. You never change. Always the kidder." Although, he had changed in so many other ways—anyone with eyes could see that.

"I've got to fly, but how about I stop by your place after my shift, around nine o'clock?"

"That'd be great. I'll just be going through Dad's office this evening with a fine-tooth comb. Hey, that reminds me, do you know anyone who can pick a lock?"

"Planning to break into someone's house?"

"Of course not. I can't open the lap drawer to my dad's antique desk, and Aunt Renee almost came out of her skin when I told her I was going to break it open. I thought that if you knew any petty criminals who could pick locks I could get their name and number from you."

"No way I'm letting you bring a criminal into your house. Geez, Jenessa. For someone so smart, you can be pretty dumb sometimes." He grinned.

That was a statement he'd made to her with some regularity when they were in high school. She responded by balling up her fist and shaking it at him playfully. "Hey, buster, you want another sock in the arm?"

Michael covered her fist with his hand. "What about a locksmith?"

"I thought about that, but I'd rather it was someone who could keep their mouth shut about anything they saw in the drawer."

"I tell you what, I'll bring my tools and I will pick the lock for you, but right now I've got to get to work." He leaned down and kissed her on the forehead.

A male, standing close by, cleared his throat.

Jenessa's and Michael's heads both turned toward the sound.

"Am I interrupting something?"

"Hello, Logan," Jenessa said, stuffing both hands behind her back, her chest tightening at his presence.

"Logan." Michael pulled upright to his full six-foot-five-inch height, towering above Logan by at least three inches. "I was just on my way out. Take care, Jenessa."

Michael pushed the door open and was gone, leaving her to deal with Logan.

"I didn't mean to chase him away," Logan said with a hint of sarcasm. "Was it something I said?"

"Don't worry, you didn't. What can I do for you?" Her voice held steady and aloof, her eyes looking toward the crowd as she stiffly rested her back against the wall and crossed her arms over her chest.

Logan rested a hand against the wall behind her and leaned in. "Can't an old friend say hello and offer his condolences?"

Her gaze shifted and met his. He was now only inches from her. Those liquid blue eyes and that wavy blond hair drew her back to her teens, as if she was standing before him as a seventeen-year-old girl, deeply in love. Her heart began to hammer in her chest and suddenly the room became stuffy and warm.

Forcing herself to look away, she searched the crowd for Ramey or Sara or Aunt Renee—anyone who could rescue her from this moment. But she couldn't make eye contact with any of them.

He must have sensed how uncomfortable he was making her, for he pushed off the wall and straightened his stance. "I'd still love to get together and catch up with you. It's been a long time since we've seen each other. A lot of things have changed, for both of us."

"I'm not so sure—"

"Listen," he cut in. "If you're going to be staying in town and working at the paper, I'd like to be friends so it's not awkward every time we run into each other."

He was right. They would keep running into each other—Hidden Valley was a pretty small town—Aunt Renee had even said as much. Perhaps if she spent more time with him, those overwhelming feelings from the past would lose their power and they could simply be friends.

"What do you suggest?" Was she out of her mind for even entertaining such an idea?

"How about you let me take you to dinner tonight?"

She started to open her mouth in protest, but he pressed a couple of fingers lightly over her lips.

"Nothing fancy," Logan promised, lowering his hand. "Just two old friends catching up over a burger and fries. What do you say?"

His engaging eyes held her gaze, her lips tingling from his touch. Should she trust him again after all this time—or run? She hated the way she felt every time she bumped into him—a cross between wanting to throw up and her heart trying to jump out of her chest. If Hidden Valley was going to be home again, maybe she should at least attempt to make peace with him, for her own sake.

If it didn't work out for them to be friends, no one could say she hadn't tried. "All right. Pick me up at six." She peeled away from him and wandered toward the crowd to find her family, leaving Logan standing alone by the door. She assumed he was watching her go, and a quick glance over her shoulder confirmed it. A nervous chill shimmied down her back at the thought of his eyes shamelessly following her. She wasn't sure whether to be pleased or irritated.

Ramey and Sara were huddled in conversation with Aunt Renee near the buffet table and she headed toward them. What would the girls think of her decision to have dinner with her old flame? Maybe it was best not to spill the beans.

~*~

It was nearly five o'clock when Jenessa planted herself at her father's desk and opened her laptop. She had promised Charles McAllister a story on her father's funeral, along with a little more background information on him. She plowed through the story, and after submitting her article via email, she sat quietly and pondered Lucy St. John's murder.

Eleven years ago, Ramey had turned eighteen and graduated from high school when her mother announced that she and her boyfriend were taking off for a more exciting life in Southern California. With no extended family that Ramey knew of, she would have been all alone in the world, if it hadn't been for the Jones family.

Jenessa closed her eyes and let her imagination run wild with theories. She liked to call it playing the *What If* game.

What if Lucy's boyfriend killed her? Lucy St. John had been a drunk most of Ramey's life and her last boyfriend had turned her on to recreational drugs. Rather than heading straight to LA, what if they had gone up to the lake for one last party? Teenagers and the college crowd were known to do that, but would Lucy and her lover have done it too?

What if she had overdosed on something? Or, what if she and this guy had fought over something and he accidentally killed her?

CHAPTER 9

IF ONLY JENESSA KNEW the name of Lucy's last boyfriend, she could research him on the internet and hopefully discover something about him. She phoned Ramey. "Hey, can you stop by my house on your way home from work?"

"Sure. What's up?"

"I'll tell you when you get here."

Within a few minutes, Ramey was knocking at Jenessa's front door. She gave her a quick hug and let her in. "Come back to the study and we'll talk."

Ramey followed her down the hallway and took a seat across from the old desk. "Why are you being so mysterious?" Before Jenessa could answer, Ramey noticed the photo of the locket sitting on the corner of the desk. "What's this?"

She picked it up and gazed at it. "This is me." She raised her eyes to Jenessa. "Why do you have a picture of my mother's locket?"

Aunt Renee was right. Ramey just confirmed it.

"Ramey, I have something to tell you. Something bad."

"What is it?" Ramey's bright blue eyes darkened as a suspicious frown swept across her face.

Jenessa drew a deep breath and leaned back in the chair. "If the little girl in this photo is you, I have reason to believe that the remains that were found at the lake belonged to—"

"My mother?" Ramey blinked a few times, then her eyes grew round and wet. "Are you saying my mother is dead?"

Jenessa rose from her seat and came around the desk. "I'm so sorry." She bent down and laced her arms around Ramey. "It certainly appears that way."

"How do you know that? Did the police tell you? Did they do some sort of DNA testing on the bones? What?"

Jenessa straightened. "This locket was found with the bones, Ramey. What else could it mean?"

Ramey studied the photo again. "How did you get this picture?"

"I can't say, but trust me when I tell you that this locket was found with the buried remains."

Ramey nodded sadly. "Here, all this time I thought my mom ran off and didn't care about me anymore—but that's not what happened at all. She didn't run off…she died." Her voice cracked on the last painful word.

"So now the question is, who killed her?" Jenessa said. "And why."

Ramey handed the picture back. "Promise me you'll find out, Jenessa. Please, promise me that."

"I'm not a detective, Ramey. I'll do all I can, but I can't make any promises."

As an investigative reporter, Jenessa would pursue every avenue available to her to find the truth. If she could continue to apply pressure on Detective Provenza, she might learn more about the case, and perhaps she could also enlist Michael's help to feed her some clues to Lucy's murder.

Jenessa took her seat behind the desk again. "Do you remember the name of your mom's last boyfriend? The one she said she was going to LA with?"

"You think he's involved?"

"I'm trying to think of anyone who may have had motive or opportunity to kill your mom, and her boyfriend was the first one that came to mind."

"It was Tony something or other. All I remember is I used to call him Phony Tony Bologna."

"To his face?"

"Not if I knew what was good for me, but that's what he used to say when he wanted me to stop doing something. 'I swear, girl, if you know what's good for you.' I can hear him screaming it in my head like it was yesterday."

"So, Tony Bologna had a temper. Did he ever hit you?"

"A few times." Ramey paused for a moment, her expression falling, as if she remembering one of those instances. "You know, I may know where I can find his name—my mom's old boxes."

"Old boxes?"

"Yeah, she was a packrat. When she left, I couldn't bring myself to throw them away. Let me poke around in them when I get home. I'm pretty sure there are photos in one of them, and there just might be a picture of the two of them. If we're lucky, mom wrote his name on the back. She used to do that—to keep her boyfriends straight, I'm guessing."

Jenessa recalled there had been quite a string of men in Lucy St. John's life. Poor Ramey.

"Do you remember anyone that your mom had trouble with? Anyone who might have wanted to hurt her?"

"Boy…that was a long time ago. I'd have to give that some thought. Let me go find that box and look through it. If I come up with anything, I can drop it by tonight."

"I probably won't be home, so just call me and leave a message."

"Where are you going?" Ramey inquired.

"I'm having dinner with a friend."

"Anyone I know? Like a certain tall and hunky police officer perhaps?"

"No, I'm having dinner with Logan. Now, don't judge."

"Logan? What on earth for?" Ramey obviously missed Jenessa's last words about judging her.

"It's no big deal, nothing fancy. He just wanted to talk, make things not so uncomfortable every time we bump into each other."

"Oh, brother. And you bought that line?"

"Well, he does have a point, Ramey. This is a small town and I work for his family now." What could it hurt to give him an hour and see if he was right? "We're going to keep running into one another. If it turns out to be a mistake, I'll make a mad dash for the door."

"Call me if you need a ride home. And even if you don't, call me when you get home. I want to hear all the juicy details." Ramey snickered.

"Please, just see if you can find that photo of Phony Tony."

~*~

Now that Ramey had confirmed she was the child in the locket, Jenessa wondered if Aunt Renee could shed any more light on Lucy St. John. She had lived in Hidden Valley for more than thirty years and knew most of what went on in that town. If she phoned her aunt now, she'd have time to talk before Logan showed up.

"Now, I can't say with a hundred percent certainty," Aunt Renee began, "but I'm pretty sure that Ramey is Grey Alexander's daughter."

Jenessa sucked in a quick breath. "Are you kidding? What makes you say that?"

"I knew Lucy St. John when she was about twenty. I had just moved to Hidden Valley with Phillip, my second husband." Renee paused. "You remember him, don't you?"

"Barely."

"Well, it doesn't matter. I met Lucy when she was working at the bank."

"The one where Grey Alexander is the president?"

"Yes, but his father was the president then, and Grey was an asset manager, I believe. Anyway, Lucy worked for him. She was a pretty girl with long red hair and bright blue eyes, like Ramey's."

Jenessa leaned closer to the phone, as if her Aunt was right in front of her. "And you think they were having an affair?"

"Oh, honey, I know they were. Lucy confided in me one day over lunch that she had been seeing Grey, but she asked me to keep it to myself. No one could know."

"Wasn't Grey married by then?"

"He was. That's why. You see, his wife was very pregnant. Some men simply can't go without sex while their wives are in their third trimester and that period of time right after the birth, so he started up with Lucy. He didn't care about her, he just wanted sex—and she knew it. It wasn't like he was ever going to leave his wife and newborn baby for her. I don't know what that girl was thinking."

"That son of a—"

"Watch your language, young lady. Lucy had a hard upbringing, and not much sense, so when a handsome, powerful man like Grey started paying attention to her, well, it must have gotten the better of her."

Jenessa knew how that felt. Those Alexander men had a way about them.

"I tried to get her to break it off with him," Aunt Renee said, "but Lucy was under his spell. She wouldn't give him up. I didn't think we should stay friends after that."

"Then how do you know Grey Alexander is Ramey's father, if you'd broken contact with her?"

There was a pause on the phone line, as if Aunt Renee was measuring her words. "As far as I knew,

Grey was the only man Lucy had ever slept with up to that point. She was obsessed with the man."

Jenessa recalled her own obsession with the younger Mr. Alexander. Her stomach knotted at the thought.

"A few months later," Aunt Renee continued, "maybe four or five, I was in the bank doing some business and I noticed Grey's wife, Elizabeth, was there with the baby. Logan must have only been two or three months old at the time. Several of the tellers were crowding around them, getting a look at the child and wishing them well. I didn't see Lucy there though, so I asked one of the girls about her. She said Lucy had been let go, but she didn't know why."

Aunt Renee let out a long sigh. "I knew something was wrong, but I wasn't sure what. A couple of days later I saw her in town, stepping out of a store, and it was obvious she was pregnant, maybe four or five months along. She turned and went the other way when she saw me coming. I called out to her, but she kept walking."

"That's odd."

"I never spoke to her after that. Maybe I should have made more of an effort."

"But you don't know for sure Grey Alexander is Ramey's father, do you?"

"No, not absolutely. But who else could it be?"

"Well, Ramey could get a paternity test," Jenessa said.

"Assuming she wants to know."

"What do you mean?"

"Well," Aunt Renee paused, "that Grey Alexander is a powerful man, and he obviously has not wanted any relationship with her. He could make life hard for her in this town if she exposed him."

"Yeah, that would be bad," Jenessa replied. Then a thought hit her like a light bulb coming on. "Oh no, that would also mean Logan is Ramey's brother—well, half-brother. I wonder if he knows." If Ramey pursued it, he would have to split his inheritance with her, which Logan would certainly be opposed to doing.

"Not likely Grey would have told him," Aunt Renee supposed, "or anyone else."

"Do you think his wife knew?"

"It's possible."

"Is there something you're not telling me?" Jenessa pressed. It wasn't like Aunt Renee to give such short answers.

"Only that Grey and Elizabeth divorced when Logan was young. There were rumors."

"What kind of rumors?"

"If town gossip at the time is to be believed, it's very doubtful Lucy was the only one. Word was that there were a number of other women Grey had been, let's just say, *spending time* with. So, yes, Elizabeth was probably aware."

"Do you think she knew about Ramey?"

Elizabeth couldn't have been pleased with that fact, not to mention the division of the Alexander wealth. Her son would no longer be Grey's only heir.

"That I can't tell you, dear."

"If she did, though, do you think she would kill Lucy to keep it quiet?"

"After all those years? Oh, my goodness, no. Ramey was already grown by the time Lucy ran off. What would have been the point?"

"Then the new Mrs. Alexander perhaps?" Jenessa asked.

"Lauren? Now that's another story. I wouldn't put it past that gold digger to do anything she had to, to protect the Alexander fortune."

~*~

It was six o'clock straight up. The doorbell rang and Logan was right on time.

Pausing before she opened the door, Jenessa gripped the brass doorknob and closed her eyes. She took a deep breath and blew it out in short puffs, the way she had learned to do in Lamaze classes. Funny how that training had stayed with her all these years. It occurred to her that she often used this method to relax in tense situations.

The butterflies in her stomach seemed to settle down—butterflies which had hatched from their cocoons as soon as she agreed to have this friendly dinner with the young man who had ruined her life. She had no choice but to open the door or he would just ring the bell again. So she forced a polite, half-hearted smile on her face and flung it open.

There stood Logan, more handsome than ever, his gaze locking onto hers. The bright summer sun was low in the sky behind him and the light from it gave his silhouette a glow, backlighting his blond hair. His alluring eyes held her gaze and seemed to be peering straight down to her soul.

Struggling to break his magnetism, "Hello, Logan," was all she could manage, flatly, no affable lilt to her voice.

"You look beautiful tonight, Jenessa," he said, giving her a winsome smile, "but then you always do."

Her back stiffened at the compliment and her smile faded as she looked away. Was this really only meant to be a friendly dinner to mend broken old fences? She fought to keep her discomfort from showing on her face, continuing to divert her eyes from his. "I'll get my purse and we can go."

"Not going to invite me in?"

His question prickled her. She didn't want to be alone in the house with him. "I'm famished, so I'd really rather go to the restaurant for that burger you promised me." She took another deep breath as she turned and snatched her purse off the entry table and stepped out the door, locking it behind her.

Logan's red BMW was parked at the curb. As they strolled together down the stone walkway to his car, his hand hugged her waist for the last few steps before he opened the door for her.

The muscles in her back tensed at his touch. Irritated, she spun around to face him. "This isn't a date."

"I know," he said with a slight nod. "Just two old friends catching up."

Jenessa slid into the tan leather seat, not sure she believed him. His words said he knew it wasn't a date, but his actions didn't quite match them.

~*~

With little conversation, they reached the burger joint and were soon seated in a red vinyl booth.

"Are you glad to be back in Hidden Valley?" Logan asked, sitting across the table from her.

"It's taking a little getting used to." Jenessa picked up her menu and read over the offerings, avoiding his probing eyes. "I'm happy to be around my family again, and Ramey."

"You and Ramey have been friends since high school, haven't you?"

"Yes." Jenessa forced her gaze to remain on the menu items. "But you've probably known her all your life, since you were both born here."

"Actually, not until high school. We didn't grow up in the same neighborhood, so we didn't go to school together until then."

Of course they wouldn't grow up in the same neighborhood. Poor Ramey was the illegitimate daughter, and Logan had the silver spoon firmly planted in his mouth.

Was it really possible Logan never knew Ramey was his sister? Would his father have ever told him?

"Too bad, she's a great girl, like a sister to me." Jenessa peeked over her menu at him. No reaction.

"The body the cops found at the lake was her mother, right?" he asked.

Jenessa dropped her menu on the table, cringing at the sharp slapping noise that rang out from it. "What do you know about that?"

"Only what I've heard around town. Why the attitude?"

She picked up the menu again. *Who could have told him that?* "Sorry, it's just that the identity hasn't been confirmed yet." She scanned the menu selections once more, then gently set it down on the table. "Did you happen to know Lucy St. John at all?"

"Not really." There was a slight hesitation in his voice, then he went on. "My father said she had worked for him at one time, before Ramey was born." Logan folded his arms on the table and leaned in.

Was it Grey Alexander who told Logan the dead woman might be Lucy? He did seem to know everything that went on in this town.

"I don't want to speak ill of the dead," Logan said, "but wasn't Lucy pretty much a drunk when we were in high school?"

"She had her problems. She certainly didn't live the charmed life the Alexanders did—neither did Ramey."

He bolted up straight in the booth. "Charmed life? Just because my family has money doesn't mean we lived a fairytale. You have no idea what I've been through, what it's like being the son of the great and mighty Grey Alexander. It was..." Logan paused and stared at Jenessa for a moment, his eyes misting. Evidently, she had struck a nerve. "It was no picnic."

"I'm sorry," she muttered, putting a hand briefly on his, a sympathetic ache stirring inside. Maybe there were things going on in that household that she didn't know about—awful things. Maybe she had been so wrapped up in her own family drama that she never noticed. "I just assumed—"

"Everyone always does," Logan cut in, pulling his hand away. He sat back against the cushioned booth and his eyes cleared. "Someday, maybe I'll tell you about it."

Would they ever get to the place in their new quasi-friendship where he would open up like that? Because he never did when they were dating. Would she ever dare to share the trials between her and her father with him?

The waitress approached their table and took their orders.

"How's your mother?" Jenessa asked after the waitress left. "Do you get to see her very much?"

He nodded. "When she's not busy with her clubs and organizations, or traveling."

"She's the president of the Hidden Valley Garden Club, isn't she?"

"No, my stepmother is. Why do you ask?"

"I'll be covering the Flower Show next week for the paper, so I thought I'd be interviewing your mother. Guess it will be Lauren instead."

"Mom will be at the high school this Sunday afternoon setting up for an auction next week. Maybe you should cover that. They're trying to raise two hundred thousand dollars to renovate the auditorium."

"I loved that old auditorium—the ornate details and the thick burgundy curtains. It was like an opera house."

"That's right. Didn't we go and see *Music Man* there?"

"We did—and *Mame,* remember?" Jenessa smiled at the memory.

"We had a lot of good times together," Logan said.

Then her thoughts turned back to his mother again. "Did your mom know Lucy St. John when you were growing up?"

"Boy, that was kind of out of the blue." Logan frowned. "Why on earth would you ask that?"

"I was thinking about the interview I want to do with her, and I figured I might as well kill two birds with one stone—" Jenessa cringed. "Wrong choice of words, I meant I might as well ask questions for the Lucy St. John case while I'm at it. To save time, you know?"

"I have no idea if she knew her. Mom and Dad divorced when I was seven. If she wasn't part of the well-to-do crowd around here, it's not likely my mother would have been friends with her."

"She could have known her other ways. She could have known her from the bank maybe." Jenessa watched for a flicker of agreement in Logan's face.

He shrugged. "No idea." He leaned in again, his brows knitting together in a serious frown. "You can't think my mother had anything to do with Lucy's death, can you?"

"I'm just gathering facts at this point." Jenessa took a sip of ice water, back-peddling while she kept her eyes from meeting Logan's so he couldn't see through her to what she was really thinking. "Besides, it's the cops' job to solve the murder, not mine."

Although, if Jenessa could help solve the murder, and be the first to publish the story, it would be a boon for her career. Maybe one day she could leave this quiet small town and go to work for another newspaper in a major city.

"So where did you end up going to college?" Logan asked, an obvious attempt to change the subject.

Jenessa shared that she had gone to Sacramento State and majored in journalism. Logan said he went to San Diego State and played football until he blew out his knee his junior year. He graduated with a degree in business, assuming his father would expect him to come back to Hidden Valley and take over the family empire. He was right.

They chatted about their college experiences and the various jobs they held, both carefully skirting around the subject of the unexpected pregnancy and the baby she had given up for adoption.

That was a discussion for later…much later.

It definitely was not a conversation she wanted to have in a public place. There would certainly be crying, maybe even some shouting and angry words. No, it was better not to bring it up in this burger joint where there was an abundance of prying eyes, and ears. No doubt just her sitting in a booth with Logan would be juicy fodder for town gossip long before morning.

Jenessa and Logan reminisced about the prom and other school activities they remembered. They even laughed a few times over the memories of some crazy antics of their classmates. She caught herself twirling her long dark hair around her finger, a lighthearted giddiness coming over her. It was almost as though she was a teenager again.

By the time the burgers and fries were consumed and conversation was winding down, Jenessa had become surprisingly comfortable with Logan. No bad memories were dug up tonight, no old wounds uncovered. Now she could at least run into him around town and avoid the spine-stiffening awkwardness they'd had up until tonight.

He drove her home and walked her to the door. It was a little after nine. They paused on the porch, under the light, and said their good-byes. Logan leaned down and unexpectedly kissed Jenessa lightly on the lips.

Before she could react, the sound of squealing tires split the air. Both Logan and Jenessa turned their heads toward the street, seeing a police cruiser racing away.

CHAPTER 10

WITH HER NERVES IN A TANGLE over having dinner with Logan, and her phone conversation with Aunt Renee, Jenessa had forgotten Michael was dropping by around nine, after his shift. *Oh, God.* He saw Logan kiss her. Now he had the wrong idea. Jenessa was mortified.

She unlocked the door, and the jingling of the keys drew Logan's attention from the street back to Jenessa. She offered him a curt smile. "Good night, Logan."

"Aren't you going to invite me in?"

Second time that night he'd asked that question.

If Michael's squealing tires hadn't broken Logan's spell over her, she might have actually considered it. They were getting along well. It had been a surprisingly enjoyable evening—then his lips were on hers, even for a brief moment, and they felt so delicious that her defenses began to melt and her body went weak. But, no! She couldn't let herself be drawn into his web again.

Thank goodness Michael had been there to rescue her from Logan's charms, but what had that saving moment done to her chances with Michael? She'd have to call him and try to salvage their budding relationship.

Jenessa thanked Logan for suggesting they get together and catch up over dinner. If he was thinking of trying to kiss her again, she wasn't going to wait around and give him the opportunity.

"Good night, Logan." Jenessa stepped inside her house and hastily shut the door. She had to call Michael, explain away what he saw, and see if he still wanted to stop by.

It wasn't like she owed Michael an explanation. They weren't dating, but there was definitely something sparking between them. Maybe it could lead to something more.

As for Logan, even now, something inside her turned to jelly when she was near him. But as for a future with that man? She couldn't see it. Not after the past they shared.

She dug her phone out of her purse and dialed Michael's number.

"Hello."

She was still surprised to hear his voice had grown so deep over the years, not the silly boy voice she had known when they were schoolmates.

"Michael, this is Jenessa."

He didn't reply right away and the air hung uncomfortably chilly between them.

"Michael?"

"Yeah, I'm here. What can I do for you?"

"You promised you'd stop by and pick a lock for me tonight."

"I did stop by, but you were otherwise occupied. I didn't want to interrupt anything."

"Logan wanted to talk to me about something, so I had a quick burger with him. There was nothing to interrupt."

"It didn't look that way to me."

Well, that confirmed it. Obviously Michael had seen Logan kiss her. Was he jealous?

"Really, Michael, that's all it was. He gave me a quick peck on the lips, which I wasn't expecting, nor did I want, then I sent him on his way. I'll be up for a while if you'd still like to come by."

"I don't think so. I'm almost at my folks' house. I need to pick up Jake and get him to bed."

It couldn't have been more than three or four minutes between when Michael peeled away and this call. How would he have had time to be close to his parents' house? He *was* jealous. "I could really use your help tonight. Pretty please."

Again, silence hung between them. Finally he spoke. "Fine. I'll call my mom and have her keep Jake overnight. See you in a few."

~*~

In less than five minutes, Michael was standing on her doorstep, ringing her bell.

She swung the door open wide and greeted him with a friendly smile. He was still wearing his navy blue uniform. Her heart fluttered at the sight of him.

"I got a call there was a woman in distress at this address, ma'am." He wore a poker face.

"That's right, Officer." Jenessa grinned as she played along and stepped to the side to let him in. "Right this way," she said with a sweeping motion toward the main hall.

He followed her to the study. "What seems to be the problem?"

She pointed to the desk. "This may sound silly, Officer, but I can't get the stupid lap drawer open."

"Well, little lady, let's see what I can do about that." Michael dragged the chair out and crouched down behind the desk to examine the lock. He whipped a small leather case out of his back pocket and unzipped it, displaying several sharp instruments. He worked a couple of them into the lock, but it wouldn't budge. He kept after it for quite a while, but no luck.

"I hoped that would be all it needed." Jenessa pursed her lips. "Just a little love from the handsome policeman."

Michael burst into a loud, deep laugh. "I've never heard picking a lock described like that."

"Well, for all your effort, how about a piece of fresh peach pie."

Michael's eyebrows arched. "Did you make it?"

She laughed as she stood in the doorway. "You really don't know me, do you?" She turned and headed toward the kitchen.

"Is that a no?" he asked, following close behind her.

"Ramey brought it to Aunt Renee's for dinner the other night. It's from The Sweet Spot. My aunt insisted I take the leftovers home." Jenessa pulled the half-eaten pie from the refrigerator and set it on the counter.

"Got any vanilla ice cream?" Michael asked.

Jenessa rifled through the utensil drawer for a knife and an ice cream scoop. "Let's look. Mom used to always keep some in the freezer for my dad. Maybe he still did too."

Michael stood behind her as she poked through the freezer side of the refrigerator. The cold air felt good on her face, which had unexpectedly grown hot at his closeness. She plucked the container of ice cream out of the freezer and spun around.

"Here it is."

He was only inches away from her. A palpable energy vibrated between them. She sensed he wanted to kiss her, she saw it in his eyes, and she would let him. Their gaze locked for a moment. Instead of a kiss, though, he went to the counter and cut the pie. Had he suddenly remembered seeing Logan kiss her?

"This thing looks delicious," he muttered.

She set the ice cream container beside the pie, the loud thumping in her chest beginning to subside, thankfully, or she was afraid he was going to hear it. "You want to do the honors?"

When Michael was finished loading the pieces of pie onto the plates, and adding a scoop of ice cream to each, they carried their dishes to the table.

Jenessa took a seat. "I haven't had a chance to ask how the review board went."

"Seemed to me like everything went well. I should hear the results in a few days, I'm hoping." He dug into his dessert.

"Soon, I'll have to call you Detective Baxter." She laughed, sticking a forkful of pie in her mouth.

He swallowed and grinned at her. "Hey, how's your story going? The one on the body that was found up at the lake?"

She explained to him about the locket that had been discovered with the body and how the photo inside looked a lot like Ramey. It was her assumption, she continued, that the body must have been Ramey's mother.

"How did you get to see the inside of the locket? I thought it was up in Sacramento at the crime lab."

She gave him a smug feline grin. "I have my ways."

"Ramey's mother, huh? Does Provenza know?"

"I called him, but I'm not sure if he believes me. He said he needs to have some way for the lab to prove it— you know, DNA, dental records, or something." She took another bite.

"Who would want to murder Lucy St. John?"

"I've got plenty of people on my list of suspects," Jenessa said.

He frowned and stopped his fork midair. "Like who?"

Ramey was the first name to pop into Jenessa's head. Not that *she* would kill her mother and bury her body up at the lake, but someone who wanted to keep Ramey's parentage a secret would have a strong motive—and there were several of them. Should she tell Michael what she knew about who had likely fathered Ramey?

"No names." She waved her hand at him. "It's too early to be putting them out there, Michael, but there is a very scandalous bit of information I discovered."

"Scandalous?" He cocked his head. "Like what?"

Jenessa shared what Aunt Renee had told her about Lucy's affair with Grey Alexander and how she was fairly certain he was Ramey's biological father.

"Grey Alexander is Ramey's father?"

"Shocker, huh?"

"Are you sure?"

"Not a hundred percent, but pretty sure. There would have to be a paternity test, that is, if Ramey wants to know."

"Haven't you told her yet?"

"Not yet, not until we get confirmation from the lab."

"That would make her Logan's sister." He stuck the last forkful of his pie in his mouth. "I never would have guessed."

"Well, half sister, but that's not for public consumption, though." If word leaked out, in this small town, Ramey would be humiliated at being the subject of widespread gossip.

"Oh, no, of course. Mum's the word."

When they were finished with their pie, she took their plates and rinsed them in the sink. "By the way, how's your little guy doing? Looking forward to kindergarten?"

"That's all he talks about—well, that and you."

"Me?" Jenessa's brow wrinkled, as she dried her hands.

"Seems you made quite an impression on him at the bakery the other day, old friend."

She laughed at the characterization, turning from the sink to face him. "He seems like a great little boy." Envy wasn't an emotion she was used to, and she pushed it down. "You're doing a good job with him, Michael."

"Thanks, I'd like to think so. It's been difficult raising him alone, with his mother gone and all. Thank God I have my mom and dad to help. I'd be lost without them."

They stood by the sink, gazing into each other's eyes. No words passed between them for a long moment. Jenessa was sure he was going to lean down and kiss her—she sensed it in his eyes and the tilt of his head. She was ready, even anxious for it. As he lowered his face to hers, she put a hand on his chest and pushed up on her toes, her lips within inches of his.

Michael was so close that Jenessa felt his hot breath on her lips. Then, he stepped back...unexpectedly.

"I can't do this right now. I have Jake to think about."

Her feet fell flat. "I don't understand."

"I saw you kissing Logan tonight. I have to be careful who I get involved with, for Jake's sake."

The romantic moment was lost.

She crossed her arms and rested her hips against the counter. "What you saw was Logan kissing me good night, and it was no more than a peck. I was as surprised by it as you were."

"Kissing you good night...so you went on a date with him?"

"I already explained that. We were just two old friends catching up over a hamburger. It wasn't a date, Michael. Please believe me."

"Listen, Jenessa, when you're nothing more than just friends, you don't kiss on the lips." Out of nowhere, Michael grabbed her by the arms and pulled her against him. His lips were on hers, kissing her fiercely, deeply, then he released her just as fast.

Her body went weak and her legs wobbly, like they were filled with hot fudge. She couldn't catch her breath. Her hands grabbed onto the counter behind her for support.

Message received.

Michael stood staring at her, like he had surprised himself by what he had done. "I have to go." He shot off down the hallway and the sound of the front door closing resonated through the house, leaving her with her mouth hanging open.

~*~

With the lap drawer of her father's desk still locked, there was nothing more to do that evening. So, after Michael left, Jenessa headed to bed, still confused by what had happened.

She sunk back against her pillows, a soft flicker of moonlight swaying through the curtains. It captured her attention momentarily, but when she closed her eyes, Michael's face came rushing into focus. The memory of his mouth so hungrily on hers caused her lips to pulsate and tingle.

Was he lying in his bed thinking about their kiss as well?

She rolled onto her side, snuggled against her pillow, and drifted happily off to sleep.

~*~

Early the next morning, the sound of the phone ringing shook Jenessa out of a dream. With her eyes half-shut and her mind still in the dream-fog, she fumbled around the top of the nightstand for her cell phone.

She offered her first word of the day—a raspy sleep-laden hello.

"Good morning, sunshine."

"Ramey?" Jenessa raised herself on one elbow, peering over at the alarm clock on her nightstand, her eyes still blurry from sleep. "What time is it?"

"It's seven thirty. Sorry, did I wake you?"

Jenessa could be polite and lie, but the sleepy sound of her voice would betray her. "I was asleep, but it's time to get up." Her father's voice echoed in her ears, admonishing her not to sleep the day away. "What's up?"

"You never called me back last night. Remember? The date with Logan? You were going to dish."

"Ugh! It wasn't a date. I keep telling everyone that." Jenessa plopped back against her pillows.

"Everyone? Who else did you tell?"

"Michael."

"Oh, girl, now you really *have* to tell me about last night. Don't leave anything out."

Jenessa gave Ramey a detailed account of her dinner with Logan, the unexpected kiss, the squealing tires, and her phone call with Michael that got him over to her house.

"He wasn't able to pick the lock, so I still have no idea what's so important in Dad's drawer that he felt he had to lock it up, but I'm not giving up. Aunt Renee forbade me to damage it, so I'll try everything else first, but I am going to get that drawer open, one way or the other."

"What do you expect to find in it?"

"I don't know, but it's obviously something Dad didn't want anyone else to see."

"Oh, before I forget, the other reason I called was to tell you I found a photo of Phony Tony Bologna with my mom."

"Did you find his name?"

"Yes, Tony Hamilton. Does that help?"

"We'll see. I'll check him out. There's likely more than one Tony Hamilton in this country, so the photo will help me identify him."

"You? What about the police?" Ramey asked.

"Of course you'll need to tell Detective Provenza you remembered his name, but I'd like to get a peek at the photo before you hand it over to him."

"I stuck it in my purse, so next time I see you, it's yours," Ramey said. "So...what happened after Michael tried to pick the lock? And don't tell me *nothing*."

"We had some pie and talked."

"And..."

"And he kissed me. Then he left."

"Woohoo! I knew it!"

"Don't get carried away, Ramey. It probably didn't mean anything."

"So it was just a little peck, like Logan gave you?"

"Not exactly."

"Spill, girl."

"It was a great kiss—"

"The kind you feel all the way to your toes?"

"Yes, but then he ran off like someone had lit his pants on fire."

"Hmm, like you?" Ramey chuckled. "Say, listen, why don't you come down to The Sweet Spot and have breakfast? We can talk more then. I've got to get back to work."

"If you'll save me a—"

"Pecan sticky bun. I know. It's already done." Ramey laughed again. "I sure don't know how you eat the way you do and stay so skinny."

~*~

After getting ready for the day, Jenessa sat down at her laptop and began searching for Tony Hamilton. She made note to check for Anthony Hamilton as well.

She came up with several possibilities, but until she got a look at Ramey's photo, she couldn't go any further.

Within the hour, Jenessa walked into the little café, dressed for the weather in a deep red tank top and slim white slacks. She took her place in line behind two others and gazed around. The tables were mostly empty, glad she had waited long enough to miss the morning rush.

Ramey was not behind the cash register or the bakery case. Jenessa figured she must be working in the kitchen. As she reached the counter, Ramey emerged with a pink box, surely filled with some delectable treat.

"Hey, Jenessa! I saved you a sticky bun in back. Order your coffee and I'll bring it out to you."

"Who's the box for?"

"That's for me," said a familiar male voice behind her.

Jenessa spun around. "Charles." She offered him a friendly smile. "What's the occasion?"

The little bells jingled and Jenessa turned toward the door.

"Dad," a boy moaned from the doorway. "What's taking so long?"

"I'm coming," Charles said to the boy, who looked to be ten to twelve years old.

"Who's this?" Jenessa smiled at the boy.

The boy glanced at her, then turned his attention back to his father. "Come on, Dad. We're gonna be late." He backed out of the doorway and let it glide shut.

"That's my son, Charlie. We're headed out on a camping trip with his troop and I'm afraid we're running a little behind. That's what these doughnuts are for." He raised the box to her before turning and striding toward the entrance. "Thanks, Ramey," he cast over his shoulder.

"You're welcome."

Charles paused in at the door and twisted back to her. "Don't forget, Sunday night."

Ramey's face lit up. "I won't forget." Her gaze followed him out the door and to his pickup, parked at the curb.

Jenessa watched Ramey's expression, her smile not fading. "What's happening Sunday night?"

Ramey continued to watch as Charles backed his truck out of the parking space and sped off. "What?"

"What's happening Sunday night? Your turn to dish."

"Oh nothing. We just have a date."

"A date?" Jenessa firmly planted her hands on both of Ramey's upper arms, effectively holding her for questioning. "When were you going to tell me?"

"He just asked me, when he ordered the doughnuts." Ramey grinned and shrugged out of Jenessa's hold, waltzing behind the bakery case. "I still can't believe it myself."

"You honestly didn't have any inkling that he liked you?"

"Well...he's always been rather friendly. I thought he was simply being a nice guy."

"Ramey's got a boyfriend," Jenessa sang, taking a seat at a nearby table.

"Stop that." Ramey swatted a hand at her. "It's not like we're in junior high."

"Oh, I'm just having fun with you." Jenessa grinned. "Charles is a great guy, from what I've seen so far. But you'll have his son to think of, too."

"I know, but I love kids. And I've known Charlie his whole life." Ramey brought Jenessa's coffee and bun to her table. "I could say the same thing about you— Michael has a son."

"That's right." In her excitement over Ramey's date with Charles, she wasn't even thinking about the similarity to her and Michael.

No sooner were the words out of Jenessa's mouth than the bells tinkled on the door, and Michael stepped through with Jake.

CHAPTER 11

"HELLO, LADIES," MICHAEL SAID with a smile as he and his son entered the café.

Jenessa jumped from her seat and stepped toward them. "Michael, what a surprise." She bent down to face Jake on his own level. "Good morning, Jake."

"Hi." Jake gave her a little grin and looked up at his father. "She's pretty."

Jenessa glanced up at Michael and stifled a giggle. She crouched down beside Jake. "Thank you. That was so sweet. I think you're a rather handsome little fellow too."

Jake pushed his little shoulders back and stood tall, pride beaming on his face. Then he intensified his gaze and cocked his head. "What about Daddy?"

Jenessa glanced up at Michael before refocusing on Jake. "I suppose he could be considered the tall, dark, and handsome type—some girls like that sort of thing."

She shot a mischievous smile up at Michael as he leaned back dramatically, his hand over his heart, looking crushed.

The subtle interaction was completely lost on Jake, who had already switched topics. "Daddy? Can she come to the fair with us?"

"Oh, Jake, I don't think she would want to—"

"I'd love to." Jenessa stood and her gaze flew from Jake to Michael. "That is, if I'm not intruding on father-son time."

A smile spread across Michael's face, lighting up his eyes. "Not intruding. Love to have you."

Jenessa peered down at her watch. "I have an interview to do in about half an hour, but I could catch up with you after that." She crouched back down to Jake's level. "Would that be okay?"

Jake nodded his head up and down in a deliberate motion. "Yes."

"Now, what can I get for you two gentlemen?" Ramey asked from behind the counter.

"Just a coffee, my usual," Michael replied.

"Nothing for Jake? One of our famous energy bars maybe."

"He's got more than enough energy, Ramey. But thanks."

"Oh, he can't leave here empty handed. That would be criminal." Ramey gave him a mock pout. "How about one of my very special chewy oatmeal cookies? On the house."

A huge smile took over Jake's face and he bounced up and down on his tiptoes. "Please, Daddy, please."

"How can you say no to that face?" Jenessa asked.

"You're not helping." Michael frowned, his gaze moving from Jenessa to Ramey. "I guess one cookie won't hurt." He took the cookie and a napkin from Ramey and handed them to his son before turning his attention back to Jenessa. "Who are you interviewing this morning? If you don't mind my asking."

"Well, Detective Baxter, I'm interviewing Lauren Alexander."

"Not detective yet. I was just curious." He leaned closer to Jenessa and lowered his voice. "Does this have anything to do with the homicide case?"

"No, Mr. Nosey. I have to write a story on the Flower Show, and Mrs. Alexander happens to be the president of the Garden Club. However, while I have her ear, I do plan to ask her a few pointed questions about what she might know about Lucy and the murder."

"Ever the investigator." A slow grin crept over his lips. "Provenza won't like you doing his job."

"It's my job too. You'd think he'd be grateful for the help."

"Just don't step on his toes. Let him think that what you're doing was his idea and you'll get along just fine."

~*~

The housekeeper seated Jenessa in the formal living room to wait for Lauren Alexander. As she waited, perched on the edge of a yellow-and-white striped chair, she surveyed the room, bright with alabaster walls and tall windows, flanked with floor-to-ceiling silk draperies—a floral design in hues of yellow, green, and red.

The décor may have changed over the years, but she could still vividly remember the last time she had been there. It was the night she and Logan had gathered both sets of parents together to break the news she was pregnant.

That night she was a scared teenager looking for help and direction from the adults. In her view, Grey Alexander had loomed large, larger than her own father even. His very presence and manner had made her knees feel like rubber. But today, she determined, she would no longer be intimidated by that man. As she gazed around at his palatial manor, a new confidence began to rise up in her. She was a professional newswoman now. She would doggedly investigate this brutal crime, she would follow the story no matter where it led her. Even if it led her to his front door.

At that moment, Lauren Alexander sashayed into the room and settled on the creamy white sofa, perpendicular to Jenessa's chair.

"Thank you for seeing me, Mrs. Alexander."

"Please, call me Lauren."

Lauren was almost forty, but she looked to Jenessa to be in her early thirties—her skin firm and young looking, her body as well. From what Aunt Renee had told her, constant trips to the dermatologist and beauty spas had kept her wrinkles, and other pesky signs of aging, at bay.

The woman was slim but shapely and her clothes fit to perfection—likely designer, definitely tailored. She was a beauty by anyone's measure—a perfect nose, full lips, long golden brown hair with blond highlights, and large round blue eyes outlined with dark lashes. It was clear how she had been able to snare Grey Alexander. Still, Jenessa wondered if it was enough to keep him faithful to wife number two.

Regardless, the woman commanded ownership of her abode. Sitting in the center of the white sofa, a myriad of colorful silk pillows behind her, legs gracefully crossed at the ankles, her hands resting in her lap, Lauren gave the appearance of a queen holding court.

"Well, Lauren, as you know, I'm here to ask you about the Garden Club and the Flower Show you are putting on in the coming week. Why don't you tell me all about it?"

Lauren's eyes lit up, and her face and hands were animated as she spoke about the flowers and what her club hoped to accomplish.

Jenessa had to scribble quickly in her notebook to keep up with the enthusiastic pace.

After thirty minutes of questions and answers about the flowers, and copious amounts of notes, Jenessa sensed her opportunity to turn the conversation toward the possible homicide. She would butter her hostess up before she launched into the questions.

"I so appreciate your time today, Lauren. You are an absolute wealth of information about flowers and gardening. Beauty and brains—it's no wonder Grey Alexander snapped you up."

Lauren offered a demure smile. "Why, thank you, Miss Jones, you are too kind. It's been my pleasure. I mean, what good is knowledge if we don't share it?"

And there was her segue. Jenessa couldn't have scripted it better herself. "Lauren, I couldn't agree more." Jenessa gathered her things, pretending to be getting ready to leave. "Actually, before I go, I wonder if I could ask you about something else."

"What would that be?" Lauren's voice turned suspicious.

"Did you happen to know Lucy St. John?"

A slight frown formed on Lauren's brow, like she was going through a mental Rolodex. "The name sounds familiar."

"Her remains were found in a shallow grave near your lake house."

Lauren's hand flew to her chest in a dramatic gesture of concern that didn't seem to quite reach her eyes. "Oh my. That's where I've heard the name—in the news. Horrible. Simply horrible." She shook her head and lowered her gaze momentarily before resuming her poised appearance. "Why do you ask?"

The reaction seemed a little over the top. And she didn't really answer the question. Jenessa played along. "I'm covering the story for the city paper—you know, building a back story—I'm trying to talk to anyone who might have known her."

"Her death was a long time ago, wasn't it?"

"Eleven or twelve years ago, I believe."

"Why would you think I knew her?"

Another evasive question.

"I have reason to believe she was acquainted with your husband. So she could have known you as well. No?"

"I guess it's possible, but I don't recall."

The woman was not going to give anything up. Time to be direct.

"I don't mean to sound indelicate, Lauren, but I've heard talk that when your husband was married to the first Mrs. Alexander, he had a reputation for sleeping with women who weren't his wife."

"What exactly are you implying, Miss Jones?"

"Lucy St. John was one of those women."

Lauren Alexander's blue eyes widened and her soft, lovely features stiffened into a glaring frown. She shot up off the sofa. "I think you'd better leave."

Should Jenessa dare tell Lauren about her husband's illegitimate daughter? Or was it possible she already knew about Ramey? Her senses were tingling, telling her this woman definitely knew something, and she didn't want to talk about it.

Jenessa rose from her chair, slowly, deliberately. "I will say, if I was able to find out about your husband's affair with Lucy St. John, you can be sure the police will too. So, if you know anything…"

"Please go." Lauren, whose face was now pinched into a scowl, flung her arm out and pointed a well-manicured finger in the direction of the foyer.

Jenessa dropped a business card on the gleaming glass coffee table. "If you think of anything at all, please call me. I'll keep your name out of my story, of course."

"Go!"

~*~

Jenessa approached the barrier surrounding the car track at the county fair just as Jake went whizzing by in a tiny motorized car. Well, maybe not exactly whizzing by, but the gleeful expression on his face as he putted by during one of his laps said he felt like he was racing.

"Daddy, Daddy! Look at me!"

She waved to Jake as he went around again.

"Hey, you found us," Michael greeted from where he stood watching his son.

"You gave me good directions." Jenessa had phoned him after her interview, before going home to change into jeans and a white t-shirt.

Jake finished his laps, hopped out of the miniature car, and ran to his waiting father. "Did you see that, Daddy? I think I came in first."

"Uh, yeah, I think you did." Michael cast Jenessa a sideways glance that said *I don't think it was a race.* "How about we get some corndogs, big guy?"

"Okay, but I gotta go potty." Jake crossed his legs with a distressed look on his face.

"Hey, why don't I go get the corndogs?" Jenessa offered. "You boys head for the bathrooms and I'll get in line." She glanced in the direction of the food court and caught sight of the Pronto Pup stand. "Looks like a long one."

Michael took Jake by the hand. "Okay. Thanks. Be right back."

They trotted off to take care of business as Jenessa took her place in line for the corndogs. It moved surprisingly fast and when she was only a few people back, someone tapped her on the shoulder.

"That was quick." She spun around with a smile on her face, assuming it would be Michael and Jake, but it was Logan that she found standing behind her.

"Fancy meeting you here," he said, peering down at her with a smile. Logan snaked a finger down Jenessa's arm. "You always did like the fair."

She was stuck in line—Jake would be expecting a corndog—she would have to talk with Logan. But she didn't have to let him touch her, especially when Michael could walk up at any moment. She took a little step away. "Yes, I did like the fair, but it's been a long time since I've been here."

"I always liked it too, particularly the fair food," he said. "What about you?"

Nervousness at Michael seeing them together caused her smile to fade, but there was a new comfort with Logan that she couldn't deny. "I liked that the week of the fair always signaled summer was almost over and we'd meet up with friends we hadn't seen since school let out. Remember?"

"Yeah, fun times." Logan grinned. "Speaking of fun times, I'm going up to the lake tomorrow, taking my boat out. How about you come with me?"

Jenessa's heart leapt into her throat. Was Logan serious? The lake?

"We could pack a picnic lunch and—"

"Next!" the corndog vendor called out.

She turned back to the young man taking orders, grateful he had saved her from having to answer. "I'll take three corndogs."

Logan chuckled. "You must be hungry."

She shot a glance over her shoulder. "They're not all for me."

As the man set the paper bag of corndogs on the small metal counter, Michael and Jake stepped up alongside Jenessa.

"Six dollars," the vendor said. "Mustard packets are in the bag."

Michael reached in his pocket and paid the guy before Jenessa could get her wallet from her purse.

"Hello, Michael," Logan said.

Michael scooped up the food and gave him a fleeting glance. "Logan."

Tension filled the air. The two had not been friends in high school, traveling in difference circles, and Michael had told her they'd only had a passing acquaintance the last few years.

But now, since Jenessa had been back in town, they had been thrown into close proximity several times. She watched as the two men seemed to size each other up, deciding she'd better step between them.

"The corndogs are going to get cold while you two stand here jawing." She tugged on Michael's arm. "Nice to see you again, Logan." She led Michael a few steps away from the line with Jake following close behind.

Michael seemed to switch gears then, looking down at Jake. "Okay, guys, where shall we eat?"

Jenessa glanced back. Logan was watching them, looking none too pleased. "Let's walk and eat." She waved a good-bye as they strolled away.

They walked down the rows of games and prizes, Jake between the two of them, as they slathered mustard on their corndogs. When the food was gone, they gave several of the games a try.

After a few hours of trying to win prizes, checking out the 4-H farm animals, and riding the Ferris wheel, the Tilt-a-Whirl, and the bumper cars, the five-year-old was tuckered out. Michael picked Jake up and carried him out to the car, the boy's head resting on his dad's broad shoulder.

Michael tucked his son in the back seat and strapped him in, then stood, looking at Jenessa across the roof of the car. "Would you like to come over tonight? We could watch a movie or something. I'm sure Jake is down for the count."

She rounded the car and stepped near him. "Sounds wonderful, but I have to work on my Flower Show story and get it in tonight. Can I have a rain check?"

"Sure…but you never mentioned how your interview went with Lauren Alexander. Were you able to sneak in a few questions about Lucy St. John?"

Jenessa breathed a laugh. "I did, and she all but ran me out of her house."

"I'd like to have seen that. Think she's hiding something?"

"Hard to tell, she puts up such a thick façade. Maybe George can get somewhere with her."

"I doubt he'd hazard going over there to question her without more reason than just your curiosity." Michael raised his eyebrows, looking for her agreement.

She nodded. "You're right."

He glanced down at his son, asleep in the car. "Jake had a great time, by the way. I'm sure he'll be talking about it for days."

Jenessa moved closer. She raked a hand through her dark tresses and raised her face to him. "How about you? Did you have a good time?"

"That goes without saying." He leaned down and gave her a soft kiss. "I'd better get him home. We're really glad you came."

A satisfied smile spread across her lips. "It was my pleasure."

~*~

On the way home from the fair, Jenessa stopped by The Sweet Spot, hoping she could pick up a sandwich for dinner before they closed. The familiar jingle rang out as she entered, giving her reason to smile. Once inside, though, her smile vanished as she came face to face with Grey Alexander, holding a pink pastry box, on his way out.

"Well, if it isn't Jenessa Jones. I'd heard you were back in town."

She read his expression as reflecting loathing and disdain. She hadn't seen this man in years, aside from noticing him at her father's funeral, and yet his dislike for her was as evident as it had been the night he'd received the news that his son had gotten her pregnant. In this moment, now, as a grown woman, there was nothing she would have liked more than to reach up and wipe that smug, self-righteous look off his face.

So why had her inner strength unexpectedly evaporated, leaving her suddenly feeling like she was seventeen again, cowering under his powerful stare?

Hadn't she just declared that morning that she would no longer be shaken by him?

"Can we step outside?" he asked. "There's something I'd like to discuss with you."

With me? Jenessa swallowed hard. Her heart rate picked up. As she followed the man out to the sidewalk, she glanced back at Ramey behind the counter, who stood staring at them with a worried expression.

"My wife called me this morning and she was extremely upset by what you said to her."

Jenessa willed her spine to hold her up. "I…I'm doing an investigative story on the remains that were discovered by your lake house last week—Lucy St. John's remains."

"Lucy St. John? The police have confirmed that?"

"Not exactly." She took a deep breath. "But I have reason to believe they will shortly."

"You think you know better than the police? You're just a cub reporter with pie-in-the sky aspirations of something more. You couldn't cut it in the big city and you've come back here with your tail between your legs—to work for me, I might add." He expelled a haughty laugh. "I would expect nothing less of you, Jenessa Jones."

"I beg your pardon," she spat back. Her eyes narrowed as renewed strength flooded her body and fortified her backbone. She straightened her shoulders and stood a little taller. "I was laid off from the paper in Sacramento due to decreasing readership. I was not fired. And I didn't come running back here with my tail anywhere—my father died, as you well know." Jenessa spoke between gritted teeth, poking a finger in the man's face. "I came back here to tend to his funeral and his estate. I've decided to stay, so I took a job at the Hidden Valley Herald. But then, you already know that, don't you. You seem to know everyone's business."

Grey's eyes widened. "Get that finger out of my face."

He obviously was not used to being spoken to like that. Sure, he owned the newspaper where she worked, and she could be jeopardizing her job right now, but the man needed to be stood up to and she needed to be the one to do it.

"You listen to me, Miss Jones." His face pinched into a scowl. "You had better be careful who you talk to like that. I could squash you like a bug. If you're smart, you'll take this warning seriously and stay away from my wife—or else." He glared at her for a moment before stomping off to his shiny black Mercedes, parked at the curb.

Or else what? Her resolve was beginning to wane. Jenessa spun around and darted back into the bakery before he could continue his threats. Once inside, she stopped and gasped for air—she hadn't taken a breath since he demanded she stay away from his wife.

"Is everything okay?" Ramey asked from behind the counter. "You look flushed."

"That Grey Alexander is a piece of work." Jenessa glanced around the bakery. Fortunately, the place was empty.

"I can't argue with you there. Anything I can do to help?"

"Can I get a turkey on whole wheat to go?"

"I was just closing up, but for you, anything." Ramey came out from behind the counter. "I'll lock up and turn off some of these lights, then we can go in the back and I'll make you whatever you want."

~*~

"The afternoon was fun, but the morning, not so much," Jenessa lamented, eyeing her friend.

While Ramey made the sandwich, Jenessa shared about her earlier interview with the current Mrs. Alexander and her afternoon at the fair with Michael and Jake.

"Here you go." Ramey stuck the wrapped sandwich in a white paper bag and set it on the worktable, in front of where Jenessa had perched on a stool. "Is that interview why you were arguing with the almighty Grey Alexander out front? I saw you guys going at it. What was going on with you two?"

"He told me to stay away from his wife—or else." Jenessa swiveled on the stool.

"He threatened you?"

"Yes, but it won't keep me from pursuing the story."

"Oh, Jen, you know he could make your life miserable if he sets his mind to it."

"I know, but I've got to get the story. This could be a big deal for my career if I can help crack this case, not to mention getting justice for your mom."

"I appreciate that, but promise me you'll be careful. Please."

"I will, I will." Jenessa nodded. "Say, besides the photo of Phony Tony, you didn't happen to find anything else in that old box of your mom's that might help solve this case, did you?"

"Like what?"

"Anything out of the ordinary—questionable photos, old letters, anything suspicious."

"Well, I hadn't been looking for anything else, but I can. I have a bunch of her old boxes in my garage. She was such a packrat."

That apple didn't fall far from the tree. Ramey could benefit from a little downsizing herself, but Jenessa was glad for that particular family trait right now. Maybe something more would come out of it. At least they'd gotten the lead on Tony Hamilton.

"Mom hated throwing anything away, especially papers. I'll have a look and let you know."

"That'd be great." Jenessa slipped off the stool and grabbed the bag. "I'd better be getting home. I've got a deadline for an article tonight."

"You know, Jen, we should all have supper at Aunt Renee's again sometime. Seems like once the funeral was over, we all went our separate ways."

"Sorry, I guess that happens. Besides, my sister can't seem to be in the same room with me without picking a fight. I'm sure she still blames me for Mom's death—she needs to get over that."

"It's more than that, Jen."

"What do you mean?" Jenessa climbed back on the stool and set the bag down.

Ramey leaned close and lowered her voice, even though the place was empty. "You never knew this, but Sara and Logan were dating a number of years back."

"What?" Jenessa gasped. The revelation was so surprising that it was a good thing she was already sitting down or she would have fallen on the floor.

CHAPTER 12

JENESSA'S HAND FLEW OVER her mouth in shock. "Sara and Logan? Oh, Ramey, you've got to be kidding." Blood was pulsing in her head.

"Nope, not kidding. They were together for about four or five months, I think."

Jenessa's hand slid down to her chest. "Wow. What happened?"

"Well...for one thing, your folks were not happy about it, as you can probably imagine."

"Mom never mentioned it."

"She wouldn't. She didn't want to hurt you. And they didn't want Sara with Logan either, not after what happed with you. I think they were afraid she'd turn up pregnant too."

"So, who broke it off?"

"Logan did. He told her the fact that your parents loathed him didn't bother him that much, but get this— he said he couldn't be with her because he was still in love with you."

"Me? What? No. He couldn't be." Jenessa's head was pounding now.

"It was before she married Travis, after Logan graduated from college and came back home. I think that's why she jumped into the relationship with Travis so quickly, to get over Logan. They got married pretty fast, remember?"

"You think that's why the marriage didn't last long? She was still in love with Logan?"

"Yeah, Sara really loved him—still does. I think she keeps holding out hope they might get back together."

Jenessa massaged her temples. "But apparently Logan doesn't share her feelings." This could make things very difficult between her and her sister.

"Exactly. That's why whenever you've been in town, it just reminds her of why they couldn't be together, because he still has a thing for you."

"I had no idea, Ramey."

In retrospect, though, how could she not have known? She recalled having told her sister after the funeral reception that she was meeting Logan for dinner. Sara had stomped off in a huff with no explanation. Now Jenessa knew why.

~*~

Jenessa went home and picked at her sandwich as she sat down to work on the computer. Pushing her thoughts of Sara and Logan aside, she spread her interview notes out on the desk. She wrote her article on the Garden Club's Flower Show and emailed it off to make the Sunday paper.

Before she could switch gears and move onto something else, Aunt Renee phoned and invited Jenessa over for brunch the next morning.

"Will Ramey be there?"

"Of course, dear. Have you told her about her father yet?"

"Not yet. I was hoping for confirmation of the remains from the crime lab."

"That's probably a good idea."

Jenessa bit her lip, considering if she should ask the next question. "Will Sara be at brunch tomorrow?"

"Yes. Why do you ask?"

Great, another chance for Sara to pick a fight. She was all-in now, so she might as well continue. "Aunt Renee, did you know Sara used to date Logan?"

"Who told you?"

"It doesn't matter, the secret is out. From your reaction, I'd say it's obviously true. I only wish someone had told me sooner."

"I'm sorry. I should have."

"No wonder Sara can't stand to be in the same room with me."

"Now that you know, dear, I hope you girls can work it out."

"I don't see how. Logan keeps pursuing me."

"Oh my, that just makes things worse now, doesn't it? How do you feel about him?"

"I'm not sure."

"What do you mean?" Aunt Renee asked.

"Michael Baxter and I have been spending some time together and things seem to be moving along nicely, but then Logan keeps inserting himself at the most inopportune times and I go all weak in the knees and my insides turn to mush like I'm a silly teenage girl again."

"Sounds like maybe you've never gotten over him."

"I thought I had. There was a time that the very mention of his name made my blood boil."

"But not now?"

"Yes, still, but in a different way."

"Well, you'd better figure it out soon, young lady, because if you choose Logan Alexander, that sweet Michael Baxter might get his heart broken, not to mention that your sister will likely never speak to you again."

"That's what I'm afraid of." Jenessa let out a sigh of exasperation. "I want to do the smart thing, Aunt Renee. Choosing Logan would only mean trouble, I'm afraid."

"But then again..." Aunt Renee said, her voice resonating with experience, "the heart wants what the heart wants."

~*~

Later that evening, Ramey phoned Jenessa with some news. "I found a box full of my mother's old bank statements."

"Bank statements? Your mom never struck me as the type to balance her checkbook and keep records." As long as Jenessa could remember, Lucy had been a falling-down drunk.

"No, she wasn't the type," Ramey replied. "She was never good with money, so it made me wonder why she would keep these things."

"Did you look at any of them?"

"Yeah, I opened up a few. The weird thing is they all showed a monthly deposit of five thousand dollars. Don't you think that's suspicious?"

"Any idea where the money came from?"

"Haven't a clue. Mom never had a job, as far as I can remember. You don't think my mom was into anything illegal, do you?" Ramey asked.

"I hope not, but you know your mom. With her drinking and her revolving door of men, she easily could have—"

"Hey, don't say that! She wasn't terrific, but she was still my mother."

"Sorry." Jenessa wished she hadn't started down that road, but it was what everyone thought—Juicy Lucy is what they called her. During Jenessa's teenage years she knew Lucy to drink like a fish, use drugs on occasion, and sleep with any man who wanted her. It wouldn't be unreasonable to think she might have gotten herself into something illegal.

"No, you're right," Ramey admitted. "But she was my mom, you know."

"I know," Jenessa said softly. She paused a moment before getting back to the matter at hand. "If she was getting regular payments, it could be an important clue, Ramey. Do you mind going through all the statements and seeing if she received a deposit every month and if it was for the same amount?"

"I'd hate to think she was doing something bad, but if it'll help find her killer, I guess I don't mind."

"No promises, but it might help."

"Well, I've got nothing better to do tonight anyway." Ramey sounded disappointed at her boring life.

"Maybe not tonight, but don't you have a date with Charles McAllister tomorrow night?"

"Ooh, yes I do!" Ramey squealed. "I'm so nervous about it, though. It's been a while since I've been on a date. Can you come over tomorrow and help me with my hair and makeup?"

"I'd love to." Jenessa was excited for her. Charles was a good guy—solid, kind, hardworking. After all Ramey had been through, she deserved a wonderful man like that in her life. "What time?"

"Five?"

"You can count on it."

"I'd better go and get busy on those bank statements," Ramey said.

"I've got nothing special going on tonight either. Why don't I come over and help?"

"Sara's on her way over. We'll have a girls' night. We can put on some music and eat cookies while we're rummaging through the boxes, hunting for clues. It'll be fun."

"Um, on second thought, maybe I'd better not." An evening bickering with Sara didn't sound inviting at all. Maybe it'd be best to steer clear of her sister until she figured out what she was going to do about Logan.

"Sure, I understand. See you at Aunt Renee's for brunch tomorrow?"

~*~

Jenessa spent a quiet evening reading and went to bed early, but she tossed and turned much of the night. Her mind was a tangle of dreams—visions of when she and Logan were high school sweethearts, her and Logan now, her and Michael now, Sara and Logan dating, and, of course, the growing mess she was finding herself in presently. She couldn't avoid her sister for long, and in this small town there was no way she could avoid Logan either.

In her half-awake dream-fogged state, Grey Alexander's scowling image popped into her mind. If she ever got back together with Logan, she would have to deal with his father too. Her stomach turned at the thought. Family dinners and holidays would be excruciating.

Stop! There were not going to be any Alexander family dinners. How could there be after what had happened between her family and his? It was too late for that.

And how could she do that to her sister? How could Sara ever move on and find love again if Jenessa brought Logan into their family?

Finally, her mind settled down and she drifted back to sleep, waking to find the digital clock on her nightstand reading nine o'clock. She flipped the covers back and slid out of bed. It was time to get ready for brunch—and going another round with Sara.

~*~

"Look what the cat dragged in," Sara quipped as Jenessa joined her and Ramey in her aunt's kitchen.

"Sara, be nice," Aunt Renee admonished, following close behind Jenessa.

"Hi, there," Ramey greeted as she checked on a dish in the oven. "Would you like something to drink?"

"She could have come earlier and helped," Sara mumbled as she went back to noisily chopping fruit on the counter.

Aunt Renee draped an arm around Jenessa's waist and kissed her lightly on the cheek. "We're happy to have you, dear."

"Thank you." Jenessa cast a smile at her aunt before turning her attention to Ramey. "I'd love some iced tea, but I can get it myself."

"Why don't you pour drinks all around then?" Ramey suggested, pulling a frittata out of the oven. "Dishes and glasses are already on the table."

Jenessa went to the enormous stainless steel refrigerator and grabbed a pitcher of iced tea and one of orange juice. "Did you get through all those bank statements last night?"

"Most of them," Ramey replied, cutting the frittata into wedges. "Funny, they all had the five thousand dollar deposit, all on the first day of the month."

Sara took the platter of cut fruit to the table. "We could have gotten through all of them, Jenessa, if you'd have come by and helped."

"You're right. I should have." Jenessa set the pitchers on the table. "I'm sorry, Sara."

Sara's gaze met Jenessa's, as if she were surprised by her sister's apology. Silence hung uncomfortably in the air for a moment, broken by Ramey's next question.

"So how do we find out where those payments came from?"

That was a very good questions. Who could have been sending Lucy five thousand dollars every single month?

Jenessa turned to Ramey at the kitchen counter. "I'll let Detective Provenza know what we've discovered and see what he can do. The police have resources to find that sort of information. Now, whether or not they'll share it with me is another story."

"Can't Michael help?" Ramey asked.

Jenessa picked up a small piece of cantaloupe from the platter and popped it in her mouth. "Maybe. Did I tell you he took his detective's test and went before the review board?"

"Hmm," Aunt Renee interjected, "Detective Michael Baxter. I like the sound of that."

Jenessa grinned. "Me too."

Conversation during the meal went better than it had in a long time. Perhaps Jenessa's simple apology had softened Sara's attitude toward her, at least for the short term.

"I can't stay long," Jenessa said once the food was gone. "I need to track down Detective Provenza and tell him about the bank deposits. Hopefully he'll think they're as important as we do. You didn't happen to bring them this morning, did you, Ramey?"

"They're in my car. The box is pretty heavy. Let me go and help you with it."

Jenessa said her good-byes and followed Ramey out to her car.

Ramey lugged the box from her trunk to the Sportster's. "Sara was sure quiet during brunch."

"Guess my apology threw her off her game."

"Seriously though, Jenessa, I hate to see you two at odds. I hope you can make things right."

Jenessa gave Ramey a forced smile. "I'll try."

~*~

It being Sunday, Jenessa phoned Detective Provenza on his cell phone. It wasn't likely he was in the office today unless he'd gotten a hot lead to follow up on.

"Hello, Miss Jones."

"How did you know it was me?"

"This new-fangled thing called Caller ID. What can I do for you?"

She hadn't expected him to have saved her number in his phone. "I'm impressed, Detective."

"Never mind the sarcasm. What's up?"

"I wanted to find out if you have a definite identification of the remains yet."

"Are you asking if it's Lucy St. John?"

"Well, yeah."

"Not yet. Hopefully tomorrow they'll be able to tell me for sure. Wanting to blab it in your story?"

"Of course, I want to be the first to report on it." That was a no brainer. "I'm doing everything I can to help you, Detective, so I hope you'll give me the heads-up first."

"I can't promise anything."

"Well, George…can I call you George?"

The detective grunted.

"George, I'm sure a man of your caliber can be counted on to do the right thing."

"Sweet talking me isn't going to help, Miss Jones."

"Can't blame a girl for trying." Jenessa chuckled. "But seriously, Detective, the reason I'm calling is I have another bit of information for you. In return, I'd like you to do something for me."

"If you have information, you'd better hand it over. I could charge you with interfering with this investigation if you don't."

"Oh, hold on to your britches there, Detective," Jenessa joked. If she could whittle her way into a more friendly relationship with him, perhaps he would be more forthcoming with information. "Lucy's daughter found some of her old bank statements that show a regular monthly deposit made to her account going back years—always five thousand dollars, always on the first day of the month."

"It could be nothing. Maybe she had been in a car accident and was getting a monthly pay out or something like that."

"I hadn't thought of that, but wouldn't Ramey know?"

"Did you know everything about your parents' finances when you were a little kid?"

"No, I guess not." Perhaps Aunt Renee would know if Lucy had been in an accident of some sort. "But it could be something totally different, couldn't it?"

"What do you think it means?" he asked.

"Blackmail, maybe." Or child support, but she wasn't ready to put that suspicion out there just yet. "We won't know until we find out who was putting that money in her account each month. Can you find that out?"

"It'll take a while. This is Sunday, so I can't even begin to dig around until tomorrow."

"Oh, and another bit of information—Lucy's last boyfriend, the one she supposedly ran off to LA with, his name is Tony Hamilton. Do you think you can track him down?"

"That could be helpful, if the woman turns out to be Lucy St. John. I'll see what I can dig up on him, once the lab gives me positive ID that it's her. Otherwise, it'll just be a wild goose chase."

"If you could let me know what you find out—"

"Depends on what I discover," George interrupted. "After all, this is an open homicide investigation."

"Remember our deal, Detective? I help you, you help me? I scratch your back, you scratch mine?"

"I never agreed to that."

"Okay, how about this? I help you solve this crime and make you the hero of Hidden Valley, and in exchange you give me first shot at the story."

"What makes you think I need your help?"

"For one thing, I'm not law enforcement, George, so I don't have the constraints you do, and I know how to dig up facts for a story. People are more likely to tell me things they won't tell the cops."

He laughed. "Like I said up at the lake—that Charles McAllister has hired himself a bulldog."

"Is that a yes?"

~*~

Jenessa stood in front of her old high school, looking up at the two-story brick building with beige stucco accents. Auction items were set on the walkway, around the circular fountain in the middle of it, and some things, like pieces of furniture and accessories, were scattered on the expansive lawn where Jenessa recalled students dotting the grassy area at lunchtime.

Elizabeth Alexander stood right outside the main double-door entrance to the building, directing people carrying items inside for the auction. She was still an attractive, elegant brunette, even in the summer heat, dressed in parchment-colored slacks and a navy blue silk tank top, her neck draped with a thick gold necklace.

Jenessa brought a contribution for the auction, a beautiful antique clock her father had purchased in San Francisco before their move, hoping it would help her garner Elizabeth's good graces. She approached the woman, holding out her gift in both hands. "Hello, Mrs. Alexander."

"Oh my. Jenessa Jones. How have you been? It's been a few years."

"Yes, twelve, but who's counting?" Jenessa forced a smile, remembering the last time she had seen Elizabeth, the night she and Logan broke the news to their parents. "I brought something for your auction. I adore that old auditorium."

"That is so sweet. Take it on inside. My assistant will show you where to put it."

Jenessa paused at the door, trying to ignore the line of people building up behind her. "Do you think we can talk later?"

Elizabeth lowered her voice and leaned in. "About what?"

"I'm a reporter now, for the Herald. I'd like to do a story on your fabulous auction."

"Oh, certainly." She sounded pleased as her voice returned to full volume and she straightened up. "Give me a few minutes. I need to give these people some direction, and we can sit down and chat."

Jenessa nodded, mustered a smile, and stepped inside.

~*~

After unloading the clock on Elizabeth's assistant, Jenessa stood in the auditorium, her gaze bouncing around at all the beautiful details, badly in need of renovating. Countless plays and musicals had been performed in this massive room, not to mention all the school assemblies and graduations.

Jenessa and Logan had come to see a few school plays here, but she had also come once with Michael. She had almost forgotten. The drama department was putting on *Guys and Dolls*, before she had begun dating Logan, and she and Michael attended the musical together to do an article for the school paper.

"There you are," Elizabeth said as she approached. "I thought you'd left."

"No, I was just admiring this old auditorium."

"She is a beauty, isn't she?" Elizabeth's gaze scanned the room. "Wait until we return her to her former glory. She'll knock your socks off."

"Shall we sit here?" Jenessa gestured toward the rows of seats.

Elizabeth filed down the row and sat.

Jenessa pulled a notepad and pen out of her bag and took a seat beside her. "Now, tell me all about your auction. Don't leave anything out."

Elizabeth's eyes lit up and she spent the next twenty minutes talking in animated fashion about when the grand fund-raising auction would be, offering great detail about what they planned to do to restore the auditorium.

"I think I've got all I need for an article. Thank you so much for your time." Jenessa stuck her pad and pen in her purse and rose from her seat. She started to turn to leave but spun back around. "By the way, I'd like to ask one more question."

"What is it?"

Jenessa sank back down on the edge of the seat, angling herself toward Elizabeth. "I'm also writing a story on the female remains found up by Jonas Lake."

"I read something about that."

"I have reason to believe the woman was Lucy St. John." Jenessa watched Elizabeth's face for a reaction.

Her eyes widened for a second then returned to normal. "What makes you think it's her? Is that what the authorities have determined?"

"I'm not at liberty to say, but I wondered if you might have known her at some point."

"Yes, I knew her. Not well, of course." Elizabeth stroked her neck, appearing a bit uncomfortable at the question. "It's no secret my ex-husband had many women on the side when we were married. Lucy was one of them."

"This question may be in bad taste, but I have to ask. Did you ever wonder if Grey was the father of Lucy's baby?"

CHAPTER 13

ELIZABETH JERKED BACK, as if Jenessa had just slapped her, and her eyes grew wide at the question. A few fingers covered her gaping mouth and she drew a quick breath. As she twisted in the auditorium chair, her startled gaze flew to the far end of the auditorium where people were arranging items on the stage.

Eventually, she dropped her hands into her lap and her features relaxed, appearing to gain control over her initial reaction. She returned her gaze to Jenessa. "Yes, I knew, eventually. But how did you find out about that?"

"I can't say."

"Does the girl know?"

"Not yet," Jenessa said, "but she will soon."

Elizabeth looked blankly toward the stage again. "Grey sent money to Lucy regularly. Did you know that? I told him it was a poor precedent to set, but he wouldn't listen to me."

"Monthly payments for child support?"

"More like hush money."

"You couldn't have been too happy that a portion of your family's income was going to his mistress."

Elizabeth's attention turned back to Jenessa. "I wasn't." Her eyes narrowed and her lips thinned. "I could have wrung that woman's scrawny neck for screwing around with my husband."

"What stopped you?"

"Knowing she wasn't the first and she likely wouldn't be the last. In fact, that Barbie doll he's married to now was once one of his affairs. That's when I'd had enough. I filed for divorce. Did you know that?"

"No, I didn't." Jenessa saw the sadness in Elizabeth's eyes.

"What's done is done."

Jenessa couldn't leave it at that. "The summer Lucy St. John was killed, were you in town?"

"What summer would that have been?"

"Eleven years ago." The exact time hadn't been determined yet, but eleven years ago was Jenessa's best guess, for that was the last time Ramey had seen her mother.

"Let's see." Elizabeth's eyes rose to the ceiling and she tapped her chin. "That would have been…ah, yes, that was the summer I spent in Italy." Her gaze set on Jenessa and a satisfied smile spread across her lips. "I had met a delicious Italian vintner and we spent a glorious three months together." Her eyes grew round. "You don't think I had anything to do with that woman's death, do you?"

Jenessa held her tongue and arched a brow.

"You do!" Elizabeth gasped. "Oh, you can't be serious."

"Sorry, Mrs. Alexander, I had to ask."

Elizabeth stood, an overt sign of her desire to end the conversation. "I'd better not find any of what I just said in your newspaper. I'll deny ever having talked to you."

Jenessa ignored Elizabeth's threat and kept the questions coming. "Does Logan know Ramey is his sister?"

"That's enough."

Jenessa continued. "Perhaps he wanted to keep Lucy from spilling the beans about her father's identity, because then he'd have to share his inheritance with her."

Elizabeth's eyes narrowed and she shot daggers at Jenessa with them. "This interview is over. Please leave."

Jenessa turned to go, then she stopped and glanced back over her shoulder. "You know the police will ask you the same questions I have. The truth will eventually come out."

Finding her way out of the school and back to the parking lot, Jenessa climbed in the Roadster. An avalanche of questions about Logan poured into her mind. She hadn't really considered him a suspect until now. It made sense though. He had the most to lose.

He would have been home from college that summer. Could he have learned about Ramey then? Had his father or mother told him, or had he overheard something? Had he somehow discovered the monthly payments—maybe heard his father talking about them? Or had he seen something about them on Grey's desk?

If so, Logan would almost certainly have confronted his father. Perhaps Grey assured Logan that Lucy had never told Ramey, that it was part of their agreement, or the payments would stop. Grey had to know that if Lucy pursued him in court he was more than able to bury her, and he would have made sure she knew it too.

Did Logan ensure the secret was kept quiet, not wanting to share his considerable inheritance with his half-sister? Had he lured Lucy to the lake house and murdered her to keep her from telling Ramey?

Jenessa hated to think Logan was capable of something like that, but then again, money can make people do things they might not otherwise do. She'd written enough news stories for the Sacramento paper to know that was true.

Was it a real possibility? Or was her writer's imagination running away with her?

Starting the car, she glanced at the clock in the dashboard. It was almost five and Ramey would be expecting her. She would have to tell Ramey about her father before someone else beat her to it.

~*~

"Oh, my gosh, Jenessa! I was about to give up on you," Ramey cried as she opened the door, dressed in her bathrobe. "Look at me, I'm a mess."

"Calm down. I'm only five minutes late." Jenessa stepped inside Ramey's cluttered little house, decorated in shabby chic with flea market finds she had refurbished.

"Sorry, I've been a basket of nerves all afternoon."

"Oh, that's typical first-date jitters. You'll be fine," Jenessa said, hoping to assure her.

Jenessa would be on the lookout for a good opportunity to break the news to her about Grey.

"Well, let's get started. You've got a lot to do, my friend." Ramey led Jenessa down the short hall to her bedroom. "What if I say something stupid? What if I get so nervous I can't say anything at all?"

"Relax, Ramey. Charles comes into the bakery all the time and you two talk, don't you?"

"Well, yes, but it's just casual, like I do with all my customers."

"Then just think of him as another customer. Make small talk like you do at the shop. Maybe that'll help."

"Okay, but what if he finds out he doesn't like me after all?"

"Oh, sweetie, just be yourself and you'll be fine." Jenessa took her by the shoulders. "Listen, you're funny and sweet and very intelligent. Your blue eyes sparkle and your smile lights up a room. If he can't see all that, then he doesn't deserve you."

When Jenessa released her hold, Ramey spun around to face a full-length mirror. She took in her image for a moment then pushed out her chest, held her head high, and smiled at her reflection. "You're right. I *am* a great catch and any man would be lucky to have me."

"That's more like it, Ramey," Jenessa assured her. "Confidence is a beautiful thing."

The two busted out laughing and gave each other a quick hug. Telling Ramey about her father at this point would only spoil her wonderful date with Charles—Jenessa couldn't bring herself to do it.

"Now, let's get busy," Jenessa ordered with determination. "We've got a date to get ready for."

Jenessa took the curling iron and styled Ramey's hair into softer, looser curls before applying her makeup, giving her smoky eyes, luscious lashes, and rosy lips. Then it was time to choose something to wear. After trying on six different outfits, she finally settled on a sleeveless summer dress with azure blue flowers on a crisp white background, which set off her eyes and her head of red waves.

Ramey stood before the full-length mirror again and admired Jenessa's handiwork. "I don't think I've looked this good in a long time—not since I was a teenager."

"Oh, it hasn't been that long." With Jenessa gone from Hidden Valley for so many years, it didn't seem so long ago that Ramey had blossomed into a beautiful slim eighteen-year-old. But something had changed in her life and she stopped paying much attention to her looks. Was it when her mother left her? Or was it all the hours and hard work she put into the bakery?

"Oh, I'm afraid it has been." Ramey turned away from the mirror and faced Jenessa. The expression on her face grew serious. "There's something I should tell you, something that happened a long time ago."

Jenessa steadied herself for what sounded like bad news. Did she already know about her father?

"When I was nineteen, I went out with Logan…a couple of times. It was the summer after my mother left."

"With Logan?" Jenessa's cheeks burned and her breath caught in her throat. It felt like Ramey had slapped her across the face. First she finds out her little sister used to date her ex—and is still in love with him— and now she finds out her best friend dated him too.

Jenessa dropped down onto the side of the bed. She raised her eyes to Ramey, her bottom lip quivering slightly. "I don't know what to say."

Logan and Ramey?

Here, Jenessa had not wanted to drop a bombshell on Ramey, yet she got blasted herself.

Ramey settled beside her on the bed. "I wanted to tell you at the time, but you were so angry at him that you didn't even want his name spoken in your presence. That's what you said, remember?"

"I'm shocked." Jenessa gave her head a shake, trying to rid herself of that feeling.

"I ran into him one day at that cute little shop The Mercantile. I was shopping for a gift for your mother's birthday and he was shopping for something for his stepmother. We got talking and he asked for my help. We chatted and we laughed about stuff—one thing led to another and he asked me out. We went to a movie and had dessert at Latiff's after that. He even kissed me good night."

"You don't need to give me the details."

"But I want you to know. The second date, he made reservations for dinner at Antonio's. After he picked me up, though, he realized he had forgotten his wallet and we stopped by his house. Logan introduced me to his father, who seemed really uneasy. It was weird."

Of course he did, he knew Logan was dating his own sister. Should she tell her now? Instead, Jenessa bit her tongue and listened.

"Grey asked if he could have a word alone with Logan and they went off into another room. When he came back, Logan wasn't the same."

"What do you mean?"

"He seemed, I don't know, aloof. Before his little talk with his father, we'd been getting along so well, conversation was easy. We laughed a lot and had fun together. But all through dinner he didn't seem to have much to say. He took me home and didn't even try to kiss me good night."

Jenessa knew why, and now she knew exactly when Logan had discovered the truth. This was the perfect time to tell her that Logan was her brother, that Grey Alexander was her father.

"Ramey, I have—"

The doorbell rang and the girls looked at each other.

"Oh, I can't go on a date now. I'm a nervous wreck," Ramey said, grimacing.

"You're not a wreck. You look beautiful. Just take a few deep breaths. I'll go answer the door while you collect yourself." Jenessa stood and started out of the bedroom door, then stopped and turned back to her friend. Telling her about the possibility Grey was her father would have to wait for another day. "Charles is a lucky man."

~*~

Charles and Ramey left on their date, and Jenessa drove home. Her conversation with Ramey played over in her mind. She could hardly believe that when Ramey was nineteen—the summer after her mother left—she'd dated Logan.

Was that the summer Lucy died?

Logan had just learned of his father's affair and that Ramey was his sister. Could he have somehow lured Lucy back to Hidden Valley? To the lake house? He would have known Ramey had no idea she was his sister, or she never would have agreed to go out with him.

This new piece of the puzzle only strengthened Jenessa's suspicion that Logan might have killed Lucy to keep her from telling Ramey who her father was. Maybe he didn't mean to hurt Lucy, only scare her into keeping quiet, but then things went terribly wrong, as they often do in situations like these.

Once she arrived home and settled in, Jenessa phoned Detective Provenza.

"Hey, George, this is Jenessa again."

"Please, call me Detective," he grumbled. "What is it now?"

"I know you don't have confirmation of the identity of the body yet, but I'm absolutely certain it's Lucy St. John."

"Yeah, I got that last time you called. Just so you know, I did a bit of checking, trying to track down Lucy St. John, but I'm not finding anything current on her. The trail goes cold about ten or eleven years ago."

"And I swear to you the locket found on her body has Ramey's childhood picture in it."

"It likely may be the St. John woman's body, but I'm still waiting for the lab results. I expect to have them tomorrow. I already told you that," the detective said. "So, why the call tonight?"

"I got confirmation that Logan Alexander discovered that his father had an affair with Lucy, and I think it was the summer she died."

"Grey Alexander had an affair with Lucy the summer she died?"

"No. He had the affair thirty years ago. But I have reason to believe that Logan found out about it the summer she died."

"How do you know that?"

"Ramey St. John told me."

"How does she know?" the detective asked.

"I can't tell you, but it turns out she's Grey Alexander's daughter."

"She is?"

"Yes, and Logan found out Ramey was his half-sister, which means that now he'll have to split his inheritance with her. Only Ramey doesn't know yet, so please don't spread that around."

"You think he'd kill Lucy over money? To keep her quiet?" George asked.

"People have killed for a lot less."

"Yeah, I have seen that."

"Maybe he didn't mean to kill her, you know? Maybe it was an accident." Jenessa couldn't help but give Logan the benefit of the doubt. "I think you should take a forensic team up to the Alexanders' lake house and scour it for clues."

"After all these years…are you looking for something in particular?"

"Lucy's blood, maybe?"

"This is Grey Alexander's place you're talking about. I'd need a really good reason to ask a judge for a search warrant."

"We have evidence that Grey had been paying Lucy five thousand a month since she had the baby."

"That doesn't prove anything."

"Oh, come on, George. There weren't that many houses near the lake around the time Lucy disappeared. With her body being found in the woods not that far from the Alexander house, don't you think it's worth a search?"

"Someone could have killed her somewhere else and buried the body there in the woods because it was remote, like that Tony Hamilton character. Likely no one would have ever found it if someone hadn't decided to build a cabin on that spot."

"I guess that's one possibility," Jenessa said. She hoped the killer was Tony Hamilton, rather than Logan.

"Miss Jones, I need a lot more than conjecture before I go to a judge and ask for a search warrant— especially for the most powerful man in this town. You bring me something concrete, and I'll see what I can do."

~*~

It was after eleven o'clock and Jenessa was crawling into bed when her phone rang. It was Ramey, home from her date with Charles.

"It was the most wonderful evening I've ever had," she gushed.

"Tell me about it."

He had taken her to dinner at a nice steakhouse and their conversation had been effortless. He told stories about his childhood, which had made her laugh. He talked about losing his wife, which brought tears to her eyes.

"I always wondered what people meant when they said they found their soul mate. Now I think I understand," Ramey said. "He's interesting and funny, and he wanted to know what I thought about things. He listened when I talked—can you believe that?"

"That's how it should be."

"And I felt a spark when he held my hand."

"Did he kiss you good night?" Jenessa asked.

"He did." Ramey giggled. "I don't have a lot of experience with that, as you well know, but I can't imagine anyone doing it better. I just wanted to melt into a puddle right there at his feet."

Jenessa could tell her about Grey now, but why ruin things? She let Ramey enjoy the night and dream about Charles's kiss.

~*~

Early Monday morning, Jenessa's phone rang, as it often seemed to do. It was Charles McAllister, asking her to meet him at the paper at ten o'clock.

"Got a good story for me to cover?" she asked.

"Not exactly. I'll tell you when you get here."

Before Jenessa left the house, Detective Provenza phoned her and told her that the CSI team estimated the woman had been dead for ten or eleven years based on the carbon dating test that the forensic anthropologist administered to the bones. They couldn't get any closer than that.

"So it could have happened any time between when Lucy left Hidden Valley and up to a year or so later," Jenessa mused, which would include the next summer after Ramey had graduated, the summer Logan learned the truth.

"Sounds about right. We'll have to search for a way to pin the timeline down a little tighter," he said. "I'll go back and try to pinpoint when the last call came in on her cell phone, if the phone company still has those records."

"Or they're still in business."

"True."

"And don't forget about her banking information. When's the last time she wrote a check or took a cash withdrawal from the ATM?" Jenessa asked.

"I've already boarded that train of thought," the detective said. "You know, Miss Jones, I appreciate your willingness to help me out, so I'll share with you what I can, but I need you to keep what I tell you under your hat."

"I understand, and don't worry, I never reveal my sources."

"No, that's not what I mean. I'm talking about not printing anything I tell you until we've got a suspect under arrest and I give you the all clear."

"Got it," she agreed. "Any luck hunting down her old boyfriend, Tony Hamilton?"

"Not yet, but we'll keep searching. He very well could be the one who killed her and buried her body," George speculated. "Probably fought over drugs or something."

"So then it's possible she never made it out of the valley at all, that she was murdered by Tony right after she told Ramey good-bye." That would clear Logan, wouldn't it?

~*~

Jenessa strolled into the Hidden Valley Herald and greeted the elderly receptionist. "Beautiful morning, isn't it, Alice?"

The woman pointed her bony wrinkled finger toward Charles's office. "Somebody's in trouble," she sang. "They're expecting you."

They?

CHAPTER 14

JENESSA KNOCKED LIGHTLY ON THE DOOR to Charles McAllister's office before pushing it open. "You want to see me, boss?"

"Yes, come in and take a seat." He gestured toward the closer of two club chairs opposite his desk. The farthest one was already occupied.

"You know Grey Alexander, don't you?" Charles asked, nodding in the man's direction.

Jenessa's back stiffened and her legs felt like rubber. She hadn't had a chance to brace herself for this encounter, but then, that was Grey Alexander's style—ambush his enemies before they have time to prepare a defense.

She drew in a deep, silent breath to steady herself and mustered her strength, focusing her gaze on the chair. "Yes, of course."

It was critical that she make it to the seat and claim it before Grey began his attack. She willed herself to the chair and sank down in it.

Head up and shoulders back. Don't let him see fear.

Charles leaned his elbows on the desk and steepled his fingers. "It seems we have a little problem, Jenessa."

"What problem?" she asked in her most innocent voice, keeping her eyes on Charles.

"Mr. Alexander says you've been harassing his family and he wants it to stop."

Jenessa forced herself to turn in Grey's direction and look him in the eye, doing her best to mask any sign of trepidation. She thought of her words to Ramey the night before about exuding confidence, and right now she needed to borrow some of it. She was not going to let Grey Alexander reduce her to a scared little rabbit again. *Grow a backbone, Jenessa!*

"What seems to be the issue, Mr. Alexander?" She willed her gaze to meet his angry eyes.

"Questioning my wife and then quizzing my ex-wife about my private life. Next thing I know you'll be interrogating my son. I demand that you stop harassing my family and stop poking around in my personal business. If you continue to try to dig up dirt on my family, I'll fire you and then I'll sue you for harassment and slander, and anything else I can think of."

"You won't get much." Her gaze broke from Grey's as she momentarily turned to Charles. She shook her head and a sarcastic smile spread across her lips. "I don't own much more than the clothes on my back."

"What about that snazzy little sports car you drive and your parents' nice house? Now that they're both gone—"

Jenessa's head snapped back to Grey and her gaze locked on his again. "Those things aren't mine. I'm only using them temporarily."

Grey leaned forward, resting an elbow on one knee, as if he wasn't already menacing enough. "I'm sure your folks left at least part of their estate to you in your father's Will. You can be sure I'll take every bit of that and more if you don't cease and desist immediately!"

Jenessa pulled back a little. "I am a news reporter, Mr. Alexander. Reporters investigate and find the truth. I wouldn't be doing my job if I did not follow the facts wherever they lead me."

Grey's attention shot to Charles. "Do you believe this? It sounds like this girl is going to defy my direct order." He bolted from his chair and turned back to Jenessa. "I'm warning you, Miss Jones—hell, I'm warning both of you—you stop harassing my family and digging into my life or you will both be very sorry you ever came to work for me."

He stomped out and slammed the door so hard the windows rattled.

Jenessa and Charles stared in silence at each other for a moment. *Now what?*

Charles was the first to speak. "I know you're questioning people for the homicide story. Are you sure you had to talk to Mr. Alexander's wives?"

"I'm doing my job."

"I know, I know, but isn't there another way?"

It was obvious he was taking Grey's threat seriously, afraid of losing his job.

Jenessa stood, shaking her head, then rested her hands on the edge of Charles's desk. "Let me bring you up to speed, boss. The dead woman was Ramey's mother."

"Are you sure?"

"I am." Yes, Detective Provenza hadn't called her with the DNA results yet, but the picture inside the locket was all she had needed to know the body was Lucy's.

"What does that have to do with the Alexanders?"

"Besides the fact that her body was found in the general vicinity of their lake house, Lucy St. John was…" Jenessa stopped before she told it all, wondering if she should spill it to Charles before she told Ramey.

"Was what?"

Jenessa leaned forward on the desk and lowered her voice. "This has to stay confidential for now, okay?"

Charles nodded his agreement.

"Lucy St. John had an affair with Grey Alexander thirty years ago and she got pregnant. There is a very distinct possibility that Ramey is Grey Alexander's daughter."

His eyes popped wide as the news hit him.

"But you can't tell Ramey," Jenessa insisted. "I haven't told her yet—I wanted to wait for DNA confirmation—but I'm not sure if I should wait. What if someone else mentions it to her?"

"She won't hear it from me, I promise. Now, tell me what else you found out."

Jenessa explained all that she had discovered so far and what she was hoping Detective Provenza would pursue. "He's trying to track down Lucy's last boyfriend, a man named Tony Hamilton. He may very well end up being our killer, but if not, maybe he can at least point the cops in the right direction. Because if it wasn't him, there are a whole host of Alexanders with about twenty million motives to get rid of Lucy."

"Including Logan? I hear you two used to date."

Ramey. "Yes, in high school."

"Do you think he's capable of murder?"

"He would have been about nineteen at the time, depending on when Lucy was killed. Under the right circumstances, with millions of his inheritance at stake, it's possible, as much as I hate to think that. Love and money are the two most common motives for murder."

"And you're certain Lucy never told Ramey who her father was?"

"Yes, I'm certain."

The thought hadn't occurred to Jenessa, though, until Charles had just brought it up, but it could be possible Ramey had found out earlier but she chose to keep it quiet all these years. Was there any chance that Ramey might have gotten into a heated argument with her mother when Lucy told her she was leaving? Had Lucy blurted out the truth? Had she ended up dead somehow, at Ramey's hand? *That's absurd—isn't it?* Jenessa felt sick at the idea of it.

"Are you okay?" Charles asked with a slight frown.

His question brought her focus back. "I'm fine." Given a few minutes to clear her head and her stomach to stop churning, she would be.

He rose from his chair, signaling their meeting was coming to an end. "Of course we want to be the first to break this story when the police find the killer, Jenessa, but please try to stay under Grey Alexander's radar—for both our sakes. My son has gotten used to three meals a day and a roof over his head."

~*~

As Jenessa was driving home, Detective Provenza phoned her again.

"I got the results back from the forensic lab. You were right—the body belonged to Lucy St. John. They were able to identify her by her dental records."

"Funny, Lucy didn't seem the type to take care of her teeth," Jenessa said, thinking about the stupor she was in most of the time.

"She'd seen Dr. Engelman since she was in her twenties. He's since retired and passed, but he was my dentist too, and I remembered seeing her there a couple of times, so I asked the office for her records. Looks like she had a couple of cavities filled and a crown on her upper molars in her thirties."

Jenessa was surprised Lucy would fork out the cash for a crown. They didn't come cheap, although, she supposed that if she was in enough pain, and with Grey's five grand every month, Lucy could have come up with the money.

"The CSI team found something else, too. I probably shouldn't be telling you this, but I can use all the help I can get with this one."

"What is it?"

"Hold your horses, I'll tell you, but like I warned you before, you've got to keep it under wraps, and promise me this goes no further, that you won't print a word of this until the case is solved—or there'll be hell to pay for both of us."

"I promise, I promise. What is it?"

"Well…" he started out reluctantly, "there was a black plastic comb found with the body. It had a few strands of light-colored hair on it. Luckily, one of the hairs still had the root attached."

"I don't remember seeing a comb." Searching her memory, she recalled seeing something that looked like a button or a cufflink, but not a comb.

"I guess it was wedged under the body, like someone might have dropped it out of his pocket as he stuck her in the hole."

"Tony Hamilton's maybe?"

"Could be. Still haven't found the sucker yet, but I'll keep looking."

"Who else do you suspect, Detective?"

"I can't say, but I know you wanted us to search the Alexanders' lake house, so maybe this is our chance. If the DNA were to match one of them, then…"

Apparently the detective suspected someone in the Alexander family too. "How do you propose getting DNA from any of them?" Jenessa asked.

"I'm not sure yet. There's got to be a way to get some without their knowing it, 'cause if they find out, we'll feel the wrath of Grey Alexander for sure. Maybe," the detective paused, as if he was hesitant to proceed, "I could enlist your help? As a civilian, you can do things I can't—that's what you said, right?"

"I'm happy to help, Detective, but I'll have to think about how we can accomplish that."

A tone pinged in Jenessa's ear, alerting her to another incoming call. Glancing down at the phone's screen, she saw it was Michael. "I've got to go, George. I'll get back to you."

She switched calls. "Hello, Michael."

"Hey, I only have a minute to talk, but I just got the news that I've been approved to start work as a detective and I wanted to share it with you."

"Oh, wow. That's fantastic!" she exclaimed. "When do you start?"

"My field training begins tomorrow. I've been assigned to work with Detective Provenza."

"Oh, yes, George. That's great."

"You're on a first-name basis with him? How'd that happen?"

"I have my ways," she replied, trying to sound mysterious, but she couldn't contain the laugh that bubbled up. "Seriously, though, we should celebrate. Any ideas?"

"How about I take you for dinner and dancing at The Brass Razoo?"

"What's that?"

"It's a cool new country-western place. They have good food, great music, and a big dance floor. It went into that old Rustler's Steakhouse that shut down a couple of years ago."

"Sounds like fun. Pick me up at seven?"

~*~

As Michael held the door to The Brass Razoo open for Jenessa, lively country-western music spilled out.

The hostess seated them right away at a table not far from the dance floor. A cover band was playing a Rascal Flatts' song over the din of conversation and the clatter of dishes and silverware. A handful of couples were dancing to the fast-paced music.

"What do you think?" Michael asked.

Jenessa's gaze roved over the room, trying to take it all in. She drew her attention back in and focused on her date, flashing him a bright smile. "I hope the food is as good as the music."

He nodded and smiled. "It is."

"You've been here before?"

"A couple of times."

It wasn't a place he would bring his young son or his parents. Had he brought another date here? *Stop that.* It was silly to be jealous. Jenessa had no claim on him. She opened a menu and stuck her nose in it.

After a little more small talk, the waitress came and took their orders.

"Would you like to dance while we wait for our food?" Michael asked.

"Sure."

He took her hand and led her to the polished, hardwood dance floor. The next song that the band began to play was a slow number. Michael slid his left arm around her waist and held her hand in his. Her body was lightly pressed against his and his nearness was exhilarating. She laid her head against his firm chest and listened to the strong rhythmic beat of his heart as they danced.

"I love this song," she muttered.

"So you want me," he said.

Jenessa pulled back and looked up at him, a little surprised by what he said. "What?"

"The name of the song—So You Want Me."

She let out a nervous giggle. "Oh, the song." She rested her head on his chest again and continued to slow dance.

The song ended, but they stayed on the dance floor for a few more. Finally, they returned to their table and waited for their food. Michael pulled out her chair, and she looked up at him briefly before she sat. She wasn't used to such chivalry.

As soon as Michael took his seat, Logan approached their table. Was this guy going to show up everywhere she went?

"Hello, Jenessa," he said, ignoring Michael's presence at the table. The smell of alcohol was heavy on his breath.

"Logan," she replied.

"Would you like to dance?"

"No, Logan. I'm here with Michael."

"Oh, he won't mind," Logan turned to Michael, "will you, buddy?"

Michael shot out of his chair and towered over Logan. "The lady said no." His voice was strong and forceful. Then, he reined it in and lowered the volume. "Keep moving, Logan."

"You don't tell me what to do!" Logan took a swing at Michael, who bobbed out of the way.

"You're drunk." Jenessa stood too. "Please leave."

"I just want one dance with you. Is that too much to ask?" Logan wobbled and stepped in close to her. "Just one lousy dance."

"Come on, Logan." Michael took hold of one of Logan's arms. "Let's call you a cab."

"She's *my* girl!" Logan yanked his arm back and took another swing at Michael.

This time, Michael wasn't ready for him and Logan hit him on the side of his jaw. Michael came back with a right hook and jabbed Logan in the eye, then another in the mouth. Logan began to sink to the floor, but Michael caught him and set him in a chair.

A crowd started to gather around their table.

"Nothing to see here," Michael called out, with his arms outspread and his hands flipping back and forth, as if he was herding cats away. "Go back to your tables."

The customers wandered away, many glancing back over their shoulders, watching the town's first son, intoxicated and bloody, slunk down on a wooden chair.

Jenessa stood between Logan and most of the crowd, trying to shield him from someone wanting to get a photo or video with their cell phones. Was that Sara she saw in the crowd?

Michael must have seen Jenessa protecting Logan, for a furrow creased his forehead as he returned his attention to them.

Logan's eye was beginning to swell and his mouth was bleeding. Jenessa grabbed a couple of heavy paper napkins and blotted the blood.

Blood! DNA.

She grabbed a few more napkins, folded them around the bloody ones, and slipped the wad into her purse. This wasn't the way a cop would preserve evidence, but it might be enough to get a DNA match to the hair that was found on the comb. The reporter in her wanted to find the truth, but part of her hoped it would prove the hair couldn't be his. She didn't want to believe he could be the killer.

When she looked up from her purse, Michael was staring at her with a quizzical expression on his face.

"I'll explain later," she said, hoping that would suffice.

He whipped out his phone. "After I settle the bill, I'm going to step outside and call for a taxi. Too noisy in here."

Jenessa nodded. "And I'll have the server box up our food to go."

Michael stalked away, leaving her to deal with Logan.

She looked up and noticed that it was Sara, a couple of tables away, moving closer, watching as Jenessa took another napkin and dabbed Logan's lip. "Logan," Jenessa shook her head, "what am I going to do with you?"

Logan grabbed her wrist when she raised her hand to dab his lip again. He looked her straight in the eye. "I love you, Jenessa," he whispered.

Stunned, no words came to her. Then, she recalled her sister had been approaching.

Sara.

Jenessa lifted her gaze and scanned the place for her sister, hoping she hadn't overheard what Logan said. She caught the back of Sara rushing toward the door. Apparently she had.

~*~

Once the taxi arrived, Logan climbed in the back. He stared out the window at Jenessa and Michael standing on the curb as the car pulled away, one side of his face bruised and swollen.

"You want to tell me what's going on?" Michael asked.

Jenessa wasn't sure if he was referring to the bloody napkins she sneaked into her handbag or the exchange between her and Logan. She chose to assume he meant the former.

"The napkins?"

"Yeah. Why did you stick them in your purse?"

"I need to capture Logan's DNA." She turned and briskly walked toward Michael's car.

He followed close behind her. "Wait up."

She slowed and he grabbed her arm to stop her. "That's not a sterile way to do it. The DNA can become compromised," he said. "Besides, you're not law enforcement, why are you collecting his DNA?"

"I know it's not sterile." She pulled her arm away. "But it's not like it's exposed to anything that could contaminate it either."

"Your hands." He arched an eyebrow at her. "If it's important, it needs to be handled with latex gloves and put in an evidence bag and tagged. Now there's no chain of evidence. If it was vital to the case, now it's useless."

"It's not useless," Jenessa argued. "I'm collecting it so…" she stopped when she recalled her promise to Detective Provenza. She couldn't tell Michael she knew about the comb and the hair, and that she was hoping to help identify the DNA. She dropped her gaze. "I can't tell you."

"What do you mean you can't tell me? I'm a cop."

"I know, and soon to be a detective." George would have to fill him in.

"That's right, so if you know something about the murder case, you need to tell me."

"You're starting your training with Detective Provenza tomorrow, aren't you?"

"That's right."

"I'll tell you then, if I can."

"If you can? You're not making any sense."

Jenessa looked him in the eye. "You're just going to have to trust me, Michael." She walked off toward his car, and with his long strides, he quickly caught up with her.

"You're killing me here, Jenessa." He opened the car door for her.

"I tell you what. Let me make a call and see what I can do."

"What you can do?" His brows furrowed in an expression of confusion.

"Why do you keep repeating me?" She pulled out her phone and tapped the numbers.

"This is Detective Provenza. What do you need, Jenessa?"

She looked across the car at Michael, who was studying her intently, obviously wondering who she was calling. "I think I have something you can match to that DNA. Where are you right now?"

"I'm at home. Meet me at the station in fifteen minutes."

"I have Michael Baxter with me," her focus held steady on him, "but I haven't told him anything. What do you want me to do?"

"Don't say a word, but you can bring him along. I'll be the one to explain it to him."

"Got it."

"So, what's going on? Who was that on the phone?" Michael asked. "I don't like being kept in the dark."

"I can't reveal my sources." Jenessa put her phone away. "Let's head to the police station. I need to see someone down there."

"Is that what your mysterious friend on the phone told you to do?"

"You might say that."

Michael started the engine and pulled away from the curb. "Woman, you can be so frustrating."

CHAPTER 15

DETECTIVE PROVENZA WAS IN THE reception area when they arrived.

"Hello, George," Jenessa said.

"That's Detec—" He raked his fingers through his white hair. "Oh, forget it," he said with a wave of his hand. "Baxter, why don't we all go back to my office?"

They followed him and took their seats around his desk.

Jenessa gingerly pulled the bundle of paper napkins out of her purse. She handed them over to Provenza. "The napkins inside have Logan Alexander's blood on them. I hoped you could use it to see if it matched the other thing, you know?"

George nodded.

Michael frowned and cocked his head. "I'm going to begin my training with you tomorrow, Detective, so I hope you'll read me in on whatever this is," he said, gesturing toward the napkins.

"Miss Jones, could you excuse us for just a moment?" Provenza asked.

"Sure, I'll step out into the hall."

When the door shut all the way, Jenessa assumed George would explain to Michael what had been discovered by the CSI team, namely the plastic comb and the hairs.

Jenessa leaned her ear against the door and listened to them.

"Why did you share that with a civilian, sir, if you don't mind my asking?" Michael said.

"She's just so darned anxious to help, and I thought she could access people and things we couldn't."

"So you're using her?"

"She offered." Provenza replied. "When you've been doing this as long as I have, son, well, let's just say sometimes you have to find creative ways to solve a case."

"Creative, huh?" Michael paused. "So you think the hair on the comb is Logan's?"

"It's a possibility, somewhere to start. The case is so old that we don't have many leads. We'll have to start with our best guesses first."

"What about the boyfriend?"

"We're still looking for him."

"Mr. Alexander will hit the roof if he finds out you're investigating his fair-haired son."

Ain't that the truth.

"That's why Jenessa and I wanted to get something to test the DNA against to see if it matched—under the radar, you know?"

"I wish you hadn't involved her, though."

228

"Why not?" Provenza asked.

Yeah, why not?

"They have a history together," Michael said.

"I see. You think that'll be a problem."

"I hope not."

~*~

Michael drove Jenessa home. He walked her to the door and paused as she unlocked it.

"Want to come in?" she invited.

"I'd better not. I've got to pick Jake up from my folks. Don't want to abuse their help."

She leaned her back against the door. "I had a wonderful time."

"You mean until Logan interrupted things."

"Even that was pretty exciting. You handled yourself like a pro—he didn't know what hit him."

"And you got your DNA sample."

"Yeah, and there's that. I hope it doesn't match though. I'd hate to think Logan was capable of killing someone."

"Under the right circumstances, anyone is capable of taking a life, Jenessa."

Was he speaking from experience, from his time as an Army Ranger or as a police officer? They had never spoken of how many people he may have killed, but she knew that was true. Under the right circumstances, even she could do it.

"It could have been an accident, though," Michael proposed, "or self-defense."

"Maybe. But if he buried the body to cover up what happened, that only made it worse."

"Enough talk about Logan, how about you and me?" he said. "What do you say we try this again on Friday night?"

"I'd love to." She couldn't help but grin at the thought of it.

Michael slid a hand around her waist, leaning down he kissed her. His kiss was so warm and moist and full of desire that she grabbed the door handle to steady herself.

When their lips parted, he gazed deeply into her eyes for a few moments. She anticipated another kiss, wanted it, but he took a step back instead.

"Are you sure you don't want to come in?" she asked.

"I'd better get going while I can." He stepped off the porch. "Sweet dreams."

~*~

Jenessa was getting ready for bed, the afterglow of the kiss still lingering on her lips. Her phone jangled on the nightstand. She picked it up and read the screen— Logan Alexander. *How did his number get saved in my phone?*

She ignored it. He was the last person she wanted to talk to right now. After what he had said to her, and with Provenza's suspicions that he might be the killer, she was determined to put a wide berth between them, especially knowing Logan's declaration of love was overheard by her heart-sick sister.

After she crawled into bed, she clicked off the lamp and pulled her bedding around her. In the morning, she had a ribbon-cutting ceremony to cover for the new City Hall building and a few obituaries to write, but right now Michael's lips on hers was all she wanted to think about as she happily drifted off to sleep.

But the phone rang again and she checked it—Logan again. A few minutes later it rang for the third time—still Logan. Irritated, she turned her phone off and snuggled against her pillow.

~*~

Jenessa awoke early, refreshed from a good night's sleep. She stretched lazily and slapped the button on the alarm clock to kill the repetitive buzzing. Before she hopped in the shower, she turned her phone back on in case someone other than Logan had tried to get hold of her.

A tone from her phone announced she had at least one voicemail. She looked at the voicemail icon—she had five. She'd better listen to them in case they weren't all from Logan.

The first one was Logan, apologizing for making a fool of himself at The Brass Razoo the night before. The second one was Logan, apologizing again. The third was Logan asking her to call him back. The fourth was from Ramey, asking how her date with Michael went, and the fifth was Aunt Renee, reminding her of the reading of the Will, scheduled for later that afternoon at the office of her father's attorney.

Jenessa tensed at the thought of running into her sister after what Sara had likely overheard. Logan had been drinking, she would tell Sara, he didn't know what he was saying.

Was this going to deepen the rift between them because of Sara's feelings for Logan? He obviously didn't love her. Jenessa or no Jenessa, Sara needed to move on. But how? The burden of that question weighed on her mind.

Jenessa stepped into the steaming shower and let the hot water beat on her shoulders, hoping to relax them. She thought of the reading of the Will, wondering what that would bring. Had her father split the assets in an equitable way, or in a way that would cause even more strife between the sisters?

~*~

When Jenessa arrived at City Hall, there was a crowd of about a hundred people already gathered around the entrance of the building. It was an attractive new structure, made of red brick with details that blended into its historic surroundings.

She snapped a few photos of the building and the crowd before a small contingency of important-looking people stepped to the main entrance, where a thick gold ribbon was draped across the oak and glass doors. One of those people was Grey Alexander. Seeing him made the hairs on the back of Jenessa's neck stand up.

The mayor stepped to a small podium to the left of the doors. Jenessa took a picture of him and his entourage before pulling out her micro-recorder. She held it toward the man to tape his address. Then the mayor introduced Grey Alexander, who was also slated to say a few words. He was a minute or so into his speech when Jenessa felt a presence close behind her, so close she felt breath on her hair.

"Dear old dad. He's quite the speech maker, don't you think?" Logan said in a low voice.

So much for a wide berth.

"I tried calling you last night," he continued. "Why didn't you call me back?"

"*Shhh*, I'm working," she whispered.

He leaned in even closer, his mouth near her ear. "I need to talk to you."

A fine layer of goose bumps rippled over her body. She didn't want him that close.

"Please, go away," she pleaded, keeping her voice down, trying to concentrate on her assignment.

"Meet me at Crane Park when this is over."

"I can't. I've got work to do."

"Then this afternoon."

"I've got an appointment this afternoon," she said.

"After that."

He wasn't going to drop it, she could see that. "Okay, but just for a few minutes."

"So, four o'clock at Crane Park?"

"Yes, yes, now go away." She waved him off. Had she just made a date to meet the devil or an old friend?

~*~

Sitting around a conference table at her father's old law firm, Jenessa admired the rich carved-wood walls and thick forest-green carpet. Her sister was there, seated across from her, as were Ramey and Aunt Renee. Mr. McCaffrey walked in with a file in his hand and sat at the head of the table. His assistant took a seat in the far corner of the room with a notepad and pen in her hands.

"This will all be rather informal, ladies. David laid out his instructions very clearly and succinctly. I'm sure you'd all like to just get to it. Shall we begin?" He glanced at each face at the table, receiving nods all around.

"To my sister, Renee Giraldy, I bequeath my antiques, except for my desk," Mr. McCaffrey read.

Aunt Renee nodded.

"To Ramey St. John, who has been like a daughter to me, I bequeath fifty thousand dollars."

Ramey's face lit up and she clapped her hands lightly.

"To my daughter Sara, I leave her mother's half-interest in The Sweet Spot Bakery & Café."

Sara smiled politely, as if it wasn't all she thought she would get.

"And to my daughter Jenessa, I leave my house, my car, and my antique desk. It was your mother's and my hope that these things would bring you back to Hidden Valley to live."

Shocked, Jenessa huffed a laugh of disbelief, incredulous of her good fortune. *The house is mine? And the Roadster?* Then the real shocker settled in—he had wanted her to move back to Hidden Valley? Well, yes, now that he was gone.

"She gets the house?" Sara asked in a voice displaying her irritation. "That's not fair."

"Sara," her aunt chided. "You now own half of The Sweet Spot, which is a very successful business. Don't be greedy."

"But the house, Aunt Renee. I love that house. I wanted to raise a family in that house."

"There are plenty of other houses, Sara," Aunt Renee said.

Sara crossed her arms and sat back with a pout.

"Is that all, Ian?" Aunt Renee asked.

"One more thing." He looked down at the Will and began to read again. "The cash, stocks and bonds, and all other assets in my estate, are to be split equally among my daughters."

"See there, dear," Aunt Renee patted Sara's arm, "your dad took care of both of you equally. He loved you equally."

Sara scowled at Jenessa. "But I was the good daughter. I was the one who stayed."

"Sara Louise Jones. You stop that right now," Aunt Renee exclaimed. "Your dad loved you girls the same, just as a good father should. You will bite your tongue and be grateful for the generous gift your father bequeathed to you. That's the way your mother would have wanted it."

"Don't bring Mom into this." Sara's eyes moistened. "She'd still be alive if Jenessa hadn't run off and refused to come home for Christmas."

Jenessa's heart thumped and her eyes misted as well. Though words were her forte, she could think of no witty comeback, no eloquent defense. As much as she wanted to argue the point, she believed Sara was right.

Ramey's eyes widened as she watched the argument, shifting back and forth between the sisters, as if she wanted to say something to make the situation better, but she didn't seem to be able to find the words either.

Aunt Renee's lips grew thin as she gathered her purse from the floor and stood up. "If that's all, Ian, I think it's time we go before we embarrass the family any further. Girls."

Jenessa couldn't agree more. She shot out of her chair and headed for the door. She didn't dare talk to Sara right now, for she would certainly end up saying something she would regret.

~*~

At four o'clock, Jenessa arrived at Crane Park, spotting Logan sitting at a picnic table waiting for her. She parked her sports car and wandered over to him.

Was this really a good idea?

"Hello, Jenessa." Logan rose and motioned for her to sit on the bench beside him.

"Hello." She met his gaze, feeling herself being pulled into the deep blue of his eyes. She lifted her wrist and checked her watch to avert her eyes and break the connection. "I don't have much time. What did you want to talk to me about?"

He sat down on the bench again, his back to the table. She followed his lead and looked out over the park.

"First, I want to apologize for how I acted last night. I must have been pretty drunk to take a swing at a cop."

"It's Michael you should be apologizing to," she said, taking a quick sideways glance at him before returning her gaze to the expansive lawn. His lip was split and one eye was blackened, but it did nothing to diminish the magnetic pull she hoped to avoid.

Was he sober enough to remember the last thing he said to her?

"You're right. I acted like a jackass."

"Hee-haw," she joked, twisting to face him.

"What?"

"That's the sound of a jackass."

He chuckled, then winced. His hand flew up to his split lip.

"I'll forgive you on one condition, Logan."

"What condition is that?"

"You let me ask you some questions, and only if you're totally honest with me."

"What kind of questions?" Apprehension colored his words.

"I'm working on a story about the remains that were found up by the lake. There are some questions I need answered. So, if you'll help me out, I'll forgive you for last night."

"You drive a hard bargain, Jenessa Jones." Logan grinned as he crossed his arms and leaned back against the table, his eyes never leaving hers. "Shoot."

"The body has been identified as Lucy St. John." She watched his face for a reaction, but there was none, at least not one that gave anything away.

"I hadn't heard that," he said. "St. John. Was she Ramey's mother?"

Jenessa couldn't decide if he was telling the truth or if his innocent demeanor was an act. "Yes, she was." Jenessa nodded slightly, continuing to study his expression. "Did you know your father had an affair with her?"

"Boy, you don't pull any punches, do you?"

"Did you know?" she repeated.

"I remember hearing something about that, a long time ago. Why are you asking?"

"Did you also know that Ramey was the product of that affair? That she's your half-sister?"

There it was—the reaction she had been expecting. His eyes flashed wide as he sat up straight and his gaze floated out over the park while he considered the question.

"Why are you bringing *that* up?" His eyes narrowed as he glared at her. "What does that have to do with your story?"

CHAPTER 16

JENESSA TWISTED ON THE BENCH of the picnic table to face Logan straight on. Was his spark of anger more than embarrassment?

"So, you did know." She worked to keep her voice cool and even.

"Yes, I knew." He looked away for a moment. "My father told me when I was nineteen. He saw us on a date and was afraid I might get involved with her. I still don't see—"

"Did Ramey know?" Jenessa interrupted him before he could change the subject.

"Not that I know of." He leaned his elbows back on the table and seemed to relax a little. "My father told me later that he had been paying her mother for years to keep it quiet, especially from Ramey. When Lucy left town, Dad was happy not to have to continue paying her. My stepmother too."

"Is that what he said?"

"Not to me, but I overheard them arguing about it— that the woman wanted more money, thousands more in a lump sum, to keep quiet. Oh, Lauren was absolutely livid."

"Did he pay it?" she asked.

"I don't know," he said. "I never heard any more about it after that, so I assumed he must have paid and she went on her way. Especially since the atmosphere at our house was icy cold between Dad and Lauren for a while after that. I think that's what made me think he must have paid."

"My guess is your father probably assumed it would be better than paying her sixty thousand a year, year after year."

"Could be, but Lauren was adamant he was not to give her one more cent."

"But he had to have paid up if Lucy went on her way, don't you think?" Jenessa asked. Or perhaps they never heard from her again because someone killed her.

"Maybe." He gave a slight nod. "From what I overheard, it was your dad who had handled the payments."

"My dad?"

"He was my father's attorney, even back then, remember?"

That's right. Grey was her dad's biggest client. But what part did her father play in all of this?

Stay focused, Jenessa.

"What about you, Logan? Didn't it bother you, knowing that if Ramey found out your father was her father that she could be entitled to half of your inheritance?"

He sat up straight. "What are you trying to infer? That I killed Lucy St. John to keep her from talking? To keep Ramey from finding out?"

"I wasn't going to ask that, but since you brought it up...yes, did you kill Lucy St. John to protect your multi-million-dollar inheritance?"

He bolted off the bench and spun around to face her, wearing a scowl she'd never seen on him before. "I may not be a choir boy, but do you really think I'm capable of murder?"

"Anybody is, Logan."

His scowl softened to a frown. Her words obviously stung him, pain was pooling his eyes. "Have you asked enough questions yet?"

"*Enough* questions?"

"Yes, for me to have earned your forgiveness?"

~*~

After Jenessa's meeting with Logan, she stopped by The Sweet Spot for a cappuccino, feeling the need for a pick-me-up. The place was busier than normal, especially since it was almost closing time.

"Hey, Ramey," Jenessa greeted her friend behind the counter.

Ramey waved at her and continued taking a customer's order.

Someone pulled on the bottom edge of Jenessa's blouse and she looked down. Two twinkling brown eyes were staring up at her, below them was a smiling mouth outlined in chocolate frosting.

"Hello, Jake." Jenessa smiled back at him, kneeling down to the boy's level. She glanced around for his father.

Michael quickly stepped from his seat at a table, a wad of napkins in one hand. "Oh, Jake," he grumbled. The frosting from his son's hand had transferred to the hem of Jenessa's blouse.

Appearing a bit embarrassed, Michael proceeded to clean Jake's fingers. "I'm really sorry."

"Don't worry, it's wash and wear." She stood up and ruffled the boy's hair. "Looks like it was delicious, Jake."

He nodded his head up and down with agreement. "Chocolate's my bestest favorite."

"Hey, there's my star reporter," Charles McAllister said as he joined them.

"Hey, boss. Calling it a day already?"

"No, I just needed to get Charlie a sandwich before I take him to football practice. After I drop him off, I'll be back at the office."

Jenessa glanced over at Ramey, who was grinning at her, apparently pleased Charles had stopped by. His son Charlie was at the bakery display, showing Ramey what cookies he wanted.

Charles was looking at Ramey too. It seemed that maybe Ramey's grin was for him instead of Jenessa.

A smile slowly spread across Jenessa's face as her gaze turned to Michael and an unexpected feeling washed over her, but what was it? Contentment? Happiness? A good-to-be-back-home feeling? Whatever it was, she relished it.

"Well, I'd better get the boy to practice. Talk to you later," Charles said as he went to pay for his son's food.

"I'm surprised you're off work so early, Michael, your first day as a detective and all," Jenessa said.

"I think Provenza got tired of my questions and having to explain things to me. He said my shift was done, so I went and picked up my son and we're celebrating my first day."

"My dad is a detective now," Jake said with pride, puffing out his little chest. "That's still a cop, right, Daddy?"

"Yes, big guy, that's still a cop." Michael took his son's hand. "We were just on our way out. You and me are still on for Friday night, right?"

"Absolutely. But with this story I'm working on, I'm sure I'll be talking to you and Detective Provenza before then."

"Jake, why don't you go and see if there's something in the cookie case we can take home to Grandma and Grandpa," Michael said, moving the boy out of earshot.

"Okay." The boy happily wandered over to the bakery case.

Michael leaned closer and lowered his voice. "You know Provenza is not supposed to be leaking information about the case to you. He could get in a lot of trouble."

"He's helping me, I'm helping him," she replied, keeping her voice down. "No one will know if you don't tell them."

"You know I won't, but I worry about him. He's retiring soon and I wouldn't want him doing anything that would screw up his pension."

"Everything is on the QT, Michael," she said in little more than a whisper, "and I never reveal where I get my information. I like George, he's a good guy. I'd never do anything to jeopardize his job either, or his pension. Trust me."

"You know he hates it when you call him George," Michael said with a smirk.

Jenessa grinned at him. "I know."

~*~

Michael and Jake left The Sweet Spot, but Jenessa decided to stick around. It was almost closing time and she had better not wait another minute to tell Ramey about who her father was. She finally had confirmation from Detective Provenza that the remains were definitely Lucy St. John. If Jenessa continued to put off telling her, someone else might, which could be disastrous for Ramey.

Once the place was empty and Ramey locked the front door and turned off most of the lights, Jenessa asked her to sit down and have a chat.

"What's going on?" Ramey asked, taking a seat. "You look so serious."

"There's something you should know."

Ramey's brows wrinkled into an odd look of puzzlement and suspicion.

"I received confirmation today that the body found up by Jonas Lake is your mother. I'm so sorry."

"You suspected as much, from the photo." Ramey's bottom lip began to quiver as her eyes grew wet. "I just hoped you were wrong."

"There's more."

Ramey grabbed a napkin and dabbed her eyes. "More?"

Jenessa took a breath and forged ahead. "Ramey, I hate to be the one to tell you this, but I believe your father is—" She hesitated for a second, the name sticking in her throat.

"Is who?"

"Grey Alexander."

Ramey's eyes popped wide open and her hands flew to her face. She sat dumbfounded for a extended moment with a dazed expression on her face.

"Are you okay?" Jenessa asked.

"Grey Alexander?" Ramey gasped.

"Now, I can't say that for sure, but I have very good reason to believe it's true. You'll need a paternity test to confirm it."

Ramey lowered her hands, still appearing quite shaken by the revelation. "Oh, my gosh. Grey I'm-king-of-the-universe Alexander?"

~*~

After sitting with Ramey for a while, making sure she was okay from the news she'd just received, Jenessa drove home in her jazzy blue sports car. She kept a sharp eye on the speedometer, trying to avoid a speeding ticket. The thing would get away from her if her mind drifted and she didn't pay close attention.

Once inside the house, she dropped her purse and keys on the kitchen table and went to her computer, which was sitting in the middle of her father's old desk. Seated before it, she ran her fingers over the carved detail in the wood, thinking about her father and how he had thought to purposely leave the piece to her. Maybe there had been moments when he cared about her, moments when she wasn't around to stir things up.

She listened to the recording she had made of the ribbon-cutting ceremony and got busy writing the story. Charles would be expecting it by six thirty so it would make the morning paper.

Charles. Visions of him and Ramey walking hand in hand down the streets of this quaint little town brought a swirl of warmth to her heart. Ramey deserved a good man. Maybe their first date would turn into a life-long love affair. Jenessa wished that for her friend, especially now.

Why not wish it for herself as well?

There was a time she was so in love with Logan Alexander that she thought she couldn't live without him. Then the unplanned pregnancy ripped their lives apart—well, hers anyway—and that dream was snuffed out.

Now Michael was in the picture. They weren't in love—not yet—but the possibility of it was definitely there.

Why did Logan have to make that outlandish declaration of love to her at The Brass Razoo last night? And in front of Sara, no less. Her head began to throb.

What was he thinking? Certainly he wasn't still in love with her, not after all the hurt and years that had passed since that pivotal night at the lake house.

Maybe her indifference to him seemed like a challenge—as if now he wanted what he couldn't have. Wasn't that just like him? Logan Alexander always got what he wanted—didn't he?

Like father, like son.

As Jenessa pushed her chair back and stood up, a pen fell off the desk and rolled under it. Getting down on all fours, she climbed beneath the desk to retrieve it. That's when she saw it—a key taped to the bottom of the lap drawer.

"Oh, my gosh." Could it be *the* key?

Picking at the tape with her fingernails, she worked the key loose. She slid it into the lock on the front of the drawer and *voila!*—it worked.

Her heart began to thump with anticipation. What was so important her father had locked it away and hidden the key?

Excited, she pulled the lap drawer open and found a manila envelope laying atop numerous office supplies. She dragged it out and set it on the desk. Her fingers nimbly worked the brad open and slid the contents out— legal documents.

Jenessa went page by page, reading through the documents—Ramey's birth certificate, an agreement between Grey Alexander and Lucy St. John, copies of cancelled checks, and more. She studied the agreement, which stated Grey would pay Lucy a sum of five thousand dollars a month, every month, as long as she kept the name of Ramey's biological father confidential.

If Lucy went public with the information, even telling Ramey about her own father's identity, the disbursements would stop.

So what happened? Why did Lucy take off and leave Ramey once she graduated from high school? Had she let it slip to Ramey who her father was? If so, Grey would have had to find out somehow to cause him to stop making payments to her.

Has Ramey actually known all this time? Did she only pretend to be shocked when Jenessa told her?

Jenessa's imagination was running wild with possibilities.

No, Ramey couldn't have known. She would never have agreed to go on a date with Logan back then if she had. Unless…could she have found out shortly after the night Grey took Logan aside and told him? Had Logan been the one to break it to her?

Or had Lucy come back to see Ramey one night and it all came spilling out? Had Ramey fought with her mother and accidentally killed her? Perhaps she took Lucy's body up to the lake and buried it in the woods behind her father's lake house, the beautiful lake house that she was never invited to, as some kind of thumbing her nose at him.

Jenessa shook her head hard, as if she could shake the horrible suspicions out of her mind.

But Logan had said he overheard his father and stepmother arguing over a large sum of money *that woman* was asking for to keep quiet. Logan had assumed they were talking about Lucy. What if they were talking about Ramey?

No, that's just plain crazy. Ramey would never do such a thing—would she?

~*~

Jenessa tossed and turned all night, playing over and over in her mind various scenarios of what might have happened to Lucy. Finally, exhausted from wrestling with her thoughts, she dragged herself out of bed and into the shower.

Standing before her bathroom mirror, she blow-dried her long, dark hair, thinking about what she had to do that day. She had three obituaries to write this morning and an interview scheduled with the high school principal regarding the students' fund-raising efforts for remodeling the auditorium. The auction Elizabeth Alexander was heading up was expected to bring in quite a haul, but the principal thought it would be good for the students to be involved as well.

Ah, small town life.

The ringing of her phone on the vanity disrupted her train of thought.

"Good morning, Charles."

"Jenessa, get down to the jail. We have a breaking story. Logan Alexander has been arrested for the murder of Lucy St. John."

"Oh, my god." The disturbing news tensed her chest and she shuddered at a zing of pain that ran down both arms. "But why?"

"That's what you need to find out. Call me when you've got something."

"I have three obits due and an appointment with the high school principal this morning that I'll need to reschedule."

"I'll do the obits and have Alice phone the principal. You get yourself over to the jail, pronto."

"Got it, boss."

Her next call was to Detective Provenza.

"I can't talk right now, Miss Jones," the detective said.

"Just give me a second." She should have waited for his agreement, but she plowed on, not allowing him the chance to shut her off. "I've been told you arrested Logan Alexander for Lucy's murder. Is that right?"

"Yes, but I have to—"

"What prompted you to do that? New evidence?"

George lowered his voice and it sounded as if he had cupped his hand over the phone. "Got the DNA results early this morning. The blood you brought in was a match to the DNA on the comb, at least close enough to link it to him."

Logan certainly had motive, likely had opportunity, and now, with his DNA being found with the dead body, the District Attorney would surely try to crucify him. There had never been any love lost between the DA and Grey Alexander.

"Thanks, George." Jenessa stuck the phone in her pocket as she ran down the stairs to grab her purse and a granola before she flew out the door.

She fired up the Roadster and raced over to the police station, hoping she could get in to see Logan before he was taken to court for arraignment.

Once inside the station, she marched up to the reception desk and asked for Detective Provenza. The middle-aged receptionist phoned him and told him he had a visitor up front. "What's your name, hon?" she asked, peering up at Jenessa.

"Jenessa Jones."

The woman repeated it to the detective. "Uh-huh." She paused. "Okay, Detective."

"Is he coming?" Jenessa asked. A nervous energy rose in her and she struggled to keep it in check.

"He said to have you cool your jets over there." The woman pointed to a row of chairs along the wall.

"How about Detective Baxter? Is he available?" She couldn't just sit and wait when there was a story to get.

The receptionist dropped her chin and glared at Jenessa over her glasses. "Hmm, let's see." She picked up the phone again, dialed and waited. "Sorry, just going to voicemail." She set the receiver down. "Anyone else you'd like me to call?"

"No." Jenessa reluctantly took a seat.

After a few minutes, the gray-haired detective came out to the reception area, followed by newly-dubbed Detective Baxter. "What can we do for you, Miss Jones?"

She started to smile at Michael, but caught herself. Detective Provenza likely wasn't aware of her personal relationship with the junior detective. She needed to keep professional decorum. "I wondered if I might be able to see Logan Alexander, as a friend."

"He's not talking," Michael said, "under the advisement of his lawyer and his father."

"Are they in with him?" she asked.

"You just missed them," George said.

Lucky me. "If he doesn't want to talk to me, I'll go away, but just ask him, please."

"All right," George reluctantly agreed. "I'll be right back." He wandered off down the hall.

Michael took the chair beside Jenessa. "Why do you want to talk to him? He's been arrested for murdering your best friend's mother."

"I know, but it's my job—what can I say?" She shrugged. "I'm hoping I have an in because we're old friends." But it was more than that. She wanted Logan to look her in the eye and tell her he didn't do it. She had to know she hadn't created a child with a killer.

Michael sat back in the chair and crossed his arms. No retort, no argument. They sat in awkward silence until Provenza returned.

"Looks like today is your lucky day," Detective Provenza announced. "Alexander agreed to see you."

Good fortune has struck twice in one day.

Michael stood. "I'll take you back there." His voice was pleasant enough, but the expression on his face told a different story.

CHAPTER 17

LOGAN WAS SEATED ON THE BED, which was little more than a cot, but jumped to his feet as Jenessa and Michael approached.

Michael held the cell door open and she slipped inside. "Just holler for the guard when you're done." He closed the door, made sure it locked, and stalked away.

Jenessa watched Michael go. When she was certain he was out of earshot, she turned to Logan.

He had dragged a metal chair to the bed and gestured toward it with his outstretched hand, as he sat on the mattress. "I wanted to spend some time alone with you, Jenessa, but this isn't how I envisioned it." He seemed to be struggling to keep his voice light and his spirits up.

"I never thought I'd be visiting you in jail, either." She glanced at the stark surroundings. It was a far cry from his usual digs.

His voice turned serious. "My father and my attorney told me not to speak to anyone."

"I'm here as your friend."

"So, whatever I say is off the record?"

"It is."

His curious gaze roved over her body. "You don't have some sort of wire or recording device on you, do you?"

"No, Logan. It's just me."

"Why did you come?" His piercing eyes searched her face, as if hoping for an encouraging answer.

"The police have evidence that you are the one that buried Lucy St. John in the shallow grave by your lake house."

"My *family's* lake house," he corrected.

"They're saying you had motive and opportunity, and with your DNA that the CSIs found at the gravesite, they're looking at you for the murder."

"Yeah, that's what my lawyer said, but I don't understand how they could have found my DNA. I was never anywhere near that woman."

"You had to be."

"But I wasn't," he shot back.

She sprang to her feet. "Then how could your DNA have been found with her body?"

He jumped up as well and grabbed her by her shoulders, locking his gaze on hers. "Listen to me, Jenessa. I did not kill Lucy St. John!"

Jenessa tried to pull away, but his grip was too strong. "Let go! You're hurting me."

His hands flew out to the sides. "I'm so sorry, I didn't realize." Fear welled up in his eyes. "You have to believe me. I did not kill that woman. They have the wrong man."

"Or woman," she muttered. Her thoughts went to those she had of Ramey the previous night, but her friend wasn't the only female that might have wanted Lucy dead. Lauren Alexander could have wanted to silence Lucy too. Maybe even Elizabeth, the ex-wife.

"Woman?" Logan's eyebrow quirked.

"I simply meant if it wasn't you, it could have been a man or a woman."

"*If* it wasn't me? So you think I could have done this?" He sank down onto the bed, running his fingers through his hair. "Oh, man."

She sat beside him. "It could have been an accident." Something inside urged her to put her arm around him and comfort him, but she held herself back. "Maybe you went to talk some sense into her and things got out of hand. Or she attacked you and it was self-defense."

Logan shook his head, then looked directly into her eyes, gently taking her hand. "No, Jenessa. I did not kill Lucy St. John—not under any circumstances. You have to believe me. I don't know how my DNA got anywhere near her dead body, but it wasn't me—I swear."

Jenessa stared deeply into his eyes, probing them for the truth. Raw fear was an expression she had never seen in them before, but today it was filling his eyes and spreading across his face. Even the night they had to tell their parents that she was pregnant was nothing compared to now.

"Say you believe me," he begged, his moist eyes pleading.

She pulled her hand back. She couldn't do it. "I want to say it, Logan, really I do, but I have to follow the facts." And she would continue to follow them, wherever they led, but for now she was satisfied that she had gotten what she had come for, to look into Logan's eyes and hear from his own lips that he did not kill Ramey's mother.

"Then follow the facts and prove me innocent." He seemed to gain strength in her resolve. "Don't let the cops stop looking for the real killer. You know how they can be. They get a suspect under arrest and they stop considering any other possibilities."

Jenessa stood to leave. "I won't stop digging, Logan."

"I believe you." He took her hand again. "I meant what I said the other night."

She pulled her hand back. "You told me at the park that you were too drunk to remember anything."

"I lied."

"And are you lying now?" she asked.

"I've never stopped loving you."

Jenessa turned toward the bars, her heart quickening its beat.

"We were too young to get married and have a baby back then," he said. "We were just kids ourselves—you know we were."

"I know."

"I was immature and self-centered. I just wanted to be a big football star and didn't want a baby to stand in the way of that."

She slowly turned and looked up at him, her eyes suddenly moist. "Not just *a* baby—our baby—our son."

"You know what I meant. I've thought about that little boy many times over the years, wondered if he looked like me, if he'd grow up liking football as much as I did."

"So, it's still all about you, isn't it?"

"I didn't mean it that way. I hope he's being raised in a good family, not a dysfunctional one like mine, with too much money and too little love."

Had he really been thinking of their son all these years? She had always believed it was just her.

"I'm not that guy anymore, Jenessa. I've tried to make something of myself, work to be a good businessman in my own right, not simply riding my father's coattails. Can't you see that?"

She studied him, wondering how much she should believe. He was always a good talker. As she stared into his eyes, something was tugging at her heart, drawing her to him—but she resisted.

"What I see is a handsome face, a hot body, and a silver tongue, all of which makes up a man that is used to getting whatever he wants. A guy who took what he wanted from me and cast me aside to fend for myself, who let his father bully me into giving up our baby."

"I already told you—that was the old Logan. He was just a stupid teenager. This Logan is a responsible, hardworking man who regrets the mistakes he made back then. And if I remember correctly, I didn't have to take anything from you. You gave it up willingly."

Her hand flew across his face before she realized what she was doing.

He froze and stared at her without saying a word. Shock widened his eyes.

"I'm sorry. I shouldn't have done that." Her cheeks flushed. "I…I don't know what came over me."

"Years of pent-up anger, I'm guessing." He rubbed his cheek. "I can't say I blame you. I didn't express myself very well. What I meant is that you gave yourself to me willingly because we were in love."

Thinking back to that night, she had to agree, but the memory suddenly made her uncomfortable. "I don't want to talk about it anymore. I need to go."

"Will you help me? Because I'm desperate to find out who really killed Lucy."

"I'll see what I can do. No promises."

"I appreciate that."

She stepped to the cell door and called out, "Guard!"

~*~

Jenessa left Logan sitting in his cell, fearing for his life. Her boss would expect a story update that afternoon, and the residents of Hidden Valley, who no doubt had already heard about the arrest through the grapevine, would want to know what was happening. She had told Logan that whatever he said was off the record, but he hadn't really told her anything except adamantly declaring that he was innocent. That she could print.

When she reached the hallway leading to the reception area, she found Michael leaning against the wall, waiting for her.

"Get what you came for?" His voice was cool, almost suspicious.

"Yes, I did."

"Care to share?"

"You know I can't."

"It's not like you have client-attorney privilege, Jenessa."

"What I can tell you is that he is unwavering in his claim that he did not kill Lucy St. John, that the police have arrested the wrong person."

"Guilty people always say that," Detective Provenza interjected as he joined them.

"Then my suggestion to you, George, is to keep digging for more evidence so you have an ironclad case. You just might find something that points to someone else."

"You have someone in particular in mind, young lady?" George asked.

"So, you believe him, Jenessa?" Michael asked.

"I want to. Logan's a lot of things, but I never thought a murderer was one of them."

Michael pushed away from the wall. "Maybe your past relationship with him is coloring your judgment."

"I am trying to keep an open mind. I need to uncover the whole story. Who killed Lucy, how she was killed, and why," Jenessa said.

"I can tell you how," Provenza spoke up. "Blunt force trauma to the head. That's the official cause of death."

"Can I print that?" she asked.

"I don't see why not," George replied. "And you'll be happy to know I've gotten a warrant to search the Alexanders' lake house."

"A search warrant for the lake house?" Jenessa's eyes lit up. "Can I tag along?" She looked from George to Michael and back.

Michael glowered at her request.

Provenza shrugged. "As long as you take your own car, Miss Jones, I guess it couldn't hurt. But you'll need to stay out of our way."

"But, sir," Michael butted in, "do you think that's wise?"

He was obviously trying to protect Detective Provenza, who, in Michael's opinion, shared too much with Jenessa.

"Baxter, relax. The crime was committed over ten years ago. It's not like she's going to walk through blood spatter or smudge any fingerprints. She'll wear gloves and stand where I tell her to stand."

"That's right." Jenessa grinned at the elder detective.

"Still…" Michael frowned at her.

"And she won't print anything we might want to hold back from becoming public knowledge, will she?" George glared at Jenessa, asking with his eyes for her agreement.

"Of course not, Detective Provenza." She was tempted to call him George again, but if she wanted to stay on his good side, she had better refrain.

"All right, I guess I'm outnumbered," Michael said. "We'll gather a couple of officers and see you up there, but you'd better watch your lead foot in that pretty little sports car you drive. Officer Ramirez is on duty on that stretch, and he isn't as likely to let you off with a warning as I was."

~*~

Michael was right. The beautiful summer day was perfect for a drive up to the lake—lots of sunshine and clear blue skies.

Jenessa carefully stayed within the speed limit until she passed the sign that announced she was leaving the Hidden Valley city limits. She eased the gas pedal down and delighted in the purr of the engine as she rounded the curves. If it wasn't for the fact that she was going to the Alexanders' lake house, and the anxiety that fact was building in her chest, not to mention the throbbing pressure it was causing in her head, it would have been a perfectly wonderful drive.

She veered onto the road that led to Jonas Lake. Before she reached the marina, she turned left toward the homes that dotted the perimeter of the shore. It had only been a week since the last time she had taken that particular road, when Charles McAllister had assigned her the story about the body that had been discovered. She breathed in deeply and blew it out, resolved to handle being in or near the Alexanders' lake house better than she had the last time.

When she reached the stunning waterfront home, there were no other cars there, thanks to her lead foot. After all, the detectives had to round up some help before heading up there.

Jenessa climbed out of her car and walked over to the spot where the remains had been discovered. Crime scene tape was still strung around the site, and construction on the new cabin had apparently been halted until cleared by the authorities.

She ducked under the tape and stood at the edge of the grave. A wave of sadness washed over her for what

Ramey had lost. Lucy hadn't been much of a mother, but Ramey had loved her anyway. Not knowing her mother was dead, Ramey had shared with Jenessa on several occasions how she pretty much felt like an orphan. That feeling was understandable, but could Ramey have known her mother was dead? Is that what really made her feel like an orphan?

Jenessa pushed the thought out of her mind, irritated at herself that she let her imagination run away with her. Sweet Ramey wouldn't hurt a fly.

Her gaze roved over the crude shallow grave. In her mind, she saw the suspicious unidentified item. Early on, when she'd inquired of her secret contact at the State's forensic lab about the locket, she'd also asked if they'd found anything else, like a button or a cufflink or something. At the time, the answer was no. Perhaps whatever it was had turned up by now. Jenessa was convinced she had seen something.

She turned at the sound of tires crunching on the dusty asphalt road. The detectives had arrived, followed by a squad car with two uniformed officers and a third person in the back seat.

Ducking back under the tape, she hurried to meet them. "Hello, boys," she greeted as Michael and George climbed out of their car.

"Why am I not surprised you're already here." Michael flashed her a quick smile, then turned to the officers and the unidentified woman. "Let's head inside."

Michael knocked hard on the front door. When no one answered, he tried the knob and found it locked. He pulled his lock-picking set out of his pocket and within seconds he had the door open.

"Why couldn't you do that on my lap drawer?" Jenessa asked, half kidding. She hadn't yet told him she had found the hidden key, but now was not the time to go into it.

Michael let Detective Provenza enter first, Jenessa close on the man's heels. The officers and the woman followed after Michael.

"Who's that?" Jenessa asked Michael in a low voice, motioning with her thumb toward the other woman.

"That's Libby from the county crime lab. Lucky for us she was in town on other business or we'd still be waiting for her."

Jenessa looked around the living room as the others fanned out, searching through the house. Most everything was as it had been twelve years ago, everything except for a new white slipcover on the sofa, the coffee table, and the area rug under it. In her mind, she saw herself and Logan, lying down on the rug that covered the hardwood floors, talking and eating ice cream the night he had brought her there. At seeing this place again, something gripped her insides, an anxiety she wasn't familiar with. It was the very spot she had given herself to Logan.

Michael must have noticed the pained expression on her face. "You've been here before, haven't you?"

She nodded, but she wasn't about to let on what she was thinking.

"Anything different from how you remembered it?"

"The rug. It was years ago, but when I was here, it had been a light blue-and-white pattern with small flowers in the border, but now it's this tan sisal. And the coffee table. It had been one of those natural slabs of burl wood with a thick resin finish—you know the kind—instead of this rectangular pine one."

"Anything else?" Provenza asked.

"The sofa always had a white slipcover," Jenessa said, "but I'm sure they've replaced it with a new one after all this time—maybe more than once."

"How do you know these things have changed?" George asked. "Mr. Alexander invite you to one of his shindigs?"

Jenessa paused for a moment, her gaze drifting from Michael to George. She pulled in a deep breath before speaking and breathed out a laugh. "Like that would ever happen. No, I used to date Logan Alexander when we were in high school, remember?"

Detective Provenza rubbed his jaw. "Yeah, I think I recall something about that. Sorry, it must be old age."

"It's probably a long shot," Michael said, "but it wouldn't hurt to check out the floor under the rug for blood, seeing how we know it's been changed. We just don't know why."

"If there had been any blood, someone would have certainly cleaned it up by now," Provenza said.

"Maybe, but what if you found a tiny bit of it in the cracks between the hardwood planks?" Jenessa raised her brows to him, suggesting what a help to their case that would be.

"That's right," Michael agreed. "Why don't we have Libby spray some Luminol on the floor, see if there's any trace of blood still there?"

"I was just about to suggest that." Provenza turned to go and find her. "Hey, Libby!" he hollered as he wandered down the hallway toward the bedrooms.

Michael watched him go. "Is it hard to be here, Jenessa?"

Even though she had tried to hide her feelings, the expression on her face must have given them away. "Some." She nodded.

"You don't have to stay." He placed a hand gently on her shoulder. "We can handle it from here."

"I'm not leaving until I see what happens with the Luminol."

George and Libby joined them. "Let's get that table and rug moved, son," he ordered.

Once the detectives had them moved out of the way, Libby bent down and sprayed the Luminol on the floor, spraying it over every inch of where the rug had been.

"Look at that!" Provenza hollered.

The chemical glowed in the cracks between a few of the slats not far from the fireplace.

Blood.

"Can you get a sample there, Libby?" he asked. "I want that taken to the lab ASAP and see if we can match it to Lucy St. John."

"Got it, Detective," Libby replied.

"If this is Lucy's blood, with Logan's DNA putting him at the burial site, and money being a strong motive,"

Michael explained, "the DA can build a solid case against him."

"Yeah," Provenza agreed. "Let's see his father and his fancy lawyers get him out of this one."

The front door burst open and all heads turned toward the noise. Grey Alexander entered and stalked over to them. "What the hell is going on here?"

CHAPTER 18

GREY ALEXANDER STOMPED INTO THE living room of the lake house. "Did you hear me?"

Michael handed the search warrant to him. "We're searching your house for clues to Lucy St. John's murder."

"I want you all out of here!" Grey yelled.

"Sorry, it's not your call, Mr. Alexander," Provenza said. "You'll need to stand aside while we finish."

"You!" Grey screamed at Jenessa. "You've got something to do with this, don't you? I warned you to stay away from my family. You'll wish—"

Michael interrupted him, stepping defensively in front of Jenessa. "You'd better hold your tongue, sir."

"Get out of my way." Grey pushed at Michael, but he did not move.

"Are you assaulting a police officer, Mr. Alexander?" Provenza asked in his unassuming way. "Because if you are, well, you do know that's a crime— right?"

"First you arrest my son on some flimsy charge," Grey said, "and now you're trying to drum up some kind of evidence to hold against him. Really, George? After eleven years you really think you're going to find anything relating to what happened to that poor woman?"

George stood a little straighter, to his full five feet nine inches, and puffed out his chest. "That's Detective Provenza to you." They had known each other for decades, but watching George stand up for himself was marvelous.

"How did you know it was eleven years?" Michael asked.

"Jenessa asked my ex-wife where she was the summer eleven years ago," Grey snapped.

Michael stepped closer and stared into the man's eyes. "Mr. Alexander, you've got to stay out of our way while we work. I don't want to have to physically remove you, but I will if you push your luck."

Jenessa peeked around Michael. Grey Alexander's lips were drawn tight and he seemed so mad he could spit nails. She swore she saw steam coming out of Grey's ears.

Grey spotted her, his angry gaze met hers and her face suddenly grew hot, as if heat was radiating from his stare.

She willed herself to straighten her shoulders, not wanting to cower in front of him, but it would take a lot for her to stand her ground with him again. In Charles's office, it was all she could do to muster enough strength to give him the illusion that she had a backbone while in his presence. If he had stayed in Charles's office a minute longer, he might have seen her dissolve.

Why did she let this man hold such power over her?

She stepped from behind Michael and faced him. "Don't blame me, I didn't instigate this search. I'm simply along as an observer. I'd appreciate it if you would stop blaming me for what's happening to your family." *That's all on you, mister.* She wished she had the courage to say that.

Grey huffed at her. "You'll be hearing from my lawyers," he said, directing his comment to Provenza. He turned and marched out the door. "Be sure to lock up when you leave," he called over his shoulder.

"Have a nice day," Provenza said with a half-hearted wave of his hand. "What a pompous jerk," he muttered.

Michael chuckled.

"Tell you what," Provenza said. "Let's call this a potential crime scene and tape off the whole house. We'll need a rotary saw to cut out these boards and take them back to the lab, take them apart, and look for more blood. I'll show that SOB."

Michael rested a hand on the older detective's shoulder. "Are you sure you want to do that? Sounds borderline to me."

"Michael's right, George," Jenessa said.

George grinned and his eyes twinkled. "I want to teach that man he can't push us around while I still can. I'm running out of time, you know, but once I retire, then you can deal with him."

"Gee, thanks." Michael grimaced.

~*~

Not long after Grey Alexander stomped out of the lake house, Jenessa left too. She couldn't take being in that house another minute.

As she flew down the road, her mind was a blur as she fought back the memories of that fateful night. She didn't even remember the drive from Jonas Lake back to Hidden Valley. When she came to a stop, she found herself parked in front of The Sweet Spot.

Jenessa leaned her head against the headrest and shut her eyes. *In and out, come on, in and out.* The rhythm of her breathing calmed her. Through the glass storefront, she could see Ramey behind the counter waiting on a customer.

It was almost noon and a sandwich sounded heavenly right about now, so she slid out of her car and pushed open the door to the café. The jingle of the bells caught Ramey's attention and she looked up, a smile lighting up her eyes when she saw it was Jenessa.

"I'll be right with you," she said.

Sara was wiping off a table. Jenessa's stomach tightened, stiffening for another conflict.

"I want a word with you," her sister said, her voice lined with anger. She took Jenessa by the arm and pushed her out the door to the sidewalk.

Jenessa yanked her arm away. "What's going on?"

"I heard you got Logan arrested."

"What do you mean? It wasn't up to me. The cops obviously think they had enough evidence to place him under arrest. Why do you care anyway?" Jenessa knew why, but she wanted Sara to say it.

Sara crossed her arms defensively and her gaze dropped to her feet. "I just do."

"Why do you think I had anything to do with it?" Jenessa asked.

"I heard you gave the cops his blood from the fight the other night at The Brass Razoo."

"Who told you that?"

Sara turned her head toward the shop and her gaze went to Ramey.

Blabbermouth.

"After he told you he loved you, this is how you treat him?" Tears filled Sara's eyes.

Just as Jenessa suspected, Sara had overheard him. "He'd been drinking, he didn't know what he was saying," Jenessa said, hoping to diffuse the situation.

The expression on Sara's face said she didn't believe that for a minute.

"We have to find out who killed Ramey's mother," Jenessa said, "for Ramey's sake."

"She was fine without her mom until the body was dug up. She'd moved on. Now she's all upset all over again. I wish it had just stayed buried."

"You can't mean that," Jenessa snapped.

"Logan would never do something like that. He's not like his father. He's kind and thoughtful. If he wasn't carrying a torch for you all these years, he would have settled down with a nice girl and had a family of his own by now."

A nice girl like you, Sara? Jenessa wanted to say it, but she couldn't bring herself to be that mean.

"If he's innocent, I'm sure his father's high-powered lawyers will find a way to get him off. But if he's guilty, Sara, he'll have to pay for what he's done. You've got to stop spending your life pining for him."

There it was—she said it, for better or worse.

"Pining for him?" Sara's voice verged on a screech. "Where did you get that idea?"

"I'd rather not say."

Sara's gaze flew to Ramey once more and her eyes narrowed. "Blabbermouth."

"Don't blame her, someone should have told me a long time ago."

"What difference would it have made?"

"Maybe if they had, we wouldn't always have this animosity between us."

"But I wanted him, and he wanted you." The tears began to spill over and down Sara's cheeks.

Jenessa calmed her voice and took a step closer to her sister, hoping she wouldn't get her head bitten off. "Sis, you need to move on, for your own sake."

Sara turned away and lowered her face, wiping her fingers over her cheeks.

A twinge of compassion pricked Jenessa and she put a hand lightly on her sister's shoulder. "There's someone else out there for you, I'm know there is—a great guy that'll love you and want a family with you." She was talking to herself as much as she was to Sara. "He'll care about what you care about, love you for being you."

Sara lifted her watery eyes to her sister. "But I can't help myself, Jen. I love Logan. I've always loved him."

Jenessa laced her arms around Sara and held her while she wept. She wanted to tell her sister that Logan wasn't worth the tears, but there was a time she had loved him too—maybe still did.

"What am I supposed to do?" Sara cried.

"Let it go, baby sister. It's the only way to move forward, just let it go."

~*~

Later that afternoon, Jenessa stopped by the police station to see if the search of the lake house had garnered the detectives any new evidence. The receptionist called for Detective Provenza and he and Michael met Jenessa in the reception area.

"We didn't find anything else of importance," Provenza said. "Just the blood on the hardwood planks. Grey Alexander is going to be pissed when he sees we cut a section out of his floor." He chuckled a little at the thought.

"Libby took it to the county lab to run it against Lucy St. John's DNA," Michael reported.

"But don't put that in your story just yet, young lady," George warned. "You can write about the fact we got a warrant and searched the premises, but not what we found—at least not yet. And nothing about the floor sample we took. Understand?"

"Yes, sir." Jenessa gave him a mock salute. "But I can write about the arrest and the charges. They're public record."

"Well, yeah, of course," Provenza replied.

"When is the arraignment?" she asked, her gaze moving from George to Michael.

"This afternoon." Michael checked his watch. "In about an hour."

"I should head over to the courthouse then and get a good seat for the proceedings," she said backing toward the main entrance of the police station. "See you later, boys."

She pushed the door open with her backside. As she turned to walk out, she bumped smack into the ominous Grey Alexander, who was followed by a couple of well-dressed lawyers, all trying to come in.

"Jenessa Jones," he grumbled with a scowl.

Her body immediately tensed and her mouth went dry. "So sorry." She couldn't get away fast enough.

She skittered down the steps to the sidewalk and rushed on foot toward the courthouse, a few blocks away. Logan's father and attorneys must have been there to prep Logan before he was transported to court.

Running into Grey Alexander twice in one day was maddening. Jenessa breathed deeply as she slowed her gait. It wouldn't do to show up in court sweaty and flustered.

She reached the courthouse and, after going through the security check, she pulled the heavy door to the courtroom open and entered. The room was teaming with reporters from around the valley, some maybe from even farther away, as well as curious townspeople.

Squeezing down the congested center aisle, she spotted Sara sitting in the second row on the defendant's side. After pressing through the noisy crowd, and climbing over the people sitting on the end of Sara's row, she reached her seat.

"Sara?"

Startled, she looked up at Jenessa and removed her purse from the space beside her without a word.

Jenessa dropped down on the hard wooden pew, next her sister. "I didn't know you'd be here."

"I just thought Logan could use some support—you know?"

Jenessa nodded. "I understand." She glanced around the room. The press, of which she was slightly embarrassed to say she was a member today, was acting like piranhas anxious to gorge on Logan's flesh.

The townspeople, as well, many of whom she recognized, seemed to be there only to glean some juicy piece of gossip to spread around. The problem with living in a small town.

Jenessa and Sara sat quietly and waited for the arraignment to begin.

Eventually Lauren Alexander filed into the first row, not seeming to notice Jenessa in the next row back. She was followed by her husband and then Elizabeth, the ex-wife bringing up the rear, apparently wanting to show their family support. That had to be awkward for all three.

After an uncomfortably long wait, the bailiff entered and gestured toward the crowd, with his hands flying up and down in unison, to be quiet and take a seat. When order was achieved, he spoke. "All rise," the bailiff commanded in a booming voice. "Judge Andrew McHenry presiding."

While the judge walked in and took his place at the bench, Jenessa retrieved her micro-recorder from her purse, clicked it on, and held it out, ready to take in the proceedings.

An officer escorted Logan in from a side door. A rush of chatter erupted at the sight of him.

He glanced at his parents on the first row, then his gaze drifted beyond them, as if he had just noticed Jenessa and Sara in the next row back. A faint smile curved his lips for a brief moment, then it quickly faded into a somber expression.

"Did you see that?" Sara said in a low tone. "He saw we were here to support him."

"I'm sure he was glad to see some friendly faces in the crowd," Jenessa replied.

Was this how Sara was letting go of him?

Logan stood beside one of his attorneys at the defendant's table, wearing the customary orange jumpsuit.

The judge banged his gavel several times. "I'll have order or I'll clear the court," the white-haired justice shouted.

The crowd fell silent.

The Deputy District Attorney, a young man in a dark gray suit with closely cropped dark hair, who appeared to be in his early thirties, stood at the prosecution's table. "Your Honor, Emilio Rodriguez for the State." He proceeded to read the charges. "Logan Alexander is being charged with murder in the first degree."

A collective gasp rose from the crowd.

First degree? Apparently the District Attorney was going to propose that Logan lured Lucy to the lake house to kill her.

"How do you plead?" the judge asked.

"Not guilty, Your Honor. Absolutely not guilty!" Logan shouted.

"Just a plain *not guilty* will suffice," the judge instructed.

"Your Honor," the DDA said, "the State respectfully requests that no bail be granted to this defendant, as we believe Mr. Alexander to be a serious flight risk. His father has considerable funds and could easily whisk his son out of the country to avoid standing trial."

"I object, Your Honor," Logan's attorney declared. "Logan Alexander has lived in this town his whole life. He has deep ties to this community, both personally and professionally. He has never been in trouble with the law. He's never had anything more than a few speeding tickets on his record. It would be grossly unfair to expect this upstanding young man to languish in the county jail until trial."

The judge eyed Logan for a prolonged moment, pursing his lips in thought, before shifting his gaze to the DDA. "The thought that this young man would be stuck in jail for months pains me."

Did that mean he'll let Logan out on bail?

"However," the judge continued, "I have known his father for several decades, and I would have to agree with Mr. Rodriguez that the potential exists that he could try to sneak his son out of the country to avoid prosecution. Bail is denied." The sound of the gavel coming down hard broke the stillness in the courtroom and pandemonium erupted from the gallery.

The judge banged his gavel a few more times and the crowd quieted. "Next case!"

Grey Alexander shot out of his seat. Reaching over the railing, he put a hand on his son's shoulder. "I'll do whatever I have to, to get you out, Son."

Jenessa held her recorder out as far, yet as inconspicuously, as she possibly could, hoping to catch something of the conversation.

Elizabeth stood as well and put her hand on her son's arm. "Stay strong, dear," she said in a strained, caring voice.

Grey leaned his head close to Logan's ear and muttered something to him. Hopefully the recorder was sensitive enough to pick it up.

Lauren rose and positioned herself beside her husband but made no effort to console her stepson. It was probably just as well, for Elizabeth would likely have bitten her head off for trying to usurp her place as his mother.

"Let's go," Sara said.

"Give me a minute." Jenessa wanted to stay as long as the Alexanders were there. Perhaps there would be something of significance she could pick up on her recorder.

Sara looked down at the device, then back up to Jenessa. "You can stay," she whispered, "but I need to get back to work."

Jenessa sat back down while Sara squeezed past her.

"Good luck," Sara said, keeping her voice low, and she continued down the row.

Elizabeth turned at Sara's voice. "Well, hello, Jenessa."

The woman's greeting drew Grey's and Lauren's attention as well.

Jenessa quickly pulled back the recorder, dropped it in her purse, and stood. "Hello, Mrs. Alexander," she said, meeting Elizabeth's eyes. "I wish we were running into each other under better circumstances."

"What are *you* doing here?" Grey growled.

"My job."

~*~

Jenessa drove back to her home office to write her story on the arraignment of Hidden Valley's number one son. Her hands were still trembling a little from her run-in with Grey Alexander.

She thought of Logan and how frightened he looked at the arraignment. His confidence and swagger were gone. If his lawyers couldn't get him out of this jam, he'd likely be spending the better part of the rest of his life in prison.

The conversation they'd had earlier in the day played in her mind. Not only had he emphatically denied any part in Lucy St. John's death, but he had also declared his love for her once more. Had Logan really been in love with her all these years? Was he truly sorry for how his parents had treated her and the situation? Her father and mother had pushed her to give up the baby as much as his parents had, but had it only been because her dad caved to Grey Alexander's pressure?

Her father was a coward. At least that's how she saw it. He hadn't stood up for her, or for his grandchild. If he had, perhaps it would have cost him his biggest client, but couldn't he have gotten others? Maybe they wouldn't have been as lucrative, but wasn't his own flesh and blood more important to him than money?

And why hadn't her mother spoken her mind that evening? Surely having had babies herself, she had to have known the emotional pain that giving up the baby would cause her daughter. Or had she truly thought it was for the best, as she had said? Jenessa chose to believe the latter.

She pulled the car into the driveway, glad to be home, giving her a mental break from the questions that could no longer be answered.

Heading straight to the office, she sat at the computer, ready to begin formulating her story. She pulled the micro-recorder out of her purse and set it on the desk. She pushed *play* to hear the proceedings once more and type up her outline as she listened.

When she got to the end of the arraignment, and she heard the judge call, "Next case!" She picked up the device and held it close, hoping to hear what Grey had said to his son.

"I'll do whatever I have to, to get you out, Son," is what she heard him say. But there had been something else, something after that, something he had whispered into Logan's ear.

Jenessa strained to hear it. There was some sound, some faint words, but she couldn't make them out. She played the recording over and over, but all she could make out were the words *sorry* and *dragged.*

What was Grey saying to his son?

CHAPTER 19

MAYBE THE CONVERSATION that the recorder couldn't pick up was nothing more than a few words of encouragement. On the other hand, perhaps Libby at the county lab could work some magic on the recording and she'd know for sure.

She had a story to write and get into the paper before too long, but if she didn't phone Libby right now, she might be gone for the day. She reached for her phone, but stopped short.

What was she thinking? Libby didn't take orders from a reporter. Jenessa would have to go through Michael or George Provenza to put in the request.

She called Michael and got his voicemail, so she phoned George next.

"Hello, Detective," she greeted in her sweetest voice.

"What can I do for you now?" George sounded a little grumpy.

"Everything okay?"

"That rascal Grey Alexander has been down here since the arraignment, angry as a hornet—chewed my butt. I guess his cleaning lady phoned him after she went to the lake house and found the hole we'd carved in the wood floor."

"Sorry to hear that, George. Wasn't it taped off?"

"It was, but she must have ignored it and gone on in. Doesn't anybody respect the law anymore? I mean, really."

"Calm down," Jenessa suggested.

"Oh, I didn't mean to go on like that. That man's got me all riled up. You must have been calling for a reason."

"Actually, I need some help—a favor really."

Detective Provenza grunted.

"Just a tiny one," she pleaded.

"What do you need?" His voice turned surprisingly obligatory.

"I was sitting behind Mr. Alexander at the arraignment this morning and overheard a little of what he said to his son. I actually had my micro-recorder going so I could record the proceedings for the story I have to write. It happened to still be on when Grey was talking to Logan and there was something on the tape that was a bit indiscernible. I wondered if you could ask Libby to see what she could do to clear it up."

"You can't be taping a person without their permission," George chided.

"I'm not expecting you to use it in court. I was just hoping it would tell me something important about the case, for my story. And if it happened to expose something significant about the case, then all the better. I know you couldn't use it, but it might point you in the right direction. It's not like they had any expectation of privacy."

"That's not the point. Besides, we already are going in the right direction. We've arrested our prime suspect, if you hadn't noticed," George retorted.

"What if Logan didn't do it?"

"You saying don't think he did?" he said with a dubious air.

"No, I'm not saying that. What I'm saying is you should keep an open mind, Detective. What if he's not the killer and you let the real killer get away because you were focusing on the wrong person? Maybe there's some other explanation for his DNA being found with the body." At least she hoped there was, for Logan's sake.

Logan had made her promise not to let the police stop looking for any other likely suspects. "Do you really want to be responsible for sending an innocent man to prison because you couldn't be bothered to pursue all other possibilities?"

"Are you trying to tell me how to do my job, princess?"

Princess? "No, I'm only asking you to keep an open mind, keep following up on leads that might point to other suspects. Logan swears he's innocent."

"Don't they all?" the detective asked.

"He could be telling the truth."

"I'm sure the captain won't go for that anyway. There's not enough money in the budget to keep working cases where we've already arrested our prime suspect."

"Then don't let him know."

"Are you trying to get me fired?" His voice rose a few decibels with the question.

"Oh, come on, Detective. It's not like Hidden Valley is a hotbed of crime and you have a stack of cases to solve."

"Maybe not murder cases, but there's still plenty to investigate," he said.

"You're a man of integrity—am I right, George?"

"I am."

"Then I have to trust that you won't let go of this case just because someone is in jail for it, not if there's a chance he's innocent. Your case isn't ironclad."

"That's true, but they aren't always. You should know that."

"Yeah, I know. But you don't have to do the work yourself, Detective. You have Michael now to help you. Use him."

"Well, I don't know…"

"Listen, all I'm saying is don't close the book on your investigation. There may be more to discover."

"Do you know something you're not telling me?" Provenza asked.

"No, George. Just a feeling." That truly was all Jenessa had to go on. "So what about calling Libby about that recording?"

~*~

After hanging up with Detective Provenza, Jenessa went back to her computer to review the photos she had taken at the crime scene where the remains were uncovered. Something about one of those photos bothered her—the unidentified tiny object she saw next to the body, near the mid-section. In the photo it looked like a button or an earring, or maybe a cufflink, still partially buried in the dirt.

When Jenessa first saw the item as she snapped a photo of the gravesite, she assumed the CSI unit would collect it and identify it. But when she had spoken to her old boss's cousin in the State crime lab earlier, she had no information about it.

Since that had been closer to the day of the discovery, perhaps by now she might have some information. Detective Provenza would likely know if they had found the item and identified it, but she had probably used up all of her grace with him for today.

She would have to phone her old boss in Sacramento and cajole him into asking his mysterious cousin to give her a call about it.

"No time like the present." Jenessa dialed his number.

"Jack Linear," he answered.

"Hey, Jack. This is Jenessa."

"So how are things in Mayberry?"

"It's Hidden Valley, Jack."

"I know, I just meant…well, never mind. What's up?"

"I need a favor."

"Oh boy. What now?"

"I had asked your cousin about something last week, which she had no information on yet. I was hoping she had something for me by now, but I don't have her name or phone number. Would you mind asking her to give me a call again? See if she's come across the button-like object and identified it?"

"She's pretty reluctant to talk to the press. She could lose her job if anyone found out."

"Even for her favorite cousin? Please ask her."

"Is this for that old murder in your neck of the woods?"

"It is. I'm doing a story on it and, well, one of my old friends has been arrested for the crime."

"Sorry to hear that. Is this a story we should be covering?" he asked.

"How about I write it for you, freelance, and you can run it—that is, if my boss at the Herald doesn't mind."

"Tell you what? You run the story in your paper first and I'll run it here the day after. The AP does that sort of thing all the time."

"I'll be in touch about it then. But first, I need to talk to your cousin. Deal?"

Jack agreed to have his cousin call her, so Jenessa went back to finishing up her story on the arraignment. There wasn't much to tell, so the story didn't take much time and she was able to email it off.

When she had spoken to Detective Provenza, in the end she had succeeded in getting him to relent and agree to ask Libby to listen to the recording, promising not to tell her what it was in regards to. He couldn't sleep at night, he had said, if he didn't pursue every possible lead in the St. John case. She had pushed his integrity button and he would come through for her.

Now to find out what that mysterious object was. Maybe Jack's cousin would call her soon.

~*~

Jenessa stuck a frozen dinner in the microwave. Tonight she would dine on herbed chicken with roasted red potatoes in a creamy honey mustard sauce. If only it tasted as good as it sounded.

As she stood before the microwave, watching her food go around and around, her phone rang. She snatched it up from the counter as the timer dinged that her dinner was done.

"Hello." She pulled the little plastic tray out of the oven with a potholder.

"Jenessa Jones?" a woman asked.

"Yes, this is she." Jenessa pushed the microwave's door closed with her elbow and moved to the table.

"I'm Jack's cousin. He told me you wanted me to call you again."

"Oh, yes. Jack's cousin." Jenessa set the hot food down and settled on a chair. "When we spoke last week, I asked if the CSIs had found a small object, like a button, or an earring, or something."

"That's right, I recall that." The volume of her voice grew low. "They hadn't at the time, but let me go through the file here. Fortunately almost everyone is gone."

The sound of shuffling papers came across the line.

"Here it is. It was a cufflink."

"Was there any DNA on it?"

"Yes, some epithelia in the crevices, but the report says it was run through CODIS and no match was found."

"Could you scan and email me the photo of it?"

"I don't know…"

"It might be important."

"I've already sent it to the Hidden Valley Police Department, to a Detective Provenza."

"Well, I can't really ask him for it, now can I?"

"I suppose not."

"Would you mind? Please." Jenessa crossed her fingers, waiting for the woman's response.

"I guess it couldn't hurt, but you have to promise you'll keep my name out of it if someone finds out you have this."

"Absolutely. Besides, I don't even know your name. I couldn't give it out if I wanted to."

"All right, I guess I could do that, but only because you're a friend of Jack's."

Jenessa ate her dinner while she waited for the email to come, keeping one eye on the computer screen. Halfway through her chicken and potatoes, the email showed up.

She clicked it open, double clicked on the attachment, and the photo filled the screen. Just as the woman had said, it was a cufflink. She'd seen it somewhere before—but where?

It was a polished gold square with rounded corners. There was a design in the middle with a black backdrop, an artistically abstract combination of an A and an E. But where had she seen it before?

She finished her meal as she stared at the screen, wracking her brain for some clue to whose cufflink it might be—but nothing came.

Frustrated, she cleared the table and threw her plastic dish in the trash. Why did it seem so familiar?

With no answer coming to mind, she moved into her office and sat at the desk. Maybe there was another clue amongst the documents she had found in the manila envelope.

Jenessa dumped the papers out on the desk and scoured them once more, hoping to see something she'd missed the first time going over them. Nothing stood out.

She opened the lap drawer and rummaged through it—nothing new there either. She slammed the drawer in frustration.

Her phone rang on the desk. "Hello."

"Hey, this is Sara. Are you free tonight?"

"Yeah, my evening is pretty open. What did you have in mind?"

"I was thinking I should come over and help you go through Dad's stuff, you know, see who wants what—if you're not busy."

Jenessa had finished her story and sent it off to the newspaper, and the search through her father's desk wasn't getting her anywhere, so sure, she wasn't busy—why not? She had tried going through his closet and drawers when she first arrived, but it was creepy and uncomfortable, with his just having passed away. "No, no, come on over. Who knows, perhaps we'll uncover some great treasures in Dad's closet."

Maybe it would be nice doing something with her sister without all the bickering and fighting that had come to define their relationship. Getting Sara to leave Logan in her rearview mirror would take some time, it seemed, but at least now they were able to talk about it. If only someone would have had the courage to tell her sooner about her sister and Logan, they could have been much further down the road by now.

~*~

When Sara arrived, they went upstairs to their parents' old bedroom and stood in the doorway. They glanced at each other without speaking, as if they were about to step onto holy ground.

Jenessa broke the silence. "This is kind of creepy, don't you think?"

"Kinda?"

"It's got to be done." Jenessa stepped into the room first and Sara followed her lead.

They went to the roomy walk-in closet first, looking through shoe boxes on shelves, round floral hat boxes on the top shelf that ran around the space, and through a jewelry case tucked behind a large ivory ceramic pot filled with a vanilla candle.

Jenessa pulled the bulky pot from the shelf and held it out to her sister. "Remember this?"

Sara ran her fingers over the intricately embossed design. "Mom loved the scent of vanilla in her closet."

"She said it made her clothes smell like a sugar cookie." Jenessa lifted it to her nose and took a whiff.

"And Dad hated it." Sara wrinkled her nose. "He used to say it didn't present a very professional image, having his suits smell like a bakery," she said, dropping her voice to imitate his.

Jenessa grimaced at her sister's portrayal. "What a stick in the mud."

"Oh, he wasn't so bad."

"Not to you." The lightness of the atmosphere disappeared, and Jenessa turned away and shoved the candle back on the shelf. "Mind if I keep the candle?"

"Knock yourself out." Sara went back to rifling through the boxes.

"I'm going to go through Dad's highboy." Jenessa walked out of the closet.

"Wait, I want to see too." Sara followed.

Was Sara afraid Jenessa might palm something she wanted? They were finally beginning to get along again. Now was not the time to start bickering over their dad's belongings like possessive dogs over a bone.

"Bring one of those shoe boxes with you so we can empty the top drawer," Jenessa said.

Jenessa pulled the top drawer open, finding a watch and a flat jewelry case. She opened it and found numerous pairs of cufflinks set in multiple little felt-lined squares. She picked up the watch. "This was his sports watch, but didn't he have another watch? That fancy expensive one Mom gave him on his fiftieth birthday."

"Oh, the Ferragamo?" Sara asked nonchalantly, studying a pair of cufflinks in her hand. "Does anyone wear cufflinks anymore?"

Was Sara trying to change the subject?

"Yes, the Ferragamo. Do you know where it is?"

"At my house." Sara's gaze rose to Jenessa for a moment, then drifted back down to the case of cufflinks. "Remember, we picked up Daddy's personal items from the morgue?"

"That was a six-thousand-dollar watch. What were you planning to do with it?" Her blood pressure began to rise. *Don't bicker now.* Her mother's voice was in her head.

"I'd forgotten about those things until you mentioned it," Sara said, her gaze still on the cufflinks as she examined them one by one.

Was that the truth? Or was she trying to pull something over? "So you have Dad's wedding ring too?"

"Of course. It was with the other stuff—his clothes and shoes. You seemed like you were only interested in getting his keys at the time. Why do you ask?" Sara inquired with an innocent lilt to her voice, flashing her sister a familiar doe-eyed look.

That was the look that got her into trouble when her little sister did something wrong and Jenessa got blamed for it. She took a breath and paused, struggling to keep her voice calm. "Why don't you bring his stuff over here so we have it all in one place? Then we can decide who gets what, what we should sell, what we should give away—that sort of thing."

"And maybe we should have Aunt Renee here as an innocent third party in case we both want some of the same things."

"Yes, so one of us doesn't try to take advantage of the other." Maybe Jenessa shouldn't have raised her eyebrows at the end of that statement.

"You mean me?" Sara asked, her voice rising with indignation. "If you're going to be like that, I'm out of here!" She handed Jenessa the tray of cufflinks as she breezed past her.

"Now, don't be like that, Sis. I was just—"

Sara was down the stairs and out the door before Jenessa finished her sentence.

"So much for getting along," Jenessa told her aunt when she phoned her and described the bit of a clash she'd had with Sara.

"You can't just say the first thing that comes into your head, dear. You've always been one to poke the bear, but you don't like it when the bear pokes back."

"Hmm…you could be right." Jenessa rubbed her hand on the back of her neck, where she felt tension building. She settled on the edge of the bed, inhaled deeply and huffed out one long breath, releasing some of her stress. "Do you mind acting as a go-between while we sort through Dad's things?"

"I don't mind, hon. I've been doing it for years."

That was true. Even before their mother had died, Aunt Renee would step in to mediate fights between the two of them.

"Now pull your big girl panties on and apologize to your sister."

~*~

After a further talking-to by Aunt Renee, Jenessa phoned her sister and apologized as instructed. She and Sara agreed to meet again when all three could be there.

Jenessa popped up off the bed and put the tray of cufflinks back in the jewelry box. As she set the tray down into the shallow top drawer, her gaze went to the one felted square that held only a single link. Where was its mate?

She plucked it from its nest and cradled it in the palm of her hand. It was an abstract A and E. *Oh, God!* It was an exact match to the cufflink in the photo.

CHAPTER 20

IT HAD BEEN HER FATHER'S cufflink down in the shallow grave. Jenessa's stomach did a backflip at the realization, causing her mouth to water. Her stomach roiled and she wanted to vomit. That was where she'd seen it before—on her father's wrists.

Her phone jingled in her pocket and she flinched at the sound. She dug it out and glanced at the screen. It was Michael. Should she tell him what she just found? It would mean her father was involved in Lucy's death somehow. But he was dead now too, so she might as well—what could happen to him now?

"Hello?"

Jenessa let him ask her how she was and how her day went before dropping the bombshell on him—she knew about the cufflink found with the body and she had a picture of it. What's more, she had the match to it and it belonged to her father.

"I'm not even going to ask how you know about it," he said.

That was just as well.

"This could mean my father is the killer—my father, Michael." The thought her dad could have killed someone sent an icy chill feathering up her spine. She shuddered to shake it off.

"We don't know that for certain, but yes, we have to look at it as a possibility. I'm coming over and we can talk more about it."

"That's a good idea, but what about Jake?"

"No problem. I'll call my mom to come by and watch him for a little while. That cufflink needs to be taken into evidence as soon as possible."

Within fifteen minutes he was knocking at her door.

After a brief exchange, she led him up the stairs to her father's bedroom. She held out the jewelry tray and he picked the lone cufflink up with a gloved hand and dropped it into an evidence bag.

"You'll find my fingerprints on it," she said.

"Shouldn't be a problem. It's DNA we're looking for to match the other link. What about a hairbrush or anything like that?" he asked.

"In the bathroom." She pitched her chin toward the bath.

"Or even an old watch might have some sweat or skin cells on the back side of it."

The sports watch in the drawer. She went to the highboy and pulled out the top drawer for Michael. "Like this?"

Michael lifted out the watch and dropped it into another evidence bag.

"What about the other cufflinks in his jewelry box?"

"Leave them. This should be enough," he said. "What do you think the A and E stand for?"

"The only thing I can think of is Alexander Enterprises," Jenessa said. "Maybe Grey Alexander had them made and gave the pair to Dad as a gift."

"If that's the case, there are probably others just like it out there," Michael surmised.

"Grey might have a pair, and maybe even Logan too," she said. "Or others in the company."

Michael gave her a slight nod. "It could be that Logan was the one who had accidentally dropped one of them in the grave when he was moving Lucy's body, along with his comb."

"Maybe," she agreed, although Jenessa had never seen him wear cufflinks, except with a tuxedo the night he took her to the prom.

"I'll get these things to the lab in the morning."

"But Michael, if my father's DNA matches the one found—"

A thick lump caught in her throat and she couldn't even get the rest of the sentence out. She blinked back the salty tears that stung her eyes.

Could the guilt over what he'd done have been the pivotal thing that changed him? Was it really what had stood between her and her father for all these years? Not only her illegitimate baby, but his part in Lucy's death as well?

It had seemed to Jenessa like it was only the relationship between her and her father that was strained, but with not having been around much, except for a couple of times a year, how could she really know? Maybe he was different with her mother and Sara too, but Jenessa just hadn't noticed because she was so caught up in her own emotional turmoil.

"Don't do that to yourself," Michael said with a soothing tone. He must have sensed her need, for his arms encircled her and he pulled her toward him. She leaned her head on his chest and he lightly kissed her temple. "You don't know he did anything. Maybe that cufflink they found isn't even his."

Michael was a doll for trying to assuage her feelings, but as a detective he had to be wondering if her father was the killer as well.

"Maybe." She could only pray it wasn't true. News headlines flashed before her eyes—*David Jones Murdered Lucy St. John.* She closed her eyes and buried her face against him.

He held her in silence and gently rubbed his hand over her back.

After a time, she pulled back. "Look at me, what a crybaby."

"No one can blame you for being upset." He tucked a couple of fingers under her chin and lifted her face. "Want some good news?"

"That would be nice." She gave him a weak smile.

"We found Tony Hamilton."

Jenessa stepped away and wiped the tears from under her eyes. "Where?"

"He was in jail in Fresno on drug charges. We got them to transport him here in the morning for questioning. If it wasn't for the comb and the cufflink, I'd think he did it."

"Yeah, I would have too, in the beginning, but now..." Thinking about her father's possible guilt, she shook her head sadly. "Let's get out of here and go downstairs."

Michael followed her out of the bedroom and down the steps. "We'll interrogate him tomorrow and see if he can at least furnish us with a date when he last saw Lucy. That'll give us a better time frame of when the murder might have taken place."

"Haven't you and George been able to see from her records when she stopped using her cell phone and her checking account?"

"We're talking over ten years ago, Jen. The bank has those records archived and they haven't gotten them to us yet, and we don't even know which cell phone company Lucy used back then. They might not even be in business now."

"And of course her landline would have continued to be used by Ramey for a while, so that won't tell us anything." She stopped at the bottom of the stairs and turned back toward Michael. "Let's hope this Hamilton character can tell you more than just the last time he saw Lucy."

"Like what?"

"Like why she ran out on Ramey, supposedly to Southern California, but then she turns up dead at Jonas Lake. She came back for a reason, but what was it?"

"Guess we'll have to wait until tomorrow to find that out." Michael slid his hands around Jenessa's waist and tugged her closer. "I need to get home and relieve my mother. Oh, and my cousin Luke is coming in tonight."

"Cousin Luke?" Jenessa rested her hands on Michael's muscular arms.

"He's driving down from Reno. He wants to check out Hidden Valley and maybe apply as a patrolman at the police department."

"I'd like to meet your cousin Luke," she said with an impish grin.

"I'm sure that can be arranged." Michael smiled down at her. "He'll be here through the weekend. Are we still on for dinner Friday night?"

She gave him a playful smile. "We are, but what about your cousin? Won't he expect you to entertain him?"

"He can have dinner at my folks' house. That's where Jake will be."

"I hope your son doesn't mind me stealing some time with his dad."

"You know, Jake still talks about our afternoon together at the fair."

"He does?" That pleased her. He was a sweet little boy.

"He wanted me to tell you that we like you a bunch."

"A bunch?" She slipped her arms around him and couldn't help but smile broadly.

"A bunch." Michael grinned. He lowered his face to hers and kissed her softly. "Both of us." He kissed her again. "But mostly me." He kissed her again, longer and more deeply than before, and she didn't want him to stop.

When he released her, her head was dizzy. "Would you like to stay?"

"Of course I'd like to, but I can't. Remember, my mom's watching Jake. I told her I wouldn't be gone long, and it's getting late." He took Jenessa's hand and kissed the back of it. "I've gotta go."

He walked to the front door, leaving her standing in the foyer, at the foot of the staircase, holding onto the balustrade.

"We'll talk tomorrow, I'm sure." Jenessa was anxious to know what Tony Hamilton would tell the detectives. "And don't forget our date Friday night."

He had opened the front door, but he returned to her with long strides and pulled her up in his arms again. He kissed her slow and long. "Wild horses couldn't keep me from it," he whispered in her ear.

His warm breath on her skin and his deliciously sensuous kiss left her lightheaded, and she grabbed hold of the banister, dropping down onto one of the steps as he went out the door with a wave.

~*~

Jenessa got up the next morning and called the Herald to bring her boss up to speed on her story.

"Mr. McAllister has stepped out," Alice said. "May I take a message?"

"This is Jenessa, Alice."

"And your phone number, Jenessa Alice?"

"No, my name is Jenessa. Your name is Alice."

"But you just said—"

"Never mind. I'll call his cell phone." Jenessa chuckled to herself as she tapped Charles's number into her phone.

"Hello, this is Charles McAllister."

"Hey, this is Jenessa. Just checking in."

"Don't forget you've got a couple of obits due this afternoon and you still need to reschedule the high school principal."

"I know, I know," she moaned. "I thought you'd like an update on the *big* story."

"Sure, but I'm having breakfast at the moment."

"At The Sweet Spot?"

"As a matter of fact, yes. How'd you know?"

"A lucky guess. I'm headed down myself to pick up a coffee. How about I meet you there and we can talk?"

There was a pause on the line. Was Charles with someone?

"I guess that'd be okay," he finally answered.

"See you in a few, boss. Oh, and say hello to Ramey for me."

~*~

Jenessa pulled her sweet little Mercedes into a diagonal parking space outside of The Sweet Spot. She slid out from behind the wheel, stepped onto the sidewalk, and glanced back at the sparkling blue sports car. What a step up from that worn-out Toyota she had been driving. She had her dad to thank for that.

The thought of her father and his possible involvement in Lucy's murder deflated the lighthearted step the beautiful car had given her. She tried to brush the uncomfortable feeling off as she reached for the coffee shop's door.

Sara was on her way out as Jenessa swung the door open.

"Good morning, Sara."

"Morning. I've got to get to the bank. Ramey's inside, making googley eyes with your boss."

Jenessa covered a giggle with her fingers. "Well, I'm happy for her."

"Me too. I just wish they'd take the show somewhere more private. You know the whole town will be talking about them by dinnertime."

"I'm sure they will." Jenessa considered telling Sara what she was uncovering about their father, but what would be the point? It was too early to accurately assess his involvement in Lucy's death. No need to weigh her or Aunt Renee down with the worry of it too. Jenessa would carry the burden of it alone, for now.

"Got to run." Sara hurried down the street.

By the time Jenessa stepped inside, Ramey was clearing the plates at Charles's table.

"There's my prize reporter," Charles said.

"Hey, Jenessa," Ramey greeted. "Nice morning, isn't it?"

Ramey's bright spirit was endearing and contagious. How could Jenessa have thought for one second that Ramey might have killed her mother?

"Can I get a small mocha cappuccino with a double spritz of whip cream on top?"

Ramey's mouth turned down. "Oh dear, a double spritz day. That can't be good."

"I'm hoping it'll turn around," Jenessa replied, trying to work up a smile. "We'll see."

"Have a seat with Charles and I'll bring it right out, poor thing." Ramey disappeared behind the counter.

"Morning, boss." Jenessa took a seat beside him.

"What do you have for me?"

Jenessa surveyed the café, dotted with townspeople enjoying their coffee and chatting away. "After Ramey brings my coffee, I think we'd better step outside to talk."

"Why?"

That was a silly question. What was Ramey doing to this man's brain? Jenessa leaned closer to him. "As if you haven't noticed, some people in this town have big ears and loose lips."

Charles looked around the place. "You may be right."

Through the bustling coffee shop, Ramey brought Jenessa's drink to the table.

Jenessa stood and hugged her friend good-bye. "Thanks, Ramey."

Charles stood and began to reach out to give Ramey a hug as well, but her gaze flashed around the crowded café and she pulled back a little, sticking her hand out instead. He took it and gently shook it. "Breakfast was great. I hope we can do it again sometime."

"I'm sure that can be arranged. I have some pull with the owner."

Ramey's face was beaming as Jenessa and Charles went out the door and stopped at the sidewalk.

"What do you have?" he asked.

"You already know I spoke to Logan in the jail and did my story on the arraignment, but what you don't know is that another piece of evidence has been found."

"What else?"

Jenessa glanced at the large windows of The Sweet Spot and saw many eyes on them. She turned her back to the storefront and continued. "What I'm telling you is not for publication—at least not yet. I have a contact in the police department, but I've promised this person I won't print any of the confidential details until I get the go ahead."

"Who is your contact?" he asked.

"I can't say."

"Not even to me?"

"Sorry, Charlie."

"It's Charles," he said gruffly. "So tell me, what is the latest?"

"Some hairs were found with the remains and the State lab has matched it to Logan Alexander. That was one of the reasons they arrested him. But you know DNA results, they really only show the likelihood that it's a match."

"True, but they must think it was close enough to arrest him."

"They did. They were also able to get a search warrant for the Alexanders' lake house, and they discovered blood in some of the floor boards. Detective Provenza sent a piece of the floor to the lab to make sure that it's Lucy St. John's."

"You can write about that, can't you?"

"Yes, and I am, but now another piece of evidence has turned up and the cops are trying to match the DNA from that to see who it belonged to."

"Any suspects?"

"Maybe, but they haven't made any definite findings yet." Jenessa couldn't bring herself to tell him it was probably her own father's. "However, they have located Lucy St. John's last known boyfriend and Detectives Provenza and Baxter will be questioning him later today. I'm headed over there to see what I can find out."

"Sounds like you've got things pretty well under control. Just get something to me by six o'clock today that I can run in tomorrow's paper. People want to know what's happening, so they're tuning into the television news. The newspaper's only advantage is that we can go more in-depth, so make sure you do that."

"I know, I know, Charles. I've been in this business long enough to get that. You really should think about having a website for the paper, though."

"I've proposed that to Grey Alexander on more than one occasion, but he continues to turn me down. Speaking of Mr. Alexander, how is he handling his son being arrested?"

"Not well. I've had a couple of run-ins with him, not including the one at your office."

"Best if you steer clear of him, if you can. That man can make a lot of trouble for you—me too."

~*~

Jenessa stopped by the police station to see if there was any word yet on Tony Hamilton.

"We're expecting him by ten," Detective Provenza said as they stood in the reception area. "You want to stick around and get a peek at him or something?"

"Actually, I was hoping I could watch the interview from the observation room."

"You sure like to push it, don't you?" He glowered at her. "You know I can't do that."

Michael approached. "Good morning," he said, directing his words to Jenessa.

She returned his greeting with a smile.

"Like I said, Miss Jones," Provenza began, "I can't let you anywhere near Hamilton and the interrogation." He leaned closer to her and dropped his volume. "I'll give you a call later and let you know if there's anything you can use in your articles."

She nodded. Maybe then she could weasel other information out of him, as well. "And what about the recording?"

"What recording?" Michael asked.

George's gaze flew to Michael for a second, then back to Jenessa. He stuck his hand out. "I'll see what I can do."

Jenessa dug the micro-recorder out of her purse and put it firmly in his hand, avoiding Michael's probing stare. "I got the words *sorry* and *dragged*. So if she can get anything else, it might be helpful to the case."

Michael must have understood what was transpiring. He took a step closer. "We can't use that," he said in a muffled tone.

Jenessa looked him in the eye. "Maybe not in court, but it might have something useful on it."

"George," Michael said, "this isn't really the way you do things around here, is it?"

"Not usually," he replied. "Normally we don't have a pretty reporter helping us out."

"I mean according to the law."

"Cool your jets, son. We're not breaking any laws," George responded, "just bending a few. I'll be retiring before long and I want to go out on a high note—you know, catch the SOB that killed that poor woman."

"That's what I want too, Michael." Jenessa had to be careful how she handled her contacts within the police department—she needed their help if she was going to write in-depth pieces on the big news stories. She had made inroads with George Provenza, and hopefully Michael would become as helpful as his mentor. "Not to change the subject boys, but what's happening with the cufflink I gave you, Michael?"

"It's already on its way to the State lab in Sacramento. They promised to let me know as soon as they have something."

"Tough break," Provenza said. "Michael gave me the low down on it being your dad's."

Jenessa offered him weak smile. "No matter what, follow the evidence wherever it takes you. Isn't that right?" *Even if it exposes your own father.*

The main doors to the station opened and the chatter of voices drew their attention as a couple of men in tan uniforms entered, ushering in a scruffy, middle-aged convict. He was dressed in the usual prison orange, tall with a thin build and long stringy brown hair that was in desperate need of a wash. It had to be Tony Hamilton, escorted by deputies from the Fresno County Sheriff's Department.

Once they got inside, out of the heat, George rushed over to them. "I'm Detective Provenza. We spoke on the phone this morning. Let's bring your prisoner back to my office and we'll take care of things there."

The deputies nodded their agreement.

"Miss Jones, I'll phone you when I have something for you." Provenza motioned to the Fresno group to follow him down the hallway.

"But can't I—" she started to call out after him.

Michael ran his hand gently down her arm. "Sorry, Jenessa. I've got to go too." He backed away toward the hall. "I'll call you later." Then he was gone.

Disappointed she hadn't gotten to learn anything from Tony Hamilton, at least not yet, she marched out the doors and back to her car. The obits wouldn't write themselves, and there was a high school principal to interview while she waited to hear back from the detectives and the lab.

It was going to be a long day—a very long day.

~*~

Once inside her car, she flipped the air conditioner on full blast. The cufflink was still on her mind. She phoned her aunt to find out how her father might have known Lucy St. John, other than writing monthly checks to her on behalf of Grey Alexander.

"I can't really say, dear," Aunt Renee replied. "She left town so long ago. Why do you ask?"

Jenessa couldn't tell her aunt about the cufflink. She'd find out soon enough, but now wasn't the time. "I'm just trying to fit the puzzle pieces together."

"He never liked her—I know that much. She wasn't much of a mother to Ramey and I remember him saying he was glad she was gone for good."

"Gone for good, huh?" How would he know for certain that she was gone for good unless he knew she was dead? "Those were his exact words?"

"I don't recall that those were his exact words, but yes, he was glad she was gone and wasn't ever coming back."

CHAPTER 21

LATER THAT AFTERNOON, when Jenessa was leaving the principal's office, she received a call from Detective Provenza. He told her that he and Michael had thoroughly questioned Tony Hamilton and that what he'd told them changed the whole ball game.

"Hamilton said Lucy agreed to go to LA with him because her sugar daddy was cutting her off. Lucy had told him Grey Alexander had been paying her each month to keep quiet about the fact he was Ramey's father."

"Yes, I found the agreement in my father's desk at home," Jenessa said.

"And you didn't think to show me?"

"Well, you already knew he had been paying her, so I didn't think you needed to see it. What else did he say?"

"When Ramey turned eighteen, Alexander told Lucy he was not going to continue to pay her, that the girl was an adult now and he was done. Lucy went nuts,

Hamilton said. However, he was able to calm her down, convincing her to tell Grey if he paid her fifty thousand dollars in cash, she'd continue to keep her mouth shut and disappear, that he'd never hear from her again."

"I guess fifty thousand would be less than paying for even one more year at five thousand a month," Jenessa said. That must have been the fight Logan heard between his father and stepmother. "What else?"

"Hamilton said Lucy had made plans to meet Grey one night to talk about it."

"Did he give you a specific date?" Jenessa asked.

"He did, but all I can share with you is that it was around the end of June, eleven years ago."

"And where was she going to meet him?"

"The lake house."

"No surprise there. So, did he see anything?" Jenessa pressed, hoping for something that would point to the killer.

"No. He said he dropped her off and then he went to the marina to have a few beers while he gave her some time to talk and get the money. He hung around down there about half an hour or so, maybe more, he couldn't really remember exactly how long it had been once he got drinking."

"Assuming Grey is who she met," Jenessa said. Maybe he had sent her father to negotiate instead, and things went horribly wrong.

"You mean like perhaps it was the junior Mr. Alexander?"

"Uh, yeah, that's what I meant." That wasn't what she meant, but it was a possibility. It could have been

Logan, but Jenessa had a sinking feeling it would more likely have been her dad.

"Logan could have overheard the conversation, I suppose, and went up there ahead of his father to confront the woman," Provenza said.

Logan *had* overheard. He had told her as much. So why was she reluctant to share that?

"Didn't Hamilton go back to get Lucy?" she asked.

"She was supposed to call him on his cell. When he hadn't heard from her after a while, he drove back to check on her. But when he got there, the house was dark and there were no cars there. He said he assumed she had gotten a ride back to town with Alexander because he had taken so long to return for her."

"What did he do then?"

"He drove to Lucy's house, but she wasn't there. He drove around town for a while, looking for her, but nothing. Said he wondered at the time if Alexander decided to make his problem go away rather than pay up."

"And the guy didn't think to report it?"

"That's what I asked," George said. "He claimed he was half drunk and who was going to believe a drunken drifter over the most powerful man in town? If something had happened to Lucy he didn't want to get pegged with it. So he got out of town as fast as he could and high-tailed it back to LA. He never heard from Lucy again after that."

"What a friend," Jenessa said sarcastically. "So, what is your gut telling you, George?"

"That any one of them could have done it—Tony, Grey, or Logan."

Or my father. "Do you think the lab might have made a mistake?" she asked. "Could the DNA from the hair on the comb have also been a close enough match to Grey Alexander? You know, what they call a familial match?"

"That is a possibility. I'll have Baxter check that out."

"I know Grey Alexander is a self-centered SOB, but do you think he would really let his own son go to prison for something that he did, knowing Logan was innocent?"

"Well, I'd have to agree, he is a pretty cold-hearted man, Jenessa, but no, I wouldn't think so. Although," Provenza paused, "I could see him putting Logan through the trial, believing his high-priced attorneys could get him off. If Johnny Cochran could get OJ off, a top-notch attorney like the kind Grey has the money to hire could very likely get Logan off too. Then neither of them would have to go to prison. That could be what the elder Alexander is counting on."

"Why don't you at least try to find out? Let's put the screws to that ogre and see if he hollers."

"The screws? What do you mean?"

"Oh, you know, George...apply some pressure to him, put the squeeze on him, see if he squeals."

Provenza chuckled. "You've been watching too many crime shows."

"With Tony Hamilton's testimony that Lucy had made plans to meet Grey, and then Tony never heard from her again, couldn't you tell Mr. Alexander you have a witness that can confirm he was with Lucy right before she died and that he is willing to point to Grey as the killer?"

"Hmm, I hadn't thought of that." Provenza paused, as if he was thinking it through. "I don't mean to sound like a bozo, but we just don't get many murders in this town, not like in Sacramento."

"You're not a bozo, George. Here, try this—drag him in and ask him if he really wants to send his son to prison for the rest of his life for something he did. Lay a heavy guilt trip on him. See how he reacts. Maybe you could offer to drop the charges against his son if he confesses to what really happened. Imply it could have even been an accident and if he admits to it, the jury would be sympathetic or something. Let him think he has a possible out and maybe he'll confess."

"Hey, that's a good idea," Provenza agreed. "I'll have to bring someone from the District Attorney's office in on it, but it might work."

Jenessa's phone began to buzz in her hand. "Hey, George, I've got another call. Let me know how it goes."

She clicked off one call and onto the next. "Hello, this is Jenessa."

"This is Ian McCaffrey. I need to see you. Do you have time to drop by my office later this afternoon? Say around four?"

She checked her watch. "I think I can make it then. What's this about?"

"I'll tell you when you get here."

~*~

Jenessa arrived home and got busy writing the obits and the story about the high school students and their beloved auditorium.

Half an hour later, Michael phoned her. "Detective Provenza filled me in on your conversation and I've got to say it was a clever idea."

"Glad I could help," she said.

"Provenza got Deputy District Attorney Rodriguez to call Mr. Alexander and ask him to come down to the station to talk, that there had been some new developments in Logan's case. Of course, Alexander said he'd be there right away, and he'd be bringing his lawyers."

"I hope the DDA didn't give anything away."

"No, he was pretty coy," Michael said. "They should all be here soon."

A smile of delight spread on her lips. "I wish I could see the interrogation." Would Michael pick up the hint she just dropped? "You do have an observation room, don't you?"

"We do, but I don't think the Captain would go for that."

"Hey, it was my idea, Detective. Besides, would the Captain have to know?"

Michael avoided the question. "I'll talk to you later."

Jenessa grabbed her purse and dashed to her car. The obits were finished and she'd emailed them off, but the auditorium story still needed a little more polish. It would have to wait, though—there was no way she was going to miss out on this interview.

~*~

Once Jenessa had slid behind the wheel, she glanced at the clock in the dash. It was going on four o'clock and she had promised her father's law partner she'd meet him at four. Maybe she could make it quick. He probably just wanted her to sign some probate documents.

There was no way for her to know how long it would take Grey Alexander to round up his attorneys and get down to the police station. Hopefully she had time to check in with Mr. McCaffrey and then scoot over to the police station before she missed all the action.

She entered the building where the law firm was and took the elevator up to their floor. The receptionist buzzed Mr. McCaffrey's assistant, who escorted her into his office.

"Jenessa, it's nice to see you." He offered his hand and she shook it. "Have a seat."

She perched on the edge of one of the club chairs across from his desk. "I can't stay long. Why did you want to see me?"

"We'll get right to it then." He pulled a small, flat package out of a drawer and set it on his desk.

Jenessa studied it with curiosity. It was about the size of a small book or maybe a framed photo she guessed, but it must have been private because it was wrapped in plastic with a wax seal on it.

"In your father's Will, there were instructions from him that I give this to you after his passing, within a week after the reading of the Will. No one but you is supposed to open it."

Now she really was curious. "What is it?"

He handed it across his desk. "Open it."

She ripped the plastic off, breaking the seal, then lifted the cover to the box. "It's a DVD." She looked up at Mr. McCaffrey. "Did you know what it was?"

He shrugged noncommittally and then rose from his seat to come around from behind the desk. "Your father's instructions said to have you watch this DVD here in my office. Shall we?" He gestured toward the other end of his office to a conference table and a television mounted on the wall.

Jenessa stood and followed, her stomach twisting with anticipation of what she was about to see. Whatever it was, she couldn't figure out why it was for her alone.

He put his hand out. "Let me put it in the DVR and get it set up for you."

Puzzled, she handed it over and took a seat at the table. "Any idea what's on the DVD?"

"Sorry, I'm not at liberty to say." He turned the television on and stuck the DVD into the device.

Not at liberty? "He's dead, Mr. McCaffrey. What difference would it make now?"

"Just watch. I'll leave you alone, but if you need me, I'll be right outside." He walked out and closed the door.

The DVD began to play. It was her father, seated behind his desk in his office at the firm, with his hands clasped in front of him.

What the heck?

"Hello, Jenessa." Her father looked away from the camera for a moment, appearing uneasy. Then, he took an audible, deep breath and focused his eyes directly forward.

It felt as if he was looking right at her and a chill shimmied down her spine, knowing he never would again. She took her own deep breath and laced her hands together in a tight grip.

"If you're watching this, it means I must have passed away. I don't know how old you are at this point, but hopefully old enough to forgive me and let the past go."

Forgive him? Was he going to apologize for all the animosity between them? It made sense now that it was for her alone.

Jenessa pressed her lips together and squeezed her hands tighter as she watched, her eyes riveted to the TV screen.

"My dear daughter, I am so sorry that I drove a wedge between us, and I am sorry that I made it seem like it was your fault. The truth is, when your mother died...well, your sister wasn't the only one that blamed you. I'm ashamed to say, I did too, even though deep down I knew it was my fault. I was the one who drove your mother to go to Sacramento that Christmas season, not you."

Tears began to form in Jenessa's eyes as she heard the words she had longed to hear all these years. Still, it angered her that he was only able to admit this in death. All those wasted years. All those misplaced feelings. She wiped at her cheek and continued watching, wondering what more he could have to say.

"I was always leery of you dating the son of Grey Alexander—even when Logan took you to the prom. I had seen how Grey treated the women in his life and I assumed Logan would follow in his father's footsteps."

She tried to get a read on her father's expression. Was it only regret or was there a hint of guilt by association on his face?

"Jenessa, when you became pregnant by Logan, my fears seemed to be coming true. There's something you need to know. Maybe you already do, I don't know, but Ramey deserves to finally know the truth. It was Grey Alexander that got Lucy St. John pregnant. Grey is Ramey's father. Though I wasn't around when Ramey was born, I was well aware of how badly Grey treated Lucy and the baby. As Grey's attorney, I was responsible for making payments to Lucy on Grey's behalf. I rationalized my actions by telling myself it was merely child support—a good thing, but the truth is, it was a payout to keep Lucy from telling anyone, especially Ramey. As such, sadly, I was also privy to Grey's demeaning comments about the woman."

Her father hung his head, shaking it side to side, wearing a shameful expression. "You have to understand, Jenessa, I didn't want that for my own daughter. I hated the thought that you would have anything to do with that family."

Knowing what she now knew, Jenessa could completely understand why her father had felt that way. Those few recent run-ins with the portentous Grey Alexander had left her feeling much the same way as her father had.

"There is no way that Grey would ever have allowed you and the baby to ruin Logan's chances of becoming a great college quarterback. He would have done anything to ensure that Logan would go on to have a successful life."

Anything?

"If you had kept the child, you would have been forever tied to that miserable family, and I couldn't chance that what happened to Lucy would happen to you."

What happened to Lucy? Did he mean the payments or what landed her in a shallow grave at the lake? Could her father really have had something to do with her death? Or was he an accessory after the fact?

"There's something else, Jenessa. I know Ramey felt abandoned, but there's more...I want to tell you what really happened to Lucy St. John."

"Oh, my gosh," Jenessa murmured. "Here it comes."

She sat up straight and held her breath, waiting for him to continue, just as a knock came at the door, startling her a little.

Ian McCaffrey pushed the door open a few inches, sticking his head inside. "Just checking to see if you're done."

She quickly pushed pause and gave her head a shake to bring herself back to the present.

"Sorry," McCaffrey said, "I can see you're not. I'll give you some more time."

He bowed out and she turned her attention back to the DVD. "Okay, Dad, you were about to tell me something important."

Her father went on to explain how he had been Grey's attorney for several years by that point, and that Lucy had contacted Grey, asking for a lump-sum settlement. "When Grey got the call from Lucy, he told me that he and Lauren argued bitterly over it," her father said. "Grey phoned me and insisted I meet them at the lake house to discuss a settlement. I agreed, of course, what choice did I really have? I hid my car in the woods, and when Lucy arrived, I stayed tucked out of the way in another room, listening, without her knowing I was there."

Jenessa stared, breathless, visualizing the scene as her father went on.

"I heard the three of them talking, then quarreling," he said. "When the argument began to escalate and become quite heated, I thought I'd better intervene. So, I stepped into the living room to find Lauren with her hands on Lucy's arms, screaming in her face, jerking her back and forth. Then Lucy pulled back from Lauren's grip and stumbled backward. She hit her head, hard, on the jagged corner of the burl-wood coffee table."

Her father paused, closing his eyes for a moment, as if the memory of it was painful. He shuffled a small stack of papers on his desk, and then continued.

"Lucy didn't get up, she remained motionless on the floor, blood beginning to pool around her head. I was frozen to the spot as Lauren began screaming hysterically. Grey bent down and checked for a pulse. But he shook his head as he stood up. She was dead."

Jenessa had predicted a similar scenario, unsure of the exact players involved, still, the confirmation sent flashes of brutal visions through her mind. She paused the DVD momentarily to collect herself.

How could her father have lived with this all these years? How could any decent person? What part did he actually play?

When she felt ready, she resumed the video, waiting for the answers. It was, as she had expected—Grey had ordered her father to take care of the mess before anyone in Hidden Valley missed them. He'd told her father that he and Lauren had to get back, and that no one could know they were involved in Lucy's death.

Her father's eyes appeared moist as he relived and confessed his deeds. "I didn't know what else to do, Jenessa. You have to believe me. Grey Alexander represented ninety-five percent of my clientele and I was certain that if I refused, Grey would fire me—or worse, blame me. And whose word would the police believe? It would be two against one. If they believed Grey and Lauren, my life would be over. I know it sounds selfish, but it wasn't—not purely anyway—I was thinking of my family. Knowing what I do about Grey Alexander, I believed I had no choice but to help them—and keep my mouth shut."

Her father dropped his head into his hands now, his shoulders rising and falling as if he were sobbing. Then his body stilled and he looked up, his eyes wet with tears and full of pleading. "It was an accident. Lucy St. John was already dead. No one could change that. What else could I do?"

"I don't know," Jenessa whispered. "But there must've been something, Dad." Shaking her head, she sat there, not shocked exactly, more like dumbfounded at the reality of it all, as her father explained how he'd reluctantly agreed to take care of the body after Grey and

Lauren left. He admitted to burying Lucy's body in a shallow grave in the woods about fifty yards from the Alexanders' lake house.

At least he'd confessed to that, told them where to locate her body. He would have had no way of knowing they had already found it, unless he'd anticipated it when he'd seen them break ground at the construction site.

"My God," Jenessa said, "his last days must have been awful, constantly worrying about the body being discovered." *It's no wonder he had a heart attack.* Or maybe that's what caused it.

Her hatred for Grey Alexander came to the forefront. Indirectly he had caused the death of both her mother and her father. Part of her wanted to get up at that moment and go throw all this damning evidence in his face, tell him what a sorry excuse for a human being he was, but no. She needed to hear the rest, and she needed to be smart about this.

Her father's confession continued on the screen. "I can admit I was a coward, Jenessa, but I wasn't stupid. I made sure I had insurance in case Grey tried to pin the murder on me. So I took a comb from the bathroom, it had several hairs still in it, and I planted it with the body. I needed to implicate Grey, too. If I was going to go down, I would take him with me."

Relief washed over her at the confirmation that Logan did not have anything to do with it. Her father couldn't have known they might have been Logan's hairs.

With the tears in his eyes now streaming down his cheeks, her father brushed them away with his hands and continued. "I don't know what you think of me right now, but I am not a bad person. I made bad decisions for the right reasons, and trust that I have been wracked with guilt for years. It ate away at me, day after day. I regret that I wasn't man enough to stand up to Grey Alexander. I only hope you can use this information to make things right, and—"

He leaned closer to the camera, the expression on his face was unlike any she had ever seen there before. "And I love you, Jenessa. I always have. I hope you can forgive me one day."

She wasn't surprised to find out her father was involved after finding the mate to the suspicious cufflink, but she hadn't expected the DVD confession. The only bright spot was that he hadn't been the one responsible for the death of her best friend's mother.

The way he had told the story, Lucy's death could possibly be considered an accident, or at the most involuntary manslaughter, but covering it up was a crime in itself, accessory after the fact. Her dad would have been guilty of that at the very least.

Coming clean after he was dead was the coward's way, but at least now she had something to take to the authorities. She looked at the clock. The Deputy DA and Detective Provenza were at the station at this very moment, questioning Grey Alexander.

Jenessa willed her tears to retreat. This was not the time to break down. She needed to get this evidence to the police station. She wiped at her cheeks, then bolted from her chair and pushed the eject button on the DVR. She slipped the disc back in the box and stuck it in her purse. Maybe the DVD could help get a confession out of the great and mighty Grey Alexander, or his ice queen.

When she opened the office door on her way out, she found Ian McCaffrey leaning on the narrow counter, talking to his assistant. He looked up as she approached. "All finished?"

"I am."

He stood up straight. "Do you want to talk about it?"

"Not right now. I've got a couple of scumbags to string up." Jenessa breezed past him and stepped into the elevator. "But you and I will talk about this later."

As the elevator doors glided shut, a thought popped into her mind and Jenessa stuck her hand between the doors to stop them from closing. When they began to open again, she poked her head out. "Mr. McCaffrey?"

"Yes," he replied, still standing near his assistant.

"Do you know who adopted my baby?"

His eyes widened a bit as he adjusted his posture, appearing a bit uncomfortable with the question. "It was a sealed adoption, Jenessa. No one can know."

"I'll definitely be back. We need to talk about that too." She let the doors close.

~*~

Jenessa had phoned Michael on her way over to tell him she had some critical new information on Lucy St. John's murder. She asked him to meet her up front so she could tell him everything.

When she arrived he met her in the reception area of the police station.

"How's the questioning going?" she asked.

"They just started."

"Well, I have a taped confession that—" she paused and glanced around, noticing the receptionist listening in, as well as an older couple sitting in the waiting chairs. "Maybe we should talk about this in private."

Michael led her to the observation room and lowered the volume of the speaker. "What is it?"

Jenessa glanced toward the two-way mirror and it drew her attention. Detective Provenza and the Deputy District Attorney had their backs to the glass and were sitting across from Grey Alexander. Seeing him there, seated between two men in dark suits, he wore a smug look on his face and it made her blood boil.

She plucked the DVD from her purse and held it out to Michael. "My father's taped confession of what happened to Lucy the night she died. His attorney just gave it to me."

"Have you watched it?"

"I have." Jenessa gave him the condensed version of what her father had said on the DVD, emphasizing who he'd claimed had been the one Lucy struggled with, but admitting he had been the one to bury her body. "That must be how his cufflink fell into the grave."

"I've got to let Provenza and the DDA know right away," Michael said.

Jenessa glanced back at the two-way window. "Wait. Look. What are they saying?"

Michael turned the speaker up.

DDA Rodriguez told Grey they had a witness who could put Lucy St. John at his lake house on the night she died. "Based on the fact that Logan had motive, opportunity, and his DNA was found on the dead woman's body, we have a pretty compelling case against your son."

Detective Provenza cleared this throat. "But someone recently pointed out to me that it could also have been your DNA, familial match and all. So, we know for sure that it was either you or Logan that killed Miss St. John."

"It was neither," Grey declared. "I'll even take a polygraph test."

One of the lawyers patted Grey on the shoulder. "Let us handle this."

"The evidence shows it was definitely one of you," the DDA said. "So, we can put your son on trial for her death, or you can confess and save him—your choice."

Grey Alexander sat stone-faced.

"How much do you love your son, Mr. Alexander?" the DDA asked. "Truthfully, would you send him to prison to save your own skin? You know what happens to pretty young boys in Lompoc, don't you?"

"Don't say a word," one of the lawyers directed. "He's just trying to scare you."

Grey shot Rodriguez a silent, hostile stare.

"If you killed her," Provenza went on, "now's the time to fess up."

Michael, looking as if he couldn't wait another minute, snatched the DVD from Jenessa's hand, turned the speaker's volume off, and dashed out the door.

Spinning back to the two-way glass, Jenessa turned it back on. "Sorry, Michael," she said, even though he was already gone. "I can't help myself. This is just too juicy to ignore."

CHAPTER 22

JENESSA STOOD AT THE TWO-WAY window and watched as Michael entered the interrogation room. All eyes turned to him. He bent down and whispered something into Provenza's ear. Provenza leaned toward the DDA and whispered something into his ear. Then they both stood.

"Wait here, please," Provenza said to Grey and his attorneys. "We'll be right back."

They seemed surprised, muttering back and forth, likely wondering what was going on.

Jenessa raised her hand to turn the speaker off, but paused. Yes, she should turn it off, she knew, because Grey was entitled to confidentiality with his lawyers after all. However, she wasn't law enforcement, so could she slide? But what if she overheard something important, something that would definitely be helpful? How would she explain how she happened to overhear it without exposing the fact that she had purposely turned the speaker on?

She forced her attention away from that tempting speaker button, wondering if Michael needed help explaining the DVD. Jenessa took a few steps toward the door, but stopped. If the DDA and Provenza saw her coming out of the observation room, Michael could get in a lot of trouble.

She bit down on her bottom lip—she was stuck. She let out a long, loud sigh of frustration. Then, against her strong reporter instincts, she made herself turn the speaker off and remain where she was.

Before long, Michael came back into the observation room. They watched Provenza and the DDA step back into the interrogation room and stand just inside the door.

"You'll be happy to know, Jen, officers are already on their way to bring Lauren Alexander in." Michael gave her a sideways look and turned the speaker back on. "Don't get used to this," he said as he came to stand beside her, both of them facing the window.

We'll see. She grinned. "This should be good."

Her fingers brushed against his and he took her hand, squeezed it lightly, then let go, which made her smile a little.

"Mr. Alexander," DDA Rodriguez began, leaning on the table with both hands, "it has just come to our attention that we have another eye-witness account of what happened to Lucy St. John at your home on Jonas Lake on the night she died."

Grey and his attorneys muttered to each other briefly, then sat silent.

Rodriguez continued. "Maybe you want to reconsider making a full confession, telling us exactly what happened, in exchange for a deal."

Grey's eyes narrowed and his lips pinched into a straight line.

"What eye witness?" one of his attorneys asked.

The DDA briefly raised one hand. "Not yet. You can be sure we will give you full disclosure before your client's trial. We'll be charging him with involuntary manslaughter, five to eight years."

"We'll need a few minutes alone to confer with our client," the other lawyer said.

Grey leaned over and whispered something into the lawyer's ear, then he muttered something to the other attorney as well. The two attorneys leaned behind Grey's back and conferred quietly.

"Are you sure?" one of the lawyers asked Grey.

Grey nodded with an air of defiance.

"Mr. Alexander does not admit to anything. He'll take his chances in court."

"Let me remind you, Mr. Alexander," the DDA said, "we have two witnesses that can put you with Lucy St. John at your lake house at the time of her death."

"That's what you keep telling me," Grey said, "but I want to know who those witnesses are. For all I know, this is nothing but a bluff."

Rodriguez and Provenza eyed each other.

"Wait here," Provenza said. "Give us a few minutes and we'll be able to tell you."

The detective and the DDA walked out.

Seeing the two men head for the door, Jenessa and Michael scooted out of the observation room before they could be spotted by the DDA. They were casually talking in the hall when Provenza and Rodriguez exited the interrogation room.

"We've got him by the short hairs, people." Provenza said as he stopped to speak with Michael and Jenessa, while the DDA kept walking. "Now, Michael, as soon as Mrs. Alexander is brought in, escort Mr. Alexander and his lawyers into the observation room. I want to make sure Grey has a front row seat for the show. Wait for my signal."

Before long, Provenza radioed Michael to move Grey and his entourage. Jenessa stepped into the observation room while Michael did as he was instructed. She hurried to the farthest corner of the dimly-lit room, trying to make herself as inconspicuous as possible, keeping her eyes focused on the two-way glass.

"What's going on?" Grey grumbled when Michael told them to come with him into the observation room.

"We need to use this room for just a little while, sir," Michael said. "Then we'll have you come back in. We appreciate your accommodating us, Mr. Alexander."

Once Grey and his legal team were in the observation room, Michael made sure the speaker was on. "It'll just be a few minutes, everyone."

At the sound of voices emanating from the speaker, they all turned and watched as Detective Provenza escorted Lauren Alexander in and asked her to take a seat.

"Why did you have me brought down here, Detective?" Lauren asked as she sat.

"I have a few questions for you about Lucy St. John's death."

"Do I need a lawyer, Detective?"

"We haven't arrested you," Provenza replied. "You're here as a possible witness."

"Oh, really?"

"We have reason to believe you and your husband were, let just say, in the vicinity when Lucy St. John was killed. Is that correct?"

"Who told you that?"

"We have a witness. Now don't get your knickers in a twist, I'm just trying to get my facts straight. Tell me, is that correct?"

Lauren crossed her arms over her ample chest and leaned back in her chair, her lips firmly clamped shut.

"Well, what if I told you that your husband has already corroborated that fact?"

"I said no such thing!" Grey shouted at the glass.

"I don't believe you," Lauren said to Detective Provenza.

"My witness said that there was arguing over money and then a physical struggle took place with Lucy losing her balance and hitting her head. Is that correct?"

Jenessa listened to the exchange between Lauren and the detective, but her gaze was riveted on Grey Alexander and his responses.

"You have a witness? How could—" Lauren caught herself. She paused for a moment, eying the detective, obviously thinking about what she would say next. Her arms relaxed and her hands drifted down to her lap as she leaned forward. "Yes, that's right. It was an accident." Tears moistened her soft blue eyes. "A horrible, horrible accident."

"Shut up, you stupid woman!" Grey yelled from behind the window.

"Calm down, Grey," one of the lawyers advised.

"I see." Provenza stood and moved to her side of the table, sitting on the corner of it. "Tell me more."

"Lucy was arguing…with Grey." Lauren went on.

"About what?"

"He didn't want to give her the money she was demanding." She folded her hands on the table.

"Go on."

"And then *Grey* grabbed her by her arms, just to get her attention, of course, and she pulled away. That's when she stumbled and crashed against the coffee table, hitting her head." Lauren buried her face in her hands. "There was nothing more we could do for her. It was a terrible accident. He didn't mean for Lucy to get hurt."

"Liar!" Grey shouted.

Michael glanced back at Jenessa and shot her a knowing look.

"Grey, silence please," the attorney reminded.

Lauren drew in a deep breath and sighed. "I told him we should call nine-one-one, get her some help, but he said it was too late, she was already dead."

"She's lying," Grey said to Michael. "Can't you see that? She's the one who was struggling with Lucy. She made her fall—not me."

"Grey, stop!" the attorney insisted. "Detective, isn't there somewhere else we can go?"

Michael ignored the lawyer, watching as Grey was riveted to every word out of Lauren's mouth.

"If it was really an accident, I still don't understand why you didn't call the police and report it?" Provenza asked the woman.

"Well, Detective, like I said, *I* wanted to, but Grey said it would be better if we just buried her. He didn't think anyone would believe us. He said no one would miss her anyway."

"I never said that! I swear!" Grey raked his fingers through his hair.

One of the lawyers put his hand on Grey's shoulder. "Listen to me. Don't say another word. You're not helping yourself."

"So you and your husband dug a shallow grave and dumped her body in it?" Provenza questioned.

"No! His attorney was there too. He buried her after we left."

"Then I'll have to talk to him to get his corroboration."

"You can't. He died last week," she said smugly, checking her manicure.

"I see. How convenient for you." Provenza stood and his gaze moved briefly to the mirror. "You do know it's a crime not to report something like this." He took his seat again.

"It is?" she asked, her words dripping with feigned innocence. "Oh, no, Detective, I didn't know."

Grey let out a low growl.

"My husband said everything would be fine. We should just go about our lives and no one would have to know. He said no one would even care."

Grey pounded his fist on the window, causing Provenza and Lauren both to jump in their seats. "She's the one who was wrestling with Lucy when the woman fell and hit her head! I wanted to pay Lucy off. It was her—it was all her!"

Then Grey spun toward the door and bolted out. Michael and the lawyers ran after him.

Jenessa watched as Grey burst into the interrogation room and lunged at his wife. "It's all lies. It was you! You're the one that pushed Lucy and killed her. I agreed to bury her to protect you!"

Michael and the lawyers pulled him off while Provenza shot out of his chair and hurried around the table to Lauren. "Are you okay?"

"I think so." Lauren's hand moved to the top of her chest.

"Then, please stand up." Provenza put a hand on her arm and helped her to her feet. "Lauren Alexander, you are under arrest for your role in the death of Lucy St. John."

"What? But I—"

Provenza clicked the cuffs on her as the absolute shock on her face melted into a mask of fear.

Michael nodded at the senior detective and then pulled handcuffs out of his pocket. "Grey Alexander, put your hands behind your back. You are under arrest as an accomplice after the fact in the death of Lucy St. John."

Jenessa continued to watch quietly as two uniformed officers entered to take the couple away.

At the sight of the officers, a pallid look of resignation washed over Grey's face. Jenessa had never seen him look so small and defeated. She had only known him as a powerful giant, a man who always got what he wanted, no matter who got hurt.

For Jenessa the rush of victory was sweet.

One of the attorneys moved close to Michael. "Who is this eye witness?"

One officer had Grey by the arm, about to lead him out, but Grey whipped his head around to hear the answer.

Michael smirked. "David Jones." Then his attention briefly flashed toward the two-way mirror and Jenessa caught his gaze. He motioned to the officers to escort the two out of the room and he and Provenza trailed behind them.

A moment later the door to the observation room opened and Michael stepped in.

"We did it!" Jenessa threw her arms around his neck and kissed him full on the mouth. Before he could fully engage in the kiss, she hopped back. "I don't know what came over me," she gasped, relieved they were alone in the room.

"Whatever it was," Michael said with a wide grin, "I'd like to see it come over you more often."

She moved closer and a mischievous smile tickled her lips. "Tomorrow night maybe?"

CHAPTER 23

RATHER THAN GO ON THEIR DATE as planned, Jenessa and Michael joined in a family celebration—a barbecue and pool party at her aunt's house. Aunt Renee had heard all about Jenessa helping to solve the mystery of Lucy St. John's death and holding the town's leading citizens responsible for the crime. She had announced to Jenessa, Sara, and Ramey that she wanted to throw a party to celebrate.

Everyone pitched in, bringing food, decorations, and inviting additional guests. Jenessa extended an invitation to Michael and Jake, and Ramey invited Charles and Charlie. Sara came alone, claiming she was happy just to be with her family.

The girls arrived early to get everything set up before the rest of the crowd arrived. The house was a beehive of activity and Jenessa loved it.

Making last minute preparations, they buzzed around the kitchen cutting up fruit and veggies and laying them on large cut-crystal trays.

"How did you manage to get Grey Alexander to confess?" her aunt asked.

Jenessa's back stiffened. Should she dare tell them what her father admitted to doing? No. What good would it do now? With Grey pleading guilty and implicating his wife, the DVD would never have to be exposed to the public. She sure wasn't going to bring it up in her article about Grey's and Lauren's confessions and the impending sentencing.

"I had some incriminating evidence that I gave to the police. A sealed package someone slipped to me."

"What was it?" Sara asked.

"Who gave it to you?" Ramey piped in.

Jenessa glanced at them both, then went back to chopping her vegetables. "Oh, ladies, you know I never reveal my sources."

They both groaned but let it go. They knew her well enough to know there was no point in persisting. She wouldn't change her mind.

A quick glance at the clock said it was almost six, just as the doorbell chimed, alerting them to the arrival of their first guest.

"I'll get it," Jenessa offered, toweling off her hands and hurrying to the door. She opened it, hoping to see Michael and Jake.

"Hello, Miss Jones." It was George Provenza, standing before her in shorts, sandals, and a Hawaiian print shirt, holding a colorful bouquet of flowers. "Am I early? I don't see too many cars out front."

George? "Uh…oh, no, you're not too early. Come on in." She turned and led him back to the kitchen. "Our first guest has arrived," she announced to the others, wondering who had invited him. Michael maybe?

Aunt Renee came out from behind the counter and greeted him with a warm smile. "I'm so glad you could make it, Detective."

Did Aunt Renee invite him?

He held out the flowers to her. "Call me George, please."

Jenessa observed their gazes interlocking. Something seemed to sizzle between them. "Shall I put those in some water for you, Aunt Renee?"

"Oh, yes, yes…please, dear." She handed the bouquet to Jenessa, her eyes remaining on the detective. "Would you like something cold to drink, George?"

Jenessa glanced at Sara and Ramey, both of whom had stopped cutting up fruit and vegetables and were watching the exchange between George and their aunt.

"Iced tea, if you have it," George said.

"I'll get it for you," Sara offered from the kitchen. "Why don't you have a seat at the breakfast bar?"

The doorbell rang again. "Oh, I'll get it," Ramey called out, rushing to answer it.

Jenessa glanced down the hallway to the front door, wondering if it was Michael. Ramey opened the door to find a smiling Charles and a deadpan Charlie.

"Did you bring your swimsuits, boys?" Ramey asked as she led them back toward the kitchen.

Charlie's face it up at the mention of swimming.

"There's a big beautiful pool out there." Ramey gestured toward the french doors between the kitchen and the great room, where the crystal blue water could be seen through the glass.

Ramey introduced Charles and Charlie to George, as George knew everyone else.

"All we need are your boys, Jen, and we can put the meat on the grill," Aunt Renee said.

My boys? Jenessa hadn't thought of them like that, but she liked the sound of it. "I'm sure they're on their way."

Before long, the doorbell chimed again. Jenessa was up to her elbows in cut-up watermelon, so Sara offered to answer the door. "I guess it's my turn anyway."

Jenessa rinsed her hands and forearms as she watched Sara move down the hall. She grabbed a towel and stood in the hallway, waiting with anticipation.

Sara swung the door open, but because the sun was shining behind them, Jenessa couldn't quite make out who was standing at the door. Three dark figures—two men and a small boy. If one was Michael, who was the second man?

She watched as Sara stood talking to them a little longer than Jenessa expected, but soon they all stepped inside and shut the door, approaching down the hall.

A smile instantly spread on Jenessa's face as Michael and Jake came into view. The other man was about Michael's age, his hair more fair and he stood a few inches shorter than Michael.

"Jenessa," Michael said, "this is my cousin Luke. Remember I told you he was coming for a few days, thinking of applying for a position with the Hidden

Valley Police Department. I hope you don't mind me bringing him."

"Of course not." Jenessa put out her hand to him. "Welcome, Luke."

Luke took her hand and shook it, but his gaze soon shifted back to Sara, who was standing beside her sister, grinning. Sara had that same glassy look in her eyes that Aunt Renee had when she was first introduced to George when he arrived at the party.

Michael seemed to notice the same thing. When his gaze moved back to Jenessa, she winked at him. "Well, now that everyone's here," she said, "let's get this party started!"

In a flash, the crowd scattered. The young boys raced to the pool and their dads followed. Ramey got busy putting the meat on the grill.

Jenessa grabbed a platter of crudité and dip for the guests to munch on. She stepped through the french doors and stood for a moment, watching everyone enjoying themselves. Sara and Luke took seats on a couple of lounge chairs under the big blue umbrella near the pool. They were laughing and seemed pleasantly engaged in conversation.

Where did Aunt Renee and George go?

Jenessa scanned the backyard and found them in the rose garden. Her aunt was showing George her prize-winning roses. They were both smiling and appeared to be enjoying each other's company.

A warm feeling of contentment settled on Jenessa. Finally, she was back in the family and loving it. Watching the men playing in the pool with their boys delighted her. Her thoughts briefly flashed to what her own son might be doing on that warm summer evening.

Jenessa set the platter down on the patio table and stepped back inside. She went to the refrigerator to stack the condiments for the hamburgers on another tray. After pulling a few items out, she bent over and reached toward the far back for the mayonnaise. Without warning, a pair of hands slipped around her waist and she flinched.

She whirled around to find Michael smiling down at her, a few drops of water dripping from his dark hair, falling onto the tile floor.

"Jake wants me to throw you in the pool. Are you game?" His toothy grin challenged her.

Her eyes widened. "Oh, my gosh, Michael—not now. But I promise, after dinner I'll put on my bikini and you are welcome to throw me in—if you dare. Deal?"

"A bikini, huh?" He pulled her to him, sliding his hands around her again. "I'm going to hold you to that."

"You can hold me to anything you like, Michael, just hold me close."

He didn't have to be asked twice. His arms encircled her and he kissed her deeply. She clung to him as her heart pounded and her legs began to go limp, overcome with desire.

"Daddy?" came Jake's voice as the little boy stood in the open french doors, wrapped in a beach towel.

Michael and Jenessa quickly dropped their passionate embrace and each took an embarrassed step back.

"Hey, buddy," Michael said as he rushed to his son.

"I have to go potty."

Michael scooped Jake up in his arms and gave Jenessa a shrug and a grin. "Duty calls."

Her lips curved into a smile as the aftereffect of his kiss lingered with her, and she grabbed onto the refrigerator handle to steady herself.

"Where's the bathroom?" Michael asked.

Catching her breath, she replied. "Through the great room, down the hall, second door on the right."

Michael dashed off with Jake and she went back to retrieving the condiments. The doorbell rang again.

Who could that be? All of the guests were already there. She padded down the hallway and opened the door.

Logan stood before her, his hair aglow from the late afternoon sun behind him. "Hello, Jenessa."

"I'm glad to see they let you out already."

"I hear I have you to thank for that."

"Well...not just me. How did you know I was here?"

"I was driving by and saw your car. It's kind of hard to miss that little gem." He smiled and his intensely blue eyes searched hers.

"Do you want to come in?" she asked.

"No." He looked past her and into the house. "I can see your aunt is having a party, I don't want to intrude. I just wanted to thank you for not giving up on me, for pushing the cops to keep working the case."

"I only wanted to get to the truth, Logan." It was the only reason she could give to him. She couldn't tell him she had hoped with all her heart that the father of her child wasn't a killer, or that every time she saw him her heart skipped a beat, or that she was forever inextricably connected to him because of their son, whether she liked it or not.

"You know, while Dad's locked up, he left me in charge of his companies. Who would have thought?"

"I can see that."

"I hope I can prove to him that I'm capable of taking over the reins of his empire one day."

"Oh, I never doubted it, Logan." In fact, she did have her doubts, but he seemed to need some encouragement and what would it hurt to give him a little?

"I meant what I said. I've never stopped loving you." He took her hand. "I hope one day you can see I am worthy of you now."

"Logan, please don't say that." She pulled her hand away.

"I've changed, Jenessa. I know now that I made a huge mistake letting you go."

"Just me?"

"And our son."

"I can't do this, Logan." She wanted to close the door, wanted him to leave. He must have seen it in her eyes.

"I'm sorry. I didn't mean to upset you. I only wanted to thank you and to…well…ask for your forgiveness. Do you think you can ever forgive me for what I did to you?"

Forgive him? For all the years of pain and heartache he caused her? She wanted to—to be set free of it—but could it really be that easy? To simply decide to forgive and then say it?

A noise behind her drew her attention and she glanced over her shoulder. Michael was taking little Jake back out to the pool. Her gaze drifted beyond them, to the others who were laughing and chatting and splashing about in the water.

She was part of a family again, a good family. It was like she had been given a second chance. That realization brought a sudden rush of warmth to her heart and it caused something hard inside of her to melt.

"Jenessa?" Logan was waiting for her answer.

She turned back to her old boyfriend and gave him a winsome smile. "Yes, Logan, I forgive you."

THE END

Thank you so much for reading my book,
The Lake House Secret.
I hope you enjoyed it very much.

Debra Burroughs

The highest compliment an author can get is to
receive a great review, especially
if the review is posted on Amazon.com.

Debra@DebraBurroughsBooks.com

www.DebraBurroughsBooks.com

Other Books
By Debra Burroughs

Three Days in Seattle, *a Romantic Suspense Novel*

The Scent of Lies, *Paradise Valley Mystery Book 1*

The Heart of Lies, *Paradise Valley Mystery Book 2*

The Edge of Lies, *Paradise Valley Mystery Short Story*

The Chain of Lies, *Paradise Valley Mystery Book 3*

The Pursuit of Lies, *Paradise Valley Mystery Book 4*

The Betrayal of Lies, *Paradise Valley Mystery Book 5*

The Color of Lies, *Paradise Valley Mystery Short Story*

The Harbor of Lies, *Paradise Valley Mystery Book 6*

The Stone House Secret,
a Jenessa Jones Mystery, Book 2

Coming in paperback in February, 2015

ABOUT THE AUTHOR

Debra Burroughs writes with intensity and power. Her characters are rich and her stories of romance, suspense and mystery are highly entertaining. She can often be found sitting in front of her computer in her home in the Pacific Northwest, dreaming up new stories and developing interesting characters for her next book.

If you are looking for stories that will touch your heart and leave you wanting more, dive into one of her captivating books.

www.DebraBurroughsBooks.com

24270098R00212

Printed in Great Britain
by Amazon